Howard Gurney was born in Sydney, Australia and is the author of six novels and multiple peer-reviewed medical journal articles. He works as a medical oncologist at Westmead Hospital in Sydney and is also a professor of medicine at Macquarie University, where he undertakes clinical trials for cancer patients. His first fantasy fiction novel, *Twin*, was published in 2015.

He lives in Sydney with his wife and their five children. He has also worked in Manchester, UK and travels extensively.

Other books by Howard Gurney

Path to Chaos series (fantasy)
Twin
The Thread Frays
Chaos

Dr Christopher Walker Murder Mystery series
Murder on the Ward
Death in a Chapel
Murder at The Rocks
Murder in The Mist

MURDER IN THE MIST

A Dr Christopher Walker Murder Mystery
Book 4

Howard Gurney

This is a work of fiction and the characters are imaginary.

Copyright © Howard Gurney 2023

ISBN 978-0-6487177-6-8

Print edition 2023

CHAPTER ONE

NO ONE HEARD Solomon Krantz die that night. A thick fog lay over the mountains and the air was cold and still. Most sensible souls were huddled inside their homes, sipping warm drinks and snuggled up in front of their fireplace for the evening.

Neither did anyone see the killer come close to Krantz in the mist, an arm outstretched, a sudden shove. Krantz cried out as he fell but the thick air muffled the howl just as good as a restless babe squeezed against a mother's breast. Halfway down, his head hit the cliff face at a bad angle, severing the spinal cord where it entered the skull. By the time his body became lodged in a fork of a tree on Federation Pass three hundred metres below, he was dead.

The murderer walked away along the road from Echo Point through pea-soup fog to reach an upmarket hotel perched on the edge of the escarpment. Through the French doors it was apparent a crowd had gathered in the lounge before one of the fireplaces, stoked high with eucalyptus and angophora logs. The fire blazed, illuminating smiling faces quaffing cocktails and beers. As the door opened, a wall of laughter tumbled out of the room but no one turned to see who entered. All attention was on the apparent originator of the mirth, a slight man with a high forehead who stood in the middle of the group. Despite the wintery weather, he held a cocktail more suited to the tropics – a yellow and green concoction with a pineapple wedge stuck on the glass edge and skewered by a little pink umbrella.

'I swear,' Christopher Walker cried. 'He wasn't even there to see me. He just stood up when I called out a name and followed me into the room. He didn't even have lung cancer. In fact, he'd never even had a scan in his life. He was there to see the endocrinologist about his diabetes. The poor fellow kept going on about how he couldn't believe his bad luck having cancer diagnosed on his birthday.'

'How did you twig that he was the wrong patient, Chris?' asked Holland Xavier, one of the medical oncologists.

'The practice manager – she interrupted the consultation. I still remember the look on her face. "Dr Walker," she said. "Why are you seeing Mr Jones?" I said, "What are you talking about? This is Mr Smith." Then the man finally said, "No, I'm Mr Jones. My GP sent me here about my diabetes."'

There was another round of chuckles although some of the audience looked uncomfortable.

'I felt terrible,' said Walker, now looking remorseful. 'Poor bloke. I even showed him his scan – which he'd never had, you remember – and phoned up myself to organise a biopsy for him.'

'You idiot, Chris,' said Xavier. 'Was the poor man okay?'

'He was a bit shell-shocked.' Walker grimaced. 'Anyway, as he left, I said, "Well, happy birthday! Good news! You don't have cancer." Strange, it didn't seem to cheer him up.'

The laughter had left the conversation.

Walker looked downcast again. 'I've always felt bad about that. Anyway, it's good to tell you lot. There's no one else I could tell such a terrible story to. Nobody else would understand.'

'Except your lawyer, maybe,' said the murderer.

'Luckily, it didn't come to that,' said Walker. He sucked the last dregs of his cocktail through the straw then plonked the glass on the coffee table. 'Anyone for another?'

Without a word, the murderer left the edge of the group, walked slowly to the elevator, caught it to the second floor and moments later was safe inside the room. A steady hand parted the curtains, the viewer hoping to catch a glimpse of the valley below, but it was already lost in darkness. The fog had cleared and, down below, the lights of the hotel illuminated the garden.

It began to snow.

CHAPTER TWO

THE NEXT MORNING the sky was crystal clear and the air freezing, and a blanket of fresh snow covered the top of the thick hedge that bordered the hotel garden. Snow was unusual in the Blue Mountains, a two-hour drive west of Sydney, although most years received a light dusting on the coldest days of winter. But the last week had been one of the coldest on record, the snowfall overnight had been unusually heavy and the temperature remained below zero, so the snow persisted on the ground now.

Hotel guests gathered on the veranda to gaze in wonder at the rare sight, smiles on faces, rubbing hands together and talking in excited tones. Most of the hotel had been taken over for a three-day conference by the medical oncology department from Western Meadows Hospital and everyone was in a good mood. Pier Mathijssen, a tall young man with fresh cheeks, red with the cold, jumped down into the garden and began pelting a few of the nurses with snowballs.

'This is how we do it back in the Netherlands,' he laughed. 'It's a tradition on the first fall of the season.'

One of the nurses who'd copped a snowball in the head shrieked with laughter and hurled her own missile back at the attacker, catching him on the side of the head.

'Great shot, Jen,' Walker cried from above. 'Get him again.'

The petite ward team leader obliged and hurled another snowball, which caught Pier in the face. Walker dearly wanted to jump down into the garden and join the mayhem but felt inhibited by his position as a consultant medical oncologist. However, one of his senior colleagues, Holland Xavier, did not have the same reservations. Xavier launched himself off the veranda with a yell and joined Mathijssen in an assault against half a dozen of the female staff.

Another tall lanky man, Peter Schäfer, attempted to come to the men's rescue. 'We must outflank them,' he cried in a thick European accent. But his shots were way off mark, missing the knot of women completely. They returned a barrage of snow that quickly covered his head and shoulders and caused him to run to the bottom of the stairs, his long arms trying vainly to protect his grinning face.

Soon it was all over. The three men retreated to the cover of the veranda, cowering together and laughing hilariously as the women continued to pelt them mercilessly from the garden below.

'Okay, I think you have made your point, ladies,' said Tania Forcett, the head of medical oncology, a fifty-something woman with short hair, thick eyebrows and a wide smile.

Still laughing and jibing each other, the group began to move inside and make their way down a corridor to a large meeting room. Tables had been placed in a U-shape and an overhead projector was positioned at the front, ready for the meeting.

'If I could get you all to take a seat, please,' Forcett called from the front of the room. 'Don't be too particular about where – I'll be moving you all around presently.'

Grumbling and murmuring, the group finally seated themselves. Walker grabbed a spot next to Madeline Piper, the new radiation oncologist. He guessed she was three or four years younger than him, fair-haired, wearing a dress with a pattern that reminded him of peacock feathers. She turned and smiled at him when he sat beside her, revealing dimples.

Forcett switched on the projector and placed a plastic sheet on the glass top. Projected onto the screen was the word 'Agenda' with a list of items beneath it.

Walker ran his eye down the text and let out a soft groan. 'Bloody role-playing. I knew it.'

Xavier, who was sitting on Walker's other side, called out gleefully, 'Excellent. I love role-playing. I want to play the part of the obnoxious consultant.'

Everyone laughed and a few exchanged smirks and whispers.

'No one wants to say the obvious, Xavier,' said Walker with a grin.

Xavier pulled his mouth down in an exaggerated fashion – 'Whatever do you mean?' – drawing another laugh from the room.

'Thank you, Dr Xavier,' said Forcett in the voice of a school mistress. 'Any more disruption and I will be forced to sit you in the corner.'

Still smiling, Xavier threw up his hands. 'Just like high school. Always being picked on.'

Walker chuckled and heard a girlish giggle from Madeline, which made him beam. After everything that had happened over the last months, it would be a relief to be with someone with a bubbly disposition who knew nothing about his horrid past.

Midmorning, Walker and Madeline entertained the room with their communication role-play, Walker playing the part of a newly diagnosed cancer patient and Madeline a bombastic surgeon with a terrible bedside manner. Madeline laid it on thick, pulling out all the terrible one-liners that surgeons were well known for (but rarely actually said).

We managed to get it all.

It won't hurt at all.

Why didn't you see me sooner?

I'll let the oncologist tell you how long you have to live.

Walker had hammed it up, pretending to be the hapless

patient. As could only happen with a group of cancer clinicians getting together, the more appalling the surgeon's comments and the more upset the patient became, the louder the laughs. Every person in the room had witnessed similar situations in reality, leaving them feeling helpless and despondent for their patient. Now was the time for catharsis. To laugh at the horror. Forcett had made sure none of the hotel staff entered the room during that time. They wouldn't understand.

Ninety minutes later, they broke for morning tea and made their way into the main lounge to congregate around a table where cakes, tea and coffee had been set for them.

Walker reached past Madeline and grabbed a slice of carrot cake. 'So what do people call you? Maddie?'

'Madeline,' she answered distractedly.

Walker followed her gaze to see a group of police officers congregated in the reception area. 'I wonder what that's all about?'

'Let's go and see,' said Madeline.

'It's probably got nothing to do with ...' he said, his voice trailing off when he realised she was already on her way to reception. He sauntered over and hung back but Madeline went to the closest officer.

'What's this all about?' he heard her say. He edged closer.

'A body,' answered the young officer. He seemed only too pleased to tell her. 'Down on the bottom. Fell off the cliff.'

'Suicide?' she asked.

'Well, if you ask me—'

'Brown, what are you doing?' barked a voice. Walker saw the speaker was an older gentleman, clearly the commanding officer.

'Nothing, sir.'

'Stand over there away from that young woman,' said the officer, gesturing towards the front door.

The older policeman came over to Walker and Madeline. 'And you two would be?'

'Drs Piper and Walker,' Madeline replied firmly. 'From

Western Meadows Hospital. Do you need any assistance?'

'And what are you doing here?'

'Team-building weekend,' said Walker.

The officer glared at the group congregated around the morning-tea table. 'Who's in charge?'

Before Walker could reply, Madeline spoke, 'What makes you think it's not one of us?'

The officer glanced at Madeline then Walker and appeared to dismiss them, then looked back towards the group.

'Dr Tania Forcett,' said Walker, pointing towards her.

The officer glanced at Madeline once more then strode to where Forcett was standing. Words were exchanged and Forcett nodded.

She turned to the group. 'Can I ask you all to return to the room immediately? Senior Constable Webb has something to tell us.'

When they were all seated, Webb said, 'A body was found on Federation Pass this morning by a bushwalker. There is evidence that the deceased had fallen from the top of the cliff, probably from Echo Point.'

A murmur arose from the group and Webb waited for them to settle. 'The deceased has been identified as,' he glanced at his notepad, 'Solomon Krantz. He was a guest at this hotel.'

This raised an even bigger commotion as people began to discuss the situation. Again, Webb waited calmly until the room was silent. 'We will be interviewing all guests at the hotel, including all of you.'

'Was he pushed?' asked Jenny. 'Or did he jump?'

Webb examined her for some moments. 'And what makes you think they're the only two options?'

'Well, I doubt he would have slipped. He would have had to be on the wrong side of the fence.'

Webb addressed the room again. 'I don't want any discussion between you. My officers will need to interview each of you individually. I ask you all to return to your rooms and to stay there until you are called.'

'So our team meeting is cancelled?' asked Pier, his Dutch accent obvious.

'What about lunch?' asked Xavier.

Forcett stood to take control. 'Our workshop will be cancelled. I'll ask the hotel staff to serve everyone lunch in their rooms. Hopefully, if all the interviews are finished by this afternoon …' she turned to Webb, who nodded, 'then we'll be able to gather for dinner in the restaurant as planned.'

With that they began to file from the room, many of them sharing excited whispers.

'Remember, no talking to each other,' Webb called, cutting the conversations short.

Walker raised his eyebrows at Madeline but kept quiet as they moved together through the door

CHAPTER THREE

THAT NIGHT THEY gathered in the hotel restaurant for dinner, sitting together at two tables on the top floor of an old colonial building separate to the main hotel. Each of them had been interviewed by the police and now everyone wanted to compare notes.

'They don't think it was suicide,' proclaimed Jenny. 'They found broken branches at the top, which he'd grabbed as he fell. Either he slipped—'

'Or he was pushed,' added Xavier, completing her story.

'How do you two know that?' asked Walker. 'They wouldn't tell me anything.'

'I just asked,' said Jenny. 'When it was clear that I had nothing to do with it, the officer was happy to spill the beans.'

'Apparently, he was a lawyer from Brisbane, of all places,' said Jenny.

'What was he doing here?' asked Walker, who was seated next to Madeline.

'On holidays, I suppose,' said Jenny.

'It's all a bit strange,' said Madeline. 'What was he doing at Echo Point at night, in the middle of the fog? He wouldn't have been able to see anything.'

'He told front reception that he was going for a walk. They didn't notice that he hadn't returned.'

Walker addressed Jenny. 'What did the cops ask you?'

'Same as you, I suppose. Why was I here? What had I done last evening? Had I left the hotel?'

'What did you say?'

Jenny rolled her eyes. 'I told them I ran down the road and threw him off the cliff. What do you think?' Those at the table laughed. 'I hadn't gone anywhere, you know that, Chris. You and I sat in the lounge all afternoon drinking tea, which led on to the cocktail party.'

'They gave me a hard time initially,' said Xavier. 'I'd walked down to Katoomba shops to buy a jacket. Didn't realise it was going to be so cold. Walked back in the pea-soup. Almost got lost.'

'I must agree, the fog was exceptionally thick,' said Peter Schäfer. 'Even in Switzerland we do not get it this thick. In winter we get the Hochnebel but it's not like this. And we have high mountains so we can take the train to get above it.'

'So you were out too?' asked Madeline.

'Yes, I went to get some fresh air. I also went for a walk to Katoomba shops.'

'Did you?' said Xavier. 'I didn't see you.'

'See *me*? I couldn't see my own hand in front of my face. I was lucky to make it back in one piece. It would have been easy to get lost.'

'What about you, Madeline?' asked Xavier. 'Did you go out?'

'Me? No. I rested in my room until the cocktail party. I was pretty beat.' She smiled and leaned forward conspiratorially. 'Well, that explains all of us.' She flicked her eyes to the end of table where Tania Forcett was engaged in conversation with a young dark-haired woman while Pier Mathijssen listened intently beside her. 'If there's anything suspicious, it's those two.'

'Which two?' asked Walker. 'You mean Pier and—'

'I agree,' interrupted Xavier quietly. 'Élodie Segal and Tania.'

'What do you mean?' said Walker. He peeked at the pair as

he sipped from his wineglass. The young woman was very pretty and petite with a sweet face and dark eyes that matched her hair.

'Why would we invite a French medical student to a team-building weekend?' said Xavier. 'She's only been in the country a few weeks.'

'Well, she's very easy on the eye for a start,' said Walker.

'That's not a reason,' said Madeline shortly.

Walker was taken aback. He felt he'd touched a nerve.

'That's closer to the truth than you think,' said Xavier in a low voice. 'Beautiful Élodie is just Tania's type.'

Walker screwed up his face. 'What?'

'What do you think I mean?' said Xavier. He widened his eyes meaningfully. 'You *know* what I mean.'

Walker stared along the table at his head of department, his mouth open. 'You mean …'

'Don't tell me you didn't know, Chris,' said Jenny in a loud voice.

Walker leaned back. 'Not at all. I had no idea.'

'You're such an idiot sometimes,' she said.

Madeline was now studying Tania Forcett carefully. 'That's very interesting. Good to know.'

'What? That Chris is an idiot or that Tania is gay?' said Jenny.

Madeline turned back to them, smiling. 'Both.'

Tania was now looking along the table towards them. 'I think we should change the subject,' Xavier said through tight lips.

'Tell us about yourself, Madeline,' said Walker, happy to oblige. 'What brings you to Western Meadows?'

'Me?' She didn't appear shy about talking about herself. 'I'm a radiation oncologist, obviously. Grew up in Brisbane. Did medicine at Mayne Medical School. Internship and RMO years at Princess Alexandra, then advanced training in radiation oncology and then worked in England for a year. Went back to Brisbane and now doing a locum at Western Meadows for the rad onc head of department, who's on long service leave for six months.'

'Nicely summarised,' said Xavier. 'I wish our trainees could be so succinct.'

'Plenty of practice lately with all the toing and froing overseas, then the interviews for the locum job.'

'So if you lived in Brisbane,' said Xavier with a grin, 'you must have known the murdered man.'

'Oh, yes,' said Madeline, matter-of-factly. 'We all know each other in Brisbane. Just like you know everyone in Sydney.'

'Don't be stupid Xavier,' said Jenny. She turned to Madeline. 'We want to know much more interesting stuff than that rubbish.'

'Oh?' said Madeline with a wry smile.

'Like, are you single? Are you here by yourself?'

Madeline didn't seem taken aback by Jenny's forwardness. 'No, still single.' She glanced at Walker. 'But not celibate.'

Walker noticed that Jenny had caught the look. The nurse smiled but thankfully said nothing.

'Any siblings?' asked Jenny.

'No,' came the fast reply. 'None. I have no relatives. My mother died recently.'

'Oh, I'm so sorry,' said Walker.

'MVA,' she said. 'A drunk hit her from behind. She died in the hospital.'

'That's terrible,' said Jenny. 'And your father?'

'Left when I was young.'

'Okay, now I think we're getting too personal,' said Walker. 'Let's stop the interrogation.'

'I don't mind,' Madeline said with a smile. 'Especially since I'm going do the same to you lot.'

To Walker's relief, the first course arrived, interrupting the conversation. Talk turned to the quality of the food and comparisons with other restaurants they'd recently visited.

After the main course, Jenny, Xavier and Schäfer became engrossed in a conversation about international holidays, leaving Walker and Madeline to themselves.

'So what about you?' asked Madeline. 'It's your turn to be hauled over the coals.'

'Don't you mean have the screws put on?'

'Maybe. So, where did you grow up?'

'Here in Sydney. In The Rocks. I still live there.'

'And did you do all your training here?'

'Mostly.' He paused. He didn't want to mention his time in New Guinea. That might lead to uncomfortable questions. 'Here and there, but mostly Sydney.'

He thought that Madeline sensed there was more to be said, but thankfully she didn't press. 'Family?'

'Like you. None.'

Madeline waited for him to elucidate.

He spoke quickly. 'I have no brothers or sisters. My father died about seven years ago from lung cancer. My mother died when I was a child.'

'Really? How old were you?'

'Four or five. Something like that.'

'That's so sad. What did she die from?'

Walker paused in thought. 'Cancer too. My father was very upset for years. Never wanted to speak about it. I remember she was very sad and then she was gone. Dad said she'd been taken to hospital and was never coming back. I don't remember much about her.'

'So we're similar in some ways. You grew up without a mother and I without a father.'

'I guess so.' He turned to her but she seemed lost in thought. He realised he felt a connection, something he hadn't experienced with Cassandra. Not even with Flea. A shared loss. He remembered what Madeline had said about her not being celibate—a strange thing to emphasise, he thought. He waited until her attention returned.

'Do you want to have a drink later?'

She shook her head. 'I don't think that's—'

'Come on, you two,' Jen interrupted loudly. 'This is not a

private party, you know. Join in. We're talking about overseas trips. Weren't you in the UK, Madeline?'

'Yes, I was. Manchester. I trained at the Christie and did some research at the Holt Radium Institute.'

'What was that like?'

'Interesting. Wet. Long summers. Lots of castles. Great research.'

'Were you there for long?'

'Over a year. I came back when my mother died.' She moved on quickly. 'I was back in Brisbane and looking around for something to do when this locum came up.' She raised her palms. 'And here I am.'

'Do you know anyone in Sydney?' asked Xavier.

'Not a soul.'

'Well, we'll have to be your new friends,' said Jenny. 'We'll show you round.' She gestured at Walker. 'I'm sure Chris here would love to take you around the sights in the city.'

'Of course,' said Walker. 'Anytime. There are some nice pubs in The Rocks.'

Madeline smiled. 'I might just take you up on that.'

CHAPTER FOUR

IT WAS MONDAY morning and Western Meadows Hospital was in full swing. It had been a busy weekend for the Emergency Department and the wards were full with new admissions. The cold weather had hung on and rain and wind had started and all the staff were feeling particularly miserable.

Christopher Walker had come to the ward early to do a round so his new registrar could settle in. Pier Mathijssen had replaced Angela Chee after she'd gone to Singapore. Her leaving halfway through the year had left them in a difficult situation. It had proved impossible to find a replacement in Australia and they were given permission to enlist from overseas. Pier had the necessary experience on paper, having completed his training in the Netherlands Cancer Institute, but Walker couldn't expect him to know the routine of an Australian hospital. To make matters worse, the junior doctors were rotating and they were due to get a new intern that day. Two new doctors on the ward was a recipe for disaster, and Walker felt obliged to oversee things closely until he was sure they were on top of things.

Walker and Pier stood near the nurses' station talking to Jenny as they waited for their new intern. Nearby was the tall figure of Peter Schäfer, the Swiss radiation oncology fellow, who was waiting for his boss, Madeline Piper. Élodie Segal arrived and Schäfer greeted her. She wore a short white coat, marking her a medical student. In the full light of day, Walker noted that she was older than he'd first thought. She had smooth skin and deep dark eyes but he guessed she was probably in her early thirties.

Schäfer welcomed her. '*Bonjour*, Élodie.' He pronounced her name with a melodic flair.

'*Salut*, Peter.' She smiled at the rest of the group. 'Good morning, everyone.'

Walker thought to himself how international the oncology team had become. Most of the doctors in the hospital were of Asian or Anglo descent but almost all were born or schooled in Australia and hearing so many European accents was a novelty.

'You know,' said Schäfer, 'I came here because of the promise of a warm country with plentiful sunshine. I wanted a break from the long Swiss winters. But I don't think I can remember being as cold as I was over the weekend. Don't you Australians know how to warm a house properly? I had to sleep with a woollen hat.'

'A beanie,' said Jenny.

'I beg your pardon?'

'The woollen hat,' said Jenny. 'It's called a beanie.'

'A beanie then. And long woollen socks. I had to wear a jacket around the house.' He shook his head. 'I thought I'd come to a civilised country.'

'Stiff upper lip, old chap,' said Pier in an exaggerated English accent.

'Excuse me?' said Schäfer.

'Chin up,' said Pier, continuing in the same voice. 'Hope for the best, and all that. Always look on the bright side of life.'

Jenny laughed.

Schäfer stared at the Dutchman. 'Are you mad? What the devil are you talking about?'

'I'm being British,' said Pier, smiling.

'What on earth for?'

He shrugged. 'Just thought it was appropriate. What about

you, Élodie? How are you coping with the antipodean winter?'

'So far, okay, I think. The hospital accommodation is well-heated.'

'Where's our new intern?' said Walker, turning his attention to the ward entrance. 'Not making a good first impression.'

'Apparently he had to go pick up his pager from switchboard,' said Jenny. 'Go easy on him, Chris. You know what happened with our last intern.'

Walker didn't answer and turned towards the door again to see Madeline Piper entering. She bounced as she walked, reminding him of an energetic teenager. He wondered whether she was putting it on. Madeline noticed the group looking at her and she came straight to them. 'What's this, a welcoming party?'

'Waiting for our new intern,' said Walker. 'I think we're sharing him so we'll have a competition to see our patients.'

'I've only got one,' said Madeline. 'Peter and I can see her by ourselves.'

'Thanks, that's appreciated,' said Walker. 'We've got four new admissions.'

'If you don't mind me saying, I've always loved the name Madeline,' said Jenny. 'In an old house in Paris,' she recited, 'that was covered with vines, lived twelve little girls, in two straight lines. The smallest one was Madeline.' She finished with a laugh.

Madeline rolled her eyes. 'Thanks, Jenny,' she said flatly, although she too was smiling.

Élodie looked confused. 'Did you live in Paris?'

Madeline frowned. 'No, it's a children's book.'

'I'll explain it to you later, Élodie,' said Schäfer. 'Everyone thinks it's French but it's actually American.'

A lanky young man with a mess of orange hair and wearing a long white coat strode up to them. 'So sorry I'm late.'

'Ah,' said Walker. 'Our new intern. And you would be?'

'Benjamin Casey.'

Walker was silent for a moment. 'Are you pulling my leg?'

'You're kidding,' said Jenny, laughing again. 'Ben Casey?'

He looked sheepish. 'I'm afraid so. My mother wanted me to be a doctor.'

'Looks like it worked then,' said Walker.

'What are you talking about?' said Pier.

'*Ben Casey*?' Jenny turned to him with glee. 'The TV show?'

Pier looked at Schäfer and Élodie, who returned blank looks.

'It's an American soapie,' explained Walker. 'The doctor was called …' He paused at the bewildered look on Élodie's face. 'Look, it really doesn't matter. Let's get on with the round.'

The first patient was an elderly man who was lying curled up in his bed with the covers pulled over his head.

'Mr Evans,' said Ben, placing his hand on the man's shoulder. 'Dr Walker has come to see you. Do you mind waking up?'

'Bugger off,' came the reply from beneath the blanket.

'What's the problem?' asked Walker of the intern. 'Check the notes.'

Ben flicked through the chart. 'Came in confused. Found on the floor of his flat by a neighbour. Known to have metastatic prostate cancer. Bilateral orchidectomy two years ago.' He flicked over the page. 'Septic screen in Emergency was negative. We're awaiting blood cultures.'

Walker nodded. 'Blood tests? Biochemistry?'

Ben flicked to the back of the folder. 'Nothing here. I'll check the in-tray.' As he scurried off to the nurses' station, Walker bent over and placed a gentle hand on the blanket where he guessed the patient's shoulder would be. 'Mr Evans, we're trying to find out why you've become ill. Do you mind talking to us?'

There was a moan, then fingers appeared on the edge of the blanket, an arm flung back, then a frowning face pointed in his direction. 'Whadaya want?'

'Do you have any pain?'

'Course I've got pain. What do ya think I came in for? Back's killing me.'

The man's hair was long and dishevelled and stuck out like an untidy bird's nest. He licked flaky lips and pointed a hooked nose at Walker accusingly. 'Are ya gonna help me or what?'

'Of course we will. We just need more information.' Walker glanced up at Pier then back again. 'How long have you had the pain?'

Mr Evans pulled the covers back over his head. 'I don't fricken know. Bugger off.'

Ben returned with a sheaf of paper. 'His blood calcium's up. Three point five.'

'Phew,' said Pier. 'That's high. Enough to make him confused.'

Walker stood up. 'Fair enough. If we treat that it might also help his bone pain.'

'He has bone mets from his prostate cancer,' said Pier, flicking through the notes. 'Probably the cause of his high blood calcium.'

'Really?' said Walker. 'Prostate cancer doesn't make your calcium go up.'

'But the bone destruction from the cancer,' said Pier, 'that's enough.'

'No, it's not. Hypercalcaemia of malignancy is not due to bone metastases. It's due to PTHrP.'

'What?'

'Jack Martin in Melbourne has just identified it. Primitive version of parathyroid hormone. It's probably involved in pregnancy. The foetus gets calcium from the mother through the placenta using PTHrP. Some cancers make it, like breast and lung cancer. I bet you prostate cancer doesn't.' Walker turned to his intern. 'Ben, take an EDTA tube of blood. We'll send it to Jack Martin. He's got an assay.'

'What's causing it then?' asked Pier.

'Just old fashioned PTH.'

'Hyperparathyroidism?'

'It's the most common cause. Probably Mr Evans already had it, then got back pain from his prostate cancer, took painkillers, got constipated then dehydrated.'

'Vicious circle,' said Pier. 'Can't excrete calcium due to the dehydration.'

'You got it,' said Walker. 'Ben, get a drip going. Who knows why he's not on IV fluids already? Rehydrate him, then we can think about pamidronate later.'

'Will do,' said Ben, who moved off to do as ordered.

CHAPTER FIVE

AFTER THE THIRD patient, Walker came out of the room and noticed Madeline, Peter and Élodie gathered together at the nurses' station.

'All finished?' he asked.

Madeline nodded. 'We're heading for a coffee. Want to come?'

'Can't. Still have a few to see.' As Madeline turned away, he called after her, 'But how about I show you one of the pubs in the city?'

She turned back. 'Sure. When?'

'I'm free tonight.'

'Why not. I've got nothing on.'

'Where are you living?'

'Epping. I'm renting a flat.'

Walker's heart dropped. Why Epping of all places? Where Angela used to live. And where Cassie still lived.

'You're in The Rocks,' said Madeline. 'I'll catch a train in.'

Walker realised he should offer to drive her but she'd probably want to go to her flat first. 'Sure. The trains are safe. I'll meet you at Circular Quay and we can walk up together. How about seven?'

'Seven it is. See you then.'

As Madeline and her team left, Walker noticed a familiar

pair coming in through the ward entrance. Curious, he waited at the station.

'Detective Barry Darling,' Jenny announced. 'What brings you here? Not another murder I hope.'

Walker nodded a greeting to the detective. 'Wendy.' He then addressed the uniformed police officer who was a step behind. 'And Constable Bianca. What can we do for you both?' Walker remembered Thelma Bianca as the constable who worked with Royce Wills on the last murder in the hospital.

'It's about the death at Katoomba,' said Darling.

'Death,' said Walker. 'If you two are involved then I guess murder is suspected.'

'Why?' asked Jenny.

'Haven't you heard?' said Walker. 'Detective Darling has been promoted and moved to the homicide squad in the city. Senior Detective Sergeant now.'

'Congratulations,' said Jenny. 'So they think it's murder?'

Darling nodded. 'We need to go back over the questions with everyone who was at the hotel. The Katoomba police are covering the locals and we have you lot to contend with. I've already met with Dr Forcett who supplied me with a list of the attendees. I thought we might as well start with you.' He consulted his notebook then glanced at Pier. 'From the description you would be Doctor ...' Darling was obviously struggling with the surname.

'It's pronounced Mat-ia-ssen.'

'Ah, yes, I can see that now. You're Dutch, is that right?'

'Yes, I am.'

Darling nodded then looked at Ben. 'Were you there also?'

'No,' interrupted Walker. 'Ben has only started today as our intern.'

'Right then,' said Darling. He flipped his notebook shut and with a swipe of his arm indicated Walker, Pier and Jenny. 'We'll start with you three.'

'We haven't finished our ward round yet,' said Walker. 'Can't it wait?'

'What about you, Jenny?' asked Darling. 'Do you have ten minutes? We need to go over your statement again.'

She threw a questioning look at Walker. 'Sure, Jenny,' he said. 'We can carry on without you.'

Two hours later, with the ward round and police questioning behind him, Walker made his way back to the medical oncology office, deep in thought. After he'd finished the formal interview where he just repeated what he'd told the Katoomba police, Wendy had walked out with him, leaving Detective Bianca alone in the interview room.

Wendy had come close to him and said in a low voice, 'There's another issue I need to talk to you about, Kit.' When Walker asked what it was about, Wendy had been circumspect. 'Something in the past. A long while ago. But I need to see you about it. Alone. I'll come to your office later.'

As Walker neared his office now, he noticed two figures further along. The corridor was over two hundred metres long and the pair halfway down but he recognised them – Madeline and Pier. They appeared to be deep in conversation, Pier standing close to her, gesticulating. He looked threatening. Madeline held her place, arms folded. As far as Walker could see, she didn't say anything. When Pier had finished he turned quickly and walked towards him. Walker pretended to fiddle with his key and waited until Pier reached him.

'Everything okay, Pier?'

'What? Oh, the police. I just told them again what I said at the hotel. I was in my room the whole afternoon.'

'No, not that. You and Madeline. You seemed to be having a serious conversation just now.'

Pier appeared taken aback and looked back up the corridor, but Madeline had gone. 'No, not at all. I think you are mistaken.' He let out a short laugh. 'I was actually telling her a joke. But she didn't get it. I think it was lost in translation.'

Walker was silent for a moment. 'Some joke. You'll have to try it on me sometime.'

Pier smiled. 'No, I am clearly not a very good comedian. I think I will leave that to the professionals.'

Walker watched until he disappeared around the next corner. He certainly was tall and good-looking. Maybe Madeline and Pier had something going on. But they'd both only arrived less than a month ago, and he'd hardly ever seen them together until now. Even on the mountain retreat, they seemed to have little to do with each other.

He entered his office, flopped down into the chair and began to check the blood test results in his in-tray. A moment later there was a knock on the door. Wendy.

Walker examined him as Wendy fiddled with his notebook – looked of Mediterranean extraction, snappy dresser. But Walker knew Wendy didn't know who his parents were. He was an orphan.

He seemed hesitant, as if he didn't know where to start. 'How's things otherwise, Kit?'

'Fine. Nothing much different.' Walker knew he hadn't come for idle conversation but gave him no help.

'I heard Angela left for Singapore.'

Walker nodded. He didn't really want to talk about her. 'Went to live with her family.'

Darling was silent again. Walker wondered what he'd really come for.

'And Cassie? You still seeing her?' Wendy finally asked.

Walker bit his jaw down. So this is what it was about. Wendy's old girlfriend. 'No, not much,' he said tightly.

'Really? I thought you'd be living together by now. You seemed pretty hot for each other.'

'No, not really. What's it to you, anyway? Still interested?'

'Me? No. I'm the happiest man in the world. I'm with a lovely woman by the name of Sally. She's a nurse. Moved in with me.'

Walker felt relieved, then also bad about being so boorish. 'Oh, that's right,' he said, trying to show interest. 'You've got yourself a place in Glebe. Any good?'

'Beautiful little terrace, two-bedder. Needs a bit of work but a good investment.'

'Good for you, Wendy.' Walker meant it. He was tired of fighting with his old friend. 'I wish you both luck. How serious is it?'

'Well, we're taking it slow for now. But you never know, she might be the one.' Darling paused then seemed to make a decision. He thrust his notebook back into his pocket. 'I really came about another issue.'

'Oh? What?'

'It's a cold case,' said Darling. 'From 1960. A dockworker was murdered.'

'What's that got to do with me?'

'Not you.' Wendy scratched his chin. He was hesitant again. 'Your father.'

'My father? What are you talking about?'

'Like I said, 1960. A fellow got stabbed in a back lane in The Rocks. High Lane.'

'I know it. Behind the Captain Cook. Who?'

'John Leremy. Also went by the name of Two-Face Leremy.'

'Never heard of him. What's that got to do with my father?'

'A crim in Long Bay has given us some information that has allowed us to reopen the case.'

'What?'

'He says he saw Lester Walker and Leremy having a heated argument in the Captain Cook Hotel on the night of the murder.'

'Lester Walker? You mean my father?'

Darling nodded.

'After thirty years? Why now?'

'He's up for parole. Wants to be seen in a good light. Wants to do a deal.'

'You surely can't believe him. My father's dead. He can't defend himself. The bloke's lying. Why should you believe him?'

'It's the reason he gave for the fight. And another con backs it up.'

'What reason?'

Darling became tentative again. 'It's about your mum. He says the fight was over your mother. They say your father started it.'

'What are you saying? 1960? That's the year my mother died.' Walker thought for a moment. 'Are you saying this jerk had something to do with my mother's death?'

Darling shook his head. 'I'm sorry, Kit, it's not about that.'

'What then? Out with it, Wendy. Stop messing about.'

'He says that your mum and Leremy were having an affair. That everyone knew. That your father had it out with him in the pub that night.'

Walker jumped to his feet. 'Bullshit! That's just bullshit, Wendy, and you know it. How can you believe such crap? You knew my mother. Tell that deadshit to crawl back into his hole and die.'

Darling had stepped back towards the door. 'Sorry, Kit. I thought you'd better hear it from me before the other plods come after you. I'm not directly involved. I heard about it and thought I should tell you first. I really shouldn't have done this.'

Walker clenched his fists and turned away, seething. 'Tell them all to get stuffed,' he said, his voice hoarse. 'This is total bullshit.'

Darling backed out through the door. 'I'm really sorry, Kit.' He closed the door behind him, leaving Walker alone.

CHAPTER SIX

WALKER MET MADELINE at Circular Quay railway station just after 7 pm that evening. He'd got there fifteen minutes early, feeling guilty that he hadn't offered to drive her, but she seemed happy when she arrived. He watched as she bounced down the stairs from the platform. Her skirt flipped as she walked, showing off toned legs, and she gave a wave and smiled brightly when she saw him. As she came close, he hesitated, unsure of whether to shake her hand or kiss her cheek.

She hung back, still smiling. 'So where are you taking me?'

'One or two pubs, as promised. The first is the Fortune.'

'Sounds good. What is it? A gambling joint?'

'Hardly. The Fortune of War. They reckon they're the oldest pub in Sydney, but so do a few others around here.'

After a short walk along George Street, Madeline paused outside. The Fortune of War was a narrow building with dark green tiles on the external walls between two open doors. 'Looks old all right. Was it a public lavatory before it was a pub?'

Inside was dark and dingy with a few old blokes dressed in singlets and shorts leaning on the bar. A bouncer stood at the door.

'Is it safe?' she asked.

'Of course. Don't worry about appearances. It keeps the riffraff away.'

They found an empty table on the edge of the room under a painting of an old sailing ship and Madeline sat and waited while Walker got the drinks. The old blokes at the bar surreptitiously examined Madeline over the lip of their schooners.

'Bit of a looker, Kit,' said one to Walker when he reached the counter.

'What happened to young Cassie?' said another.

Walker ignored them.

He returned with their drinks and they clinked their glasses – his a schooner of pilsner, hers a Cinzano and Coke.

'Long time since I've had one of those,' said Walker, pointing to her drink.

'Just felt like it.' She took a sip. 'Reminds me of my teenage years.'

'Oh yeah? I bet you were a tearaway.'

'No, not at all. I was a good girl. Studied hard. I was close to my mum. She needed looking after.'

'Was she sick?'

Madeline laughed. 'Not at all. Fit as a Mallee bull. Too fit, that was her problem. She worked so hard to care for me. I tried to get her to limit how much time she spent on her business. After I started work, I kept telling her that we didn't need the money anymore. Didn't do any good. I think she loved her work.'

'Father?' he asked before remembering she'd already said he left when she was young.

She didn't seem to mind. 'Just Mum and me. Never met my father.'

Walker wanted to ask more about her father but held back. The conversation was getting too deep, too quickly. 'What did your mum do?'

'She had her own business. Interior design. Quite successful.'

A musician had set himself up in the corner near the door and began strumming a few distinctive chords. The pair turned their attention to him.

'Crowded House,' said Walker.

'"Don't Dream It's Over",' she said. 'It was one of Mum's favourites.' She paused, thoughtful. 'I've played it a lot lately.'

'You said it was a car accident.'

'Drunk driver. She was driving home from Southport from one of her suppliers. Died soon after in hospital. Ruptured spleen.'

'Shocking.'

'Mm.' She took a sip. 'But what about you? You said your mother died when you were young.'

Walker took a long gulp of his schooner. He didn't want to talk about his mother, especially after what Darling had said about her. He looked over at the musician. 'Getting pretty loud in here. Do you want to move on? The Orient's just up the road. Has a beer garden out back.'

Madeline glanced at her drink which was only half gone. 'Okay. If you like.' She reached out a hand. 'We don't have to talk about your mother if you don't want to. I know what it's like with everyone prying.'

He looked down out her outstretched hand. He wanted to take it but something was stopping him. 'No, it's not that.'

The hand went up to her glass. 'What then?' The compassion she had shown in her voice was now gone.

'Wendy.'

'Was that her name?'

'What? No. I mean Barry Darling. You know, the copper who came and interviewed us at the hospital.'

'What about him?'

'He and I go back a long way. Grew up together. That's the nickname I gave him. Can't seem to lose it.' He was silent as he thought about Cassie. 'Annoys some people.'

'So, what's he got to do with your mother?'

'He said something about her yesterday. Thrown me off.

Total bullshit.' He stood up abruptly. 'Anyway, should we go?'

'Looks like it.' She took another sip then put her bag over her shoulder. 'You lead the way.'

That night, for the first time in a long while, Walker couldn't sleep. The rest of the evening with Madeline was uneventful, mostly small talk about living in Sydney versus Brisbane. He knew he'd killed the mood with his reaction about the business with Wendy and his mother. By nine, Madeline had said she needed to get to bed early since she had an early start, so he walked her to the station and they waved their goodbyes.

Lying in bed, he stared at the reflected headlight of cars on the ceiling as they drove along Lower Fort Street. He tried to remember his mother. He had vague memories, feelings rather than images. He was only five at the time, maybe younger. He remembered she had thick wavy hair to her shoulders. Auburn. Or was it black? She'd been sad a lot of the time. Crying. His father had been upset. They hadn't fought. Never shouted at each other. Surely if his father had caught her having an affair, they'd have argued. The house wasn't big. Walker would have heard.

The sadness had dragged on for a long time. Then she was gone. His father said she'd been admitted to hospital, that she was sick. That she wasn't coming back anymore. The neighbours were kind, cooking them meals and babysitting him when his father was at work. His father had gone to church a few times, something Walker had never seen him do before. And not since, for that matter.

Walker had started school around then. Or was it before? It was all a jumble. But around that time he met Barry Darling and they became close friends. Darling didn't have a mother either, not like the other kids at school. They felt like brothers. Orphans. Walker's father was hardly ever home, having to work most of the time, so all he'd had was his brother. Later, there was Flea, but for a long time there was only Wendy.

Maybe his mother did have an affair?

He heaved himself upright on the side of his bed. 'This is bullshit.' His dad had said she'd died of cancer. The neighbours said it too.

He could remember going to be the beach with his father – Palm Beach. He remembered the sign as they drove in. They'd thrown stuff into the sea. Flowers. Ashes. He remembered sitting on the rocks and watching the waves wash the flowers in and out on the sand while his father wandered up to the lighthouse. Some of the flowers got caught in a rip and drifted out to sea. He'd followed them for a long time. First time he'd ever seen a rip.

No, she'd died all right. But maybe she also had an affair. But did people do that? Have affairs when they were dying from cancer? He didn't think so. He'd cared for hundreds of dying cancer patients but he couldn't remember any of them having an affair just before they died.

He laughed out aloud. 'Why would they tell me?'

Maybe he should start asking them? For some reason, this ridiculous thought comforted him and he slumped back into bed, a half-smile on his face. Soon he was asleep.

CHAPTER SEVEN

DETECTIVE SERGEANT BARRY Darling, hands in his pockets, stood at the second-floor window of the Parramatta Police Station staring at the deluge of rain that had started falling half an hour ago. On the street below, a man ambled past wearing shorts and sneakers and a large garbage bag over his upper body with a hole torn in one end for his head. A woman with an umbrella, wearing a long yellow raincoat and high heels, dashed along in the opposite direction leading a dark-haired poodle on a leash and splashing water up onto her ankles as she went. A bedraggled man with a fag hanging out of his mouth – one of the homeless by Darling's reckoning – stood on the curb opposite, staring down at the rainwater that rushed along the gutter, heedless of the rain that soaked his long, matted hair and dirty tracksuit. It looked cold out but Darling felt snug and warm. He wished he had a cigarette to puff on but he'd given them up years ago. After Felicity died. He laughed to himself. *What does that have to do with anything?* He wondered what Kit was up to. Probably swanning around the hospital, as usual. He stirred and scratched his head, knowing he was being unkind. He had made his peace with Walker but old habits died hard.

Darling had recently been promoted to the homicide squad housed at head office in the CBD of Sydney but had moved back to the Parramatta station to investigate Krantz's murder.

He was glad he'd got away. The politics of the place was starting to become oppressive. The Queensland Police had just been gutted by the Fitzgerald Inquiry and there was talk of a similar corruption inquiry for New South Wales. Barriers were going up left, right and centre and no one was talking about anything contentious. The tension was painful.

He turned and walked to where Thelma Bianca stood before a bare corkboard, the same one that Darling had used on previous cases. He felt at home. Back then it was Constable David Jones doing the hack work but now he had Thelma Bianca. He wondered how Jones was going with his promotion. He felt sorry for him since he had to work with Senior Detective Sergeant Royce Wills, who'd been moved sideways into the cold cases section after Darling's success. Wills would never forgive him, and Darling just hoped he didn't take it out on Jones.

He looked at his new subordinate – petite, blonde and pretty in her own way. She was also proving to be very sharp.

'What have we got, Bianca?'

She pinned a photo in the top left corner of the board – a middle-aged man with dark curly hair, slightly oiled. 'The deceased is Solomon Krantz, a solicitor from Brisbane. He fell from the clifftop at Echo Point and fractured his neck, dying almost immediately.'

'So the killer had to be strong,' said Darling. 'The fence meant he had to be thrown over.'

Bianca nodded. 'So probably a man. He had arrived at the hotel that day and, according to the front desk staff, had not gone out until the evening.'

'There was no record of phones calls in or out of his room and no one saw him meet anyone, so the killer is most likely a guest in the hotel.'

'Or one of the staff,' added Bianca.

Darling grunted agreement. 'Most of the hotel was booked out by the Western Meadows group. The local team is questioning the six other guests but they say they all have alibis.'

'Meaning the killer might be one of the staff of Western Meadows,' said Bianca.

'Or one of the staff,' added Darling with a smirk.

Bianca gave a gracious nod then continued. 'Krantz did mostly general legal work – contracts, business planning and estates, that sort of thing. He didn't do criminal law.'

Darling frowned but said nothing.

Bianca next tacked a piece of paper that appeared to be a photocopy. On it were a few lines in black pen. 'The deceased had this note in his coat pocket. A handwritten letter. It was not in an envelope and there was no address.'

'Hopefully forensics will give us something on the handwriting,' said Darling. 'Read it out again.'

'Vengeance is mine,' read Bianca, 'for the day of your calamity is at hand. If any harm is done to you, then you shall give an eye for eye, a life for a life. PS. I'll never forgive you for what you did.' She looked up. 'At least, that's what I think it says. The writing is atrocious.'

Darling laughed. 'Maybe a doctor's writing.'

Bianca didn't return the laugh. 'Maybe. What we don't know is whether he brought the letter with him from Brisbane or whether someone gave it to him just before his death. And we don't know what Krantz was doing in Sydney.'

'Or, more specifically, why he was staying in Katoomba in the same hotel as the crowd from the cancer unit at Western Meadows.'

'I've spoken to his secretary on the phone,' said Bianca. 'Krantz told her he was going on a holiday, not business. He didn't have any legal documents with him in his hotel room. And he doesn't have any family that we can find. Certainly no wife or children. Never been married, according to his secretary. Didn't have a girlfriend.'

'Gay?'

'Apparently not. I asked the secretary. She said no. She even asked him once herself. He'd said that he just liked to live alone.'

'Do we have any professional links with any of the cancer staff or any other guests at the hotel?'

'Krantz's secretary has faxed me a list of his clients for the last year. I'll cross-reference with the hotel guest list.'

'Good. What else?'

'He was wearing casual clothes and comfortable shoes, the sort you'd wear around a hotel room. Not made for walking a long distance. And there was a heavy fog, so not good weather for sightseeing. Echo Point was probably deserted. We can't find any witnesses.'

'Perhaps he organised to meet someone and quickly nipped out of the hotel, not expecting to be gone long.'

'The person who gave him the letter?'

'Maybe.'

'And the hotel staff said he hadn't met anyone nor talked to anyone in the lobby.'

'Correct. He'd only arrived that afternoon and went straight to his room, then told the staff he was going for a short walk.'

'Did he say where?'

'Not to reception.'

'Isn't there someone at the front door?'

'Yes, there's the porter. He remembers him arriving but doesn't remember him leaving. The porter could have been helping someone, or Krantz could have taken one of the other exits.'

'What about his luggage?'

'As I said, no legal paperwork. Just clothes, a novel and toiletry items. He was booked for two nights. His flight arrived about midday and he caught the train to Katoomba then got a taxi to the hotel. He had cash and a few credit cards in his wallet and a return air ticket for the Monday.'

'Quick holiday. And didn't even bother to go into the city. I'd say that's a bit unusual for a tourist from Brisbane.'

'Not everyone likes Sydney,' said Bianca.

'Better than Brisbane though. You'd think he'd have a look, at least, after coming all that way. Opera House, Harbour Bridge, the beautiful harbour, Kings Cross.'

'Are you a travel agent now, sir?' Before Darling could answer she continued quickly. 'Not everyone likes cities. The Blue Mountains are unique. Overseas tourists make a beeline for them.'

'But not from Brisbane. I still think it's strange. It seems to me he came for a purpose other than sightseeing. I think he specifically came to meet someone.'

'Someone at the hotel?'

'Or at least someone who was in Katoomba on that weekend.'

Bianca drew her lips tight and nodded at the corkboard. 'And someone who gave him a note threatening vengeance for something he'd done.'

'The note sounds religious.'

'An eye for an eye?'

'I think we should get further advice from an expert.'

'Who?'

'The reverend from the church near where I grew up. I'll give him a call and set up a meeting.'

'Right you are, sir. I'll start on the lists of the solicitor's clients and the hotel guests.'

CHAPTER EIGHT

THAT SATURDAY MORNING, Walker woke to a thumping sound. Some dickhead was pounding on his front door. He dragged on a dressing-gown and stomped down the stairs, holding onto the rail. His legs didn't work so well in the mornings these days.

It was Bruce Rowntree, dressed as usual in a shabby suit, the stub of a rolly hanging out the corner of his mouth. The morning sunlight bounced off his balding pate.

'What the fuck is Wendy up to, Kit?'

Walker groaned then threw open the door and went into the lounge room to slump into a chair. Bruce followed him.

'That bullshit about your mother is total bullshit.'

Walker rubbed his eyes with the palms of his hands. 'Nice to know you care, Bruce, but what's it to you?'

'I knew your mother. She was a lovely lady and I won't have her name besmirched like that.'

'Besmirched. That's a big word for a union bagman, especially so early in the day.'

'Fuck off, Kit. I'll have you know I've a fuckin' fantastic vocabulary when the occasion calls for it.'

'Thanks for the info.' Walker had to admit that having Bruce so outraged buoyed his heart.

'You might have gone to a fancy-schmancy selective school and Sydney University,' he said, stabbing Walker's chest with his thumb, 'but I've gone to the university of life. Just as bloody good.' He sucked on the cigarette perched on his bottom lip then blew out the smoke. 'Better, in fact.'

'University of New South Wales,' corrected Walker.

Another suck, another cloud. 'That fuckin' explains it.'

Walker wondered what he meant but didn't have the strength to ask. Or the interest. His vision was blurred and he was seeing double again. He hadn't even been drinking. Probably the lack of sleep.

He squinted. 'Bruce, it's Saturday. Why are you wearing a suit?' Bruce was wearing the same crumpled oversized suit he'd seen on him last time. 'Don't you have any casual clothes?'

'That's right, Kit, it's a fuckin' Saturday, not fuckin' Christmas Day. I've got work to do.'

'Can't you at least change your suit?'

Bruce looked down at this jacket. 'What do you mean? I've got six of these. New one every day.'

'Don't you ever send them to the laundry? Or at least pull out an iron?'

'I can't help if I sweat a lot. I'm a very active man, all right.' He took the fag out of his mouth and pointed it at Walker. 'For your information, I get these laundered by Mrs Chow every fuckin' week.'

Walker laughed. 'I hope you don't pay her.'

'What I give her's more valuable than money.'

Walker grimaced. Whatever it was that Bruce gave to Mrs Chow, he didn't want to know about it. 'Bruce, how old were you when you knew my parents?'

'I was only a whippersnapper. About twenty-one, if my memory serves me correctly. I started out in the docks with your dad. He was good to me. Showed me the ropes. Then I got more into the unions. Became a shop floor rep.'

'How did my folks seem? Did they get on?'

'Your dad worked long hours. And like most of the wharfies, he liked to knock back a few drinks after work. But on weekends they'd go out together, mostly to the pub.'

Rowntree smiled to himself, remembering. 'Your mum was a real looker. You know, snappy dresser, latest fashions. Looked like a real model when she went out.'

'What about later? Walker was uncertain how to put it. 'When she got sick?'

Rowntree shook his head sadly. 'Bad news that. They were both pretty morose. We didn't see them at the pub for a while. Then I heard from Lester that she'd gone into hospital. Can't remember if it was Sydney or Prince Alfred. Cancer. There wasn't much they could do. The next thing you know she was gone. Poor thing. Your dad was devastated.'

'Did you go to the funeral?'

'No funeral in Sydney. She was a country girl and she was buried back home. Armidale, I think.'

'I don't remember a funeral. My dad would have taken me to it.'

'Maybe he didn't want you upset. He had a service at Palm Beach. He took you to that.'

Walker perked up. 'Yes, I remember that. You were there?'

'Just a few friends. Threw some flowers into the sea and said a few words.'

'And ashes?'

Bruce frowned. 'Don't remember that. She was buried, remember. There wouldn't have been ashes.'

Walker let Bruce's words and his memories wash over him. 'Makes sense,' he said after a while.

CHAPTER NINE

ON MONDAY MORNING, Walker got to work late. He'd slept badly again, with memories of his mother swirling around in his mind all weekend. He couldn't work out which ones were real and which were imagination. At least he hadn't imagined the ceremony at the beach. But he had to find out what had happened to his mother, and he realised there was only one way to do that. He'd have to go to Armidale and search for her grave.

As he entered the ward, he saw Élodie and Pier standing together in the corridor, deep in conversation. As he approached, he realised they made an attractive couple, both dressed in what Walker imaged to be the latest European fashion, both young and beautiful. They looked like actors out of a television soapie. He could see them getting together during their stay at Western Meadows.

He reached them and caught the last bit of their conversation. It sounded like a teaching session. They were talking about one of their patients who had suffered a lung clot and Pier was asking Élodie basic medical student–type questions.

'So, always be suspicious of a cancer patient with dyspnoea or tachycardia for no obvious reason,' said Pier. 'Pulmonary embolism is always top of the list.'

Élodie nodded and made a note in her pad.

Pier gave a nod of recognition to Walker, then went back to his questioning. 'So, what complications of pulmonary embolism and its treatment do we have to look out for?'

She gave a blank look, then flicked back through her notes.

'Élodie, you shouldn't have to look at your notes. You should know this. You're in your final year, aren't you?'

'Yes,' she said. 'It's just not something I've studied well.' She gave a disarming smile. 'It's easy for you, you're so clever.'

Pier seemed impervious. He didn't smile in return. 'Give it a try.' He seemed to be struggling to sound reasonable. 'Just think logically using your basic knowledge.'

'Well,' said Élodie slowly, 'if she has a thrombosis in her leg that has broken off and lodged in her lung ...'

'Yes?'

'She could have a stroke?'

'A stroke?' Pier was frowning. 'How?'

'You know, the blood clot lodges in the brain.'

Pier threw a questioning look at Walker. Walker could tell he was struggling to be patient. 'How is a blood clot going to get from the leg to the brain?'

'Oh, you know,' said Élodie breezily. 'Up through the heart then through the blood vessels in the neck and into the brain.'

Walker intervened. 'That's possible, Élodie,' he said. 'But what special conditions does the patient need to have for that to happen?' He was trying to be gentle. When she remained silent, he added, 'How would the thrombus bypass the lungs from the right heart to the left heart, then into the brain?'

Élodie bit her bottom lip and gave a cute smile. She shrugged her shoulders. 'I'm sorry, I don't know. Don't think bad of me.'

Her charms appeared to have no effect on Pier. 'We don't think bad of you, Élodie, but it appears you need to do a bit of reading. Look up patent foramen ovale and VSD and tell us about them tomorrow.'

Élodie seemed contrite and scribbled in her pad. Peering

over her shoulder, Walker noted she had written 'paint tint for valley'.

Pier threw Walker another look as they joined together to visit the patient.

The women with the pulmonary embolism appeared to be in her seventies and was lying comfortably in bed, a drip in her arm and an I-med pump running. She had pulled the oxygen mask down so it covered her mouth and chin but left her nose free. Élodie looked on as Pier listened to her chest and heart then examined her legs, the left one slightly swollen, while Walker flicked through the bed chart.

After he reassured the patient that everything seemed fine, she asked, 'Am I having any more chemotherapy?'

'I don't think so,' said Walker. 'You've had a hard time of it. This chemo regimen is pretty hard going, as you now know. I think we've got the most out of it.'

'What about the cancer that's spread to my lung?'

'We'll do a scan but hopefully that should have shrunk.'

'But not cured,' she said.

'That's right. I'm sorry about that. This cancer tends to come back even if you get a good response.'

As they walked away, Walker said to Pier and Élodie, 'This MVAC is a miserable regimen. It requires us to give chemo when the blood counts are low. Hardly anyone can get through it. You have to ask whether it's worth it.

'Hopefully, G-CSF will help,' said Pier, and Walker nodded his agreement.

Pier spoke to Élodie, 'I wrote the protocol for the study that got G-CSF approved in the States and Europe. Just published in *Blood*. I put about a third of the patients on the study.'

'G-CSF?' Élodie said.

'Granulocyte colony stimulating factor. Discovered by an Australian team, in fact. It boosts the white blood cell count after chemotherapy and makes it safer to give.'

'We did some of the initial clinical studies here at Western

Meadows,' added Walker. Then he addressed Pier. 'That study of yours published in *Blood*? Wasn't that out of the Christie Hospital in Manchester?'

'Mmm,' said Pier. 'It'll be a while before we can use it in bladder cancer patients though. It will mostly be used in the curative setting – lymphomas and such.'

'And it will be years before it's on the PBS in Australia,' said Walker.

CHAPTER TEN

AFTER THE WARD round, they dispersed and Walker went to the cafeteria for lunch. Afterwards, as Walker ambled back to his office, he wondered about Élodie's lack of knowledge. The French medical course couldn't be that bad. Maybe she was just a poor student. As he approached Tania Forcett's office, he noticed that the door was ajar and decided he should ask her about Élodie. She must have got a recommendation from someone before Élodie had been allowed to take up an elective at Western Meadows.

He tapped softly on the door. 'Tania.'

There was no answer. He could have sworn he'd heard someone moving around the office before he knocked.

He pushed the door open and was immediately bowled over by someone who shoved past him. Walker yelled as he was bashed backwards into the wall then fell sideways onto the floor. The person was running away.

Walker recovered quickly and pushed himself up. 'Hey you! Stop.'

He started running after him — he was sure it was a man. The figure disappeared around the next corner — someone dressed in surgical scrubs and mask with a head covering.

Walker sprinted to the corner and grabbed the edge of the wall as he skidded around. The man was halfway across the airbridge that led to the pathology building.

'Stop him!' yelled Walker but there was no one there to hear.

Walker ran in pursuit. He prided himself on being a fast runner, winning the four-hundred metres trophy in the regional competition in high school. He felt he was gaining as the man burst through the stairwell doors ahead, which went down to the ground floor. He had to get him before he reached the external door. Walker flung the door open then scooted down the stairs, taking them three at a time. One false move and he would end up in a heap at the bottom of the stairs, but he managed to negotiate them safely then flung himself at the door, which was slowly swinging closed.

The man, dressed in blue scrubs and easily seen, seemed to be getting away along the road between the buildings. He'd been faster on the stairs, but now they were in the open, Walker could run unfettered. He was on his toes, sprinting madly, his long legs like coiled springs. The other man was fast but Walker was faster. He'd catch him. The man would have to pause at top of the steps that led down to the oval. He'd get him there.

Snap! Walker crumpled. An excruciating pain in his left calf. It felt like he'd been shot! Grabbing his leg, Walker rolled onto his side and looked backwards, searching for a gunman. He couldn't see anyone. Tentatively, he felt down his leg, expecting blood. But there was none. Carefully, he pulled up his trouser and examined his calf. He pushed his finger on where it hurt and the pain got acutely worse.

He slumped back on the ground with a moan. 'I've done my bloody monkey muscle.' He peered in the direction the man had run. He was nowhere to be seen. He'd got away.

'You okay, Chris?'

It was Madeline. She stood over him, a stack of folders under one arm. 'I saw you chasing that man. Who was he? You look like you've hurt your leg.'

'A thief. He was in Tania's office. I caught him at it and he ran for his life.'

'What did he steal? Is Tania okay?'

'Don't know. Almost got him.' He cradled his calf. 'If it wasn't for this.'

'A cramp?'

'No, not a cramp. I ripped a muscle. Plantaris longus.'

Annoyingly, she giggled. 'Your monkey muscle? Bad luck.'

Walker said nothing. He sat up and rubbed his calf. He was beginning to feel like a fool.

'That was very brave of you chasing him, though.'

He looked carefully at her face but she seemed sincere. 'Yeah?'

'I'll say. He could have been a killer. He could have had a gun.'

'A gun? I didn't see one.'

'Or a knife. He could have been a druggie.'

'He didn't look like a killer.'

'You never know what a killer looks like.' She was towering over him, her voice soft. 'For all you know, I could be a murderer.' Then she laughed.

Walker went back to rubbing his calf. The acute pain had gone but it was really starting to ache. He imagined the torn muscle filling with blood and all the tissue around starting to swell. Madeline was probably right. What if the man had been armed? What would he have done if he'd caught him? He looked up at her. 'You going to help me?'

'Of course. Here, give me your arm.'

Madeline seemed surprisingly strong as she helped him to his feet. She pulled his arm over her shoulders and grabbed him firmly around the waist. 'Come on then, gently now.'

With her help, they made it to the lift, caught it to the first floor, then made their way back towards Tania's office. He probably could have made it by himself, limping, but he enjoyed the feeling of her body against his. His hand was on her hip. 'You've got muscles,' he said.

'I like to keep fit.'

Tania's office was a mess. The drawers of the filing cabinet were all open and the folders were scattered on the ground. The desk drawers were also open and loose papers were spread over the desktop. Tania stood in the middle of the room, looking annoyed. She looked him up and down. 'What happened to you?'

'Someone was in your office. I chased him.'

'Did you see who it was?' asked Tania. 'A drug addict?'

'Couldn't see his face. He was wearing surgical scrubs and had his head covered. Tall, I think. Young. He was a fast runner. I don't think he was a drug addict. If he was, he was unusually fit.'

'Did you get in a fight with him?'

'Tore a muscle,' said Madeline. 'I saw it. Chris almost had him. He was very brave.'

'Could you tell who it was, Madeline?'

Madeline shook his head. 'Too far away, and as Chris said, he was wearing a mask and a surgical cap.'

Tania looked around at the mess. 'Didn't steal anything of value as far as I can see.' She pointed to a silver clock on her desk. 'My purse was in the top drawer and he didn't take that.'

'After something else then,' said Walker. 'Some sort of document by the looks of it. It appears as if he concentrated on the filing cabinets. What's in there?'

'Mostly information about our medical staff – CVs, references, HR information, that sort of thing.'

'Can you tell if anything is missing?' asked Madeline. She began to flick through the folders that had been dumped on the desk. 'Mine's here, at least, so he didn't get that.'

Tania reached past Madeline, grabbed the folders and neatened them into a pile. 'I'd better get those if you don't mind.' She placed them into the top drawer of the filing cabinet and locked it.

'Will you notify the police?' asked Madeline.

'I'll phone Barry Darling if you wish,' said Walker.

'That would be great,' said Tania. 'I'm already late for my clinic.'

Tania began to shoo them out of her office but Walker caught sight of something down the back of the desk. 'What's that?'

Tanis stood back and let Walker fish the object from the space between the desk and the wall. It was a buff manila folder with 'Élodie Segal' written on the cover.

'Do you think this is what he was after?' said Walker. He flipped open the cover but Tania firmly pulled it out of his hands.

'I don't think so,' said Tania. She opened the drawer and placed Élodie's file in with others, locking it again.

Walker wondered how she could be so sure. It could easily have fallen behind the desk when the culprit dumped all the folders onto it.

Tania waved them out of her office then locked the door and strode away, leaving Madeline and Walker standing together in the corridor.

For a moment, neither of them spoke.

Then Madeline said, 'That was weird. Did you get the feeling that Tania was hiding something? She seemed quick to dismiss that it was Élodie's file he was after.'

'I agree. But who would want to look at Elodie's file?'

'And why?'

'I'll mention it to Barry when I see him.'

'Barry? I thought you called him Wendy.'

'I've been thinking that I should call him by his proper name, especially at work.'

'Doesn't bother me. He's your friend.'

'Yes. Yes, he is. A good friend. But he's also a senior police officer and I've decided I should start showing him due respect.' Then Walker thought about his surly mood the other evening in the pub.

'Listen, Madeline, I'm sorry about the other night.'

She flapped her hand. 'Don't worry about it. You were

upset about your mother, I understand.'

'So you'll forgive me? I don't want us to fall out over a silly thing like that.'

'Nothing to forgive.' She noticed him wince when he straightened his leg. 'You need help getting back to your office?'

'I'll be fine. I've done worse than this. Should be better in a few days.' He began to limp towards his office.

'Okay, I'm heading this way,' she said pointing in the opposite direction.

He waved, then called out to her. 'Shall we try again sometime?'

'Of course. When your leg's better.'

CHAPTER ELEVEN

DARLING PARKED HIS Commodore at the bottom of Argyle Street just outside the Orient Hotel. As he got out, he could see across George Street down to the international passenger terminal where a huge cruise ship was moored – *Fairstar*, according to the name displayed in black print on the white bow. Darling wondered what sort of people could afford to go on an ocean cruise.

Thelma Bianca pulled herself out of the passenger side and straightened her skirt then put on her hat. She looked up at the clear blue sky then at the ship. 'Nice weather for it.'

'If you like that sort of thing,' grumbled Darling. He suspected Bianca's parents were well off and, for all he knew, she'd actually been on a pleasure cruise. 'Do you have the letter?'

She tapped her pocket briskly and squared her shoulders. 'Yes, sir.'

Darling noticed her change of demeanour. Had she sensed his mood? If so, she was pretty switched on.

'Read it out again, please, Bianca,' he ordered. 'We should get it clear in our heads before we talk to Father Wesley.'

Bianca looked around to make sure they were alone then raised the sheet of paper up to the light. Darling could see the long lines in the paper where it had been folded. Spidery handwriting showed through the page.

She began to read, pronouncing the words crisply and in a strong voice as if she was reading for an audience. 'Vengeance is mine, for the day of your calamity is at hand. If any harm is done to you, then you shall give an eye for eye, a life for a life.' She lifted her eyes then looked back at the page. 'PS. I'll never forgive you for what you did.'

'I agree, it sounds religious, at least the first part,' said Darling.

'I'm sure part of it's from the New Testament,' said Bianca.

'We'll see what this priest has to say.' Darling started up the hill and Bianca fell in beside him.

'He can't be a priest. They're Catholic,' said Bianca. 'Isn't he a vicar or a pastor or something?'

'I knew him as a priest when I was a kid. I think vicars are English. Maybe we should ask him.'

'Don't do that, it's embarrassing. And don't tell him I'm Catholic.' Her eyes were wide and her brow furrowed.

'Why?'

'He might kick me out. It's Church of England.'

'We're not in Ireland, Bianca. And I think the correct term now is Anglican.'

'Well, they don't like Catholics.'

'Really? Perhaps we should ask him that as well.'

'Don't you dare. You must promise not to. If you don't, I won't come in with you.'

He raised his hands, trying not to grin. 'Okay, I promise.'

'And don't tell him I'm Catholic. You have to promise.'

'I promise.'

They walked beneath the Argyle Street arch with the distant rumble of traffic overhead. When they reached the other side, Darling said, 'I'm glad we've had this conversation, Bianca. It's very illuminating.'

'What do you mean?'

'It's important for me to know that as far as Anglican priests are concerned, you're just a big scaredy cat.'

'I'm not a scaredy cat. It's just my upbringing, all right?'

'Loreto College, I know. Heavy-duty Catholic.' They walked on in silence until they reached the rear of the church, an historic sandstone building set on the corner of Argyle and Lower Fort Streets. 'Which makes me ask, how are you getting on with our Constable David Jones?'

'What do you mean getting on?'

He noticed her cheeks had reddened and he regretted bringing up the subject. 'Oh, you know, are you getting along?'

'That's none of your business,' she snapped.

He put his hands up again. 'Okay, okay. I'm sorry. Just trying to show some interest. I think you're good for him. I just hope he's good for you too.'

She huffed. 'I don't know what you mean by that.'

Darling stopped walking and waited until she also stopped and turned back towards him. 'Bianca, I want to be clear, I'm not implying anything. Please don't take it the wrong way. Perhaps we should stop talking about your relationships.'

She began walking again towards the church. 'Yes, please.' After a few more steps she stopped and turned to him. 'And remember what you promised about the vicar. Or priest, or whatever you call him.'

Reverend Horace Wesley looked to be in his late fifties, with scruffy greying hair, balding at the front, and dressed in black trousers and woollen jumper with the knitted pattern of crossed golf clubs on the front. They met on the front porch of the church. Darling knew that out of sight, just behind the church, was Darling House, the nursing home where he had been raised as a child and which had given him his name. He also knew that Reverend Wesley was one of a few people who knew that fact. Wesley led them inside.

It was a small church with arched columns supporting a timber roof and a row of tall stained-glass windows on each side. In the corner was an old pipe organ and one wall was decorated with wooden plaques commemorating those lost in the various wars.

After introductions and a short explanation, Darling showed Wesley the handwritten note. 'This sounds to us like it could be from the Bible and we'd appreciate your expert opinion.'

Wesley silently read the note. 'Terrible handwriting.' He pursed his lips thoughtfully. 'Follow me.'

He led them to the front of the church where a lectern stood in the shape of a golden eagle with outstretched wings on which sat a large leather-bound Bible. He opened it, selected a page then pointed to a passage. 'Most people associate the eye-for-an-eye quote with the New Testament. See here, Matthew 5:38 in the Sermon on the Mount.'

He pointed to a line and Bianca and Darling peered over his shoulder.

'Jesus said, *You have heard that it was said, An eye for an eye and a tooth for a tooth.*' He stopped reading and looked at them. 'But that was actually Jesus quoting the Old Testament.'

Wesley then turned to the front of the Bible and flicked back and forth for a few moments.

'Here we are. Exodus 21:23. *But if any harm follows, then you shall give life for life, eye for eye, tooth for tooth, hand for hand, foot for foot, burn for burn, wound for wound, stripe for stripe.*'

'Does it mean what it sounds like?' asked Darling.

'Oh yes. In ancient times it was a common rule that the punishment should exactly equal the crime. The Romans believed it but so did societies before them, including the Jews.'

'Not very Christianly,' said Bianca. 'Whatever happened to let bygones be bygones.'

'Ah yes. I think you'll find that was Shakespeare. And you're right about the eye for an eye. That is not Christian. Which is exactly the point Jesus was making on the Sermon on the Mount. What he said in full was, *You have heard that it was said, An eye for an eye and a tooth for a tooth. But I say to you, Do not resist the one who is evil. But if anyone slaps you on the right cheek, turn to him the other also.*' He looked up. 'You know – turn the other cheek?'

'So the letter is actually a misquote,' Bianca said. She pointed to the line in the Bible. 'Here it says life for life, eye for eye, but the letter says eye for an eye, a life for a life. The letter puts more emphasis on a life for a life.'

'Murder,' said Darling.

'And that's a mortal sin,' said Bianca. 'Much worse than an eye for an eye.'

Wesley turned to the young officer. 'Ah, a Catholic, I see.'

Bianca appeared horror-struck, her face noticeably paling. Darling had to stop himself from smiling.

Wesley seemed not to notice. 'But I agree, murder is a grave sin.'

'What about the first line in the letter?' asked Darling. 'Is that a quote from the Bible as well?'

Wesley looked down, frowning as he read, 'Vengeance is mine, for the day of your calamity is at hand.' He pushed a thumb into his bottom lip. 'It rings a bell. It certainly reminds me of the Old Testament. Deuteronomy, I think.' He turned the pages, his finger running down the verses. 'Oh, of course. Here it is. Deuteronomy 32:35. *Vengeance is mine, and recompense; their foot shall slip in due time; for the day of their calamity is at hand, and the things to come hasten upon them,*' he quoted.

'Whoever wrote the letter used a shortened version of that,' said Bianca.

'Obviously someone who knew their Bible,' said Darling.

'Not necessarily a Christian though,' said Wesley. 'Both quotes are from the Old Testament but they are also in the Jewish Torah. And in fact, anyone could flick through and pull out pieces to back up a threat. The Old Testament is full of terrible lines. The threatening tone of the letter is definitely not Christianly, although I know a lot of so-called Christians who think like that. They selectively quote the Bible for their own selfish purposes.'

'However, whoever wrote the letter, the fact they used the

Bible, or Torah, says something,' said Darling. 'It points to someone with a religious education, even if it was just in school.'

Wesley made a noncommittal noise. 'Maybe. The bit after the postscript is not biblical.'

'Agreed,' said Darling. 'Just a straight threat. Thank you, reverend, you've been very helpful.'

'Not at all. Glad I could help. Will I be seeing you in church on Sunday in the future, Barry?'

'Ah, maybe. I've got a lot on my plate with this murder. We tend to get called out at all hours.'

'It would be lovely to see you if you can make it,' said Wesley. 'And bring Chris with you, perhaps.'

'Perhaps. We're both pretty busy.'

'But I've heard you're friends again. At least that's good news.'

CHAPTER TWELVE

WALKER TOOK THE lift up to the ward, his calf muscle still in no shape to take the stairs. At least the pain had settled but he had to limp to make sure he didn't bring on the sharp jab when the torn muscle was stretched.

A cleaner coming out of the ward held the door open for him and he thanked her as he limped through.

'Argh, me hearty,' Jenny called from near the nurses' station. 'You forgot yer parrot, Capt'n.'

'Ha, ha,' stated Walker in a flat voice. 'You're a real comedian, Jenny.'

'Will ye be doin' a ward round, Capt'n?'

Walker didn't engage in her attempt at humour. 'Just waiting for Ben. I saw Pier on the way through. He's carrying out the midazolam clearance study and I thought I'd leave him to it. I'll round with Ben.'

'Okay, I'll wait with you.' Walker was glad she'd dropped the accent. 'How was your date with Madeline?' she asked.

'It wasn't a date. Anyway, it was a disaster. I was in a foul mood and ruined the evening. She must think I'm a jerk.'

'Not what she said. She had a lovely time, according to her.'

Walker perked up. 'Did she say that? Maybe it wasn't as bad as I thought. She did help me when I hurt my leg the other day and told me not to worry about the evening.'

'Keep trying,' said Jenny. 'You seem well suited if you ask me.'

'Maybe,' said Walker, trying to sound noncommittal. Then he smiled at her. 'At least I know you'll never give up on me. I get the feeling you won't rest until I've found my soul mate.'

'Don't get too excited. I don't think about you that much.'

There was a bang at the end of the corridor and they looked around to see the doors thrown open. Ben Casey rushed through. 'Call an arrest!'

Jenny immediately picked up the phone, dialled a number and calmly gave orders.

'It's Pier,' yelled Ben. 'He's been poisoned.'

Walker limped towards the door and followed Ben through. Behind him, he could hear multiple beeping pagers going off as the cardiac arrest was called.

Pier was lying in the doorway of the treatment room that adjoined the chemotherapy unit. It was normally used as an overflow on busy days and Pier had been using it for the research project.

He looked dead.

He was lying face down and Walker got Ben to help turn him over. He wasn't breathing. Walker felt the artery in his neck. 'I can feel a pulse,' he said.

The arrest team arrived, the cardiology nurse and registrar pushing a silver trolley between them. When they saw Walker over the body, they waited.

Walker listened with his stethoscope. 'He's got a heartbeat but I can't see him breathing.'

The cardiology registrar knelt, placed the resuscitation mask over Pier's nose and mouth then began to pump the bag. Walker could see his chest rise and fall. The nurse opened Pier's shirt and placed the paddles on his chest.

They all turned to the ECG monitor.

'Sinus rhythm,' pronounced the cardiology nurse.

'What happened?' asked the registrar.

Ben moved forward. 'I was walking past the door and saw

him stumble out of the room, then collapse. I went to help and he told me he'd been poisoned. Then he stopped breathing.'

The anaesthetic registrar arrived and took over the bag.

'Poisoned?' said the cardiology registrar, still kneeling beside the patient. She peeled back an eyelid and shone a torch. 'Equal and reactive. Normal size pupils. Doesn't look like a narcotic.'

'Seems like a sedative of some sort,' said the anaesthetic registrar. 'Benzodiazepine maybe.'

'What was he doing in here?' asked the cardiology registrar, looking into the room. There was a single treatment chair and next to it was a trolley and a tray with a number of vials and syringes.

'Midazolam clearance,' said Walker. 'Part of a research project. He was injecting patients with tiny doses of midazolam then taking blood for metabolites. I wrote the protocol. It's his main project this year.'

'Midazolam,' said the anaesthetic registrar, with a grunt. 'That'd do it. Great short-term benzo. Wears off faster than Valium.'

'But how would he have been injected with it?' asked Ben.

The cardiology registrar stood up and examined the trolley Pier had been using. 'There's about ten empty ampoules here,' she said. 'Five milligrams each.'

'Fifty milligrams would knock him out, all right,' said the anaesthetic registrar. 'And you don't have to inject it. Same effect if you take it orally.'

All eyes went to a mug that sat on the edge of the trolley. The cardiology registrar sniffed it. 'Coffee. And it's empty.'

'Will he be all right?' asked Jenny.

'Should be,' said the anaesthetic registrar. 'Wears off quickly. That's why we're starting to use it in anaesthetics. If it was fifty milligrams, he'll be asleep for an hour or so.' He took the bag off and watched him carefully. 'See. He's already started to breathe himself. Anyway, let's get him down to ICU so we can monitor him until he's awake.'

Walker watched the trolley leave, loaded with the still

unconscious Pier. He closed the door of the treatment room and stood outside it with Jenny. 'I guess we have to wait. This is a crime scene.'

Walker had called Darling, who said he'd be there shortly. True enough, a few minutes later, Darling and Thelma Bianca turned the corner coming from the lifts.

They listened to Walker's report.

'You mean a Mickey Finn?' said Darling. 'But who'd do that? And why?'

'Isn't that why we called you?' said Jenny.

'Was it enough to kill him?' asked Bianca.

'Not sure,' said Walker. 'He wasn't breathing when I arrived. If that lasted long enough he would have arrested due to the lack of oxygen.'

'And you think it was administered in this cup?' Darling asked, sniffing the mug without touching it. 'Has anyone moved this?'

'The cardiology registrar,' said Walker. 'No one else. We guarded the door.'

'Good,' said Darling. 'We'll get his prints to exclude him.'

'Unless he was involved,' warned Bianca. 'Who is he?'

'She,' Walker corrected. 'She's one of the cardiology trainees. Been here for years. Very dependable. Doesn't even know Pier, as far as I can tell.'

'We'll check her out anyway,' said Bianca. 'Does she have a partner?'

'How would I know?' said Walker. 'What's that got to do with anything?'

'Maybe she's after Pier,' said Bianca. 'He's quite a looker.'

'Maybe,' said Walker. 'He doesn't have a girlfriend, as far as I know.'

Jenny let out a snorting laugh.

'What's wrong with you?' asked Darling.

'Chris, that's what.' Jenny laughed again.

'What do you mean?'

'Don't you pay attention to anything, Chris? Pier is gay.'

'Gay? No, he's not.' He paused. 'Is he?'

'Yes, you idiot. If you could keep your eyes off all the young ladies and take an interest in your male staff, you'd know. He hasn't been hiding it.'

'Oh.' Walker felt stupid. 'Are you sure?' But now that it was pointed out to him, he realised it was the truth. Many women had shown interest in Pier since he'd started and Walker had never seen him reciprocate. 'I just thought he was reserved.'

'Reserved,' said Jenny. 'That's a new word for it.'

'We'll get her prints anyway,' said Bianca.

Three hours later, Darling and Bianca were permitted to interview Pier in the ICU. Pier requested that Walker be present and he obliged.

Pier was sitting upright in the bed and looked perfectly well. If anything, he seemed perky, thought Walker, more talkative.

'I finished my coffee and all of a sudden, I became very drowsy. I don't remember anything after that. There's a whole part of my life that's just disappeared. No memory, no dreams. The next thing I knew, I woke up in this bed and a nurse was offering me a cup of tea.' He threw up his hands, oblivious to the drip in one arm. 'I don't know how I got here. It's amazing.'

'Can you remember events before you had your coffee?' asked Darling.

'Perfectly. I'd finished testing one patient. I'd given her the midazolam injection a few hours before. She was perfectly fine. I'd taken her blood for the drug level and was about to let her go home. I was setting up for the next patient when I noticed that all the midazolam ampoules were empty. I thought someone had made a mistake and sent me empty vials.'

'Had anyone come into the room while you were there?'

'No,' he said slowly as he thought. 'I did need to use the bathroom and asked someone to watch the patient for me.'

'Who was that?'

He paused before answering. 'Peter Schäfer. But I was only gone for two minutes or so, five at most. The bathroom was just across the corridor. And I'm sure he was there the whole time.'

'Do you know Peter Schäfer well?'

'Not very well. He arrived after me less than two months ago. We share an office but I wouldn't call us friends.'

'Did you know him from before?'

'No. He's from Switzerland and I'm from the Netherlands.' He smiled. 'I know you think Europe is small in comparison to Australia but it's not that small.'

'You've never worked together before?'

'No, never.'

'Okay,' said Darling. 'I think we have enough.' He turned to Bianca. 'I suggest we go and see Peter Schäfer. Kit, do you think you can find him for us?'

CHAPTER THIRTEEN

WALKER LED DARLING and Bianca to the tearoom in radiation oncology where they found Peter Schäfer. He was a tall serious-looking man who stated that he'd started at Western Meadows a few months previously as the radiation oncology fellow. He'd come straight from Geneva, where he had completed his training, and had decided to spend a year in Australia before taking a permanent job back in his home country.

Darling watched as he fussed over his coffee, which he made in a plunger using a supply of ground coffee – Ethiopian, according to the packet. He wore a slight frown, as if the task was particularly difficult, but when he looked up, his face broke into a wide smile with dimples that almost made him look girlish. Darling considered that women would find him attractive.

He didn't look like a murderer.

'You love your coffee by the looks of it,' said Bianca.

'As do all Swiss.'

'I guess the Europeans drink coffee like we drink beer,' Darling said with a smile.

'Yes, but we're not the biggest coffee drinkers.'

Darling nodded but said nothing. He wasn't really interested.

'No, that crown belongs to Brunei. Last year Brunei's coffee consumption per individual was the world's highest.'

'You don't say.'

'Do you know that the richest man in the world is Sultan Haji Waddaulah of Brunei? Makes his money out of oil and gas. He has two wives – one the Queen of Brunei, the other a former airline stewardess – and he alternates nights with them.'

'Sounds exhausting,' said Walker.

Schäfer raised his eyebrows as he poured the coffee into a small ornate cup. 'Well, if you've got the money?'

'You know what they say,' said Walker, trying to change the subject. 'Money is the root of all evil.'

'Actually, that's not correct,' said Schäfer. He offered the coffee pot to Walker and the police officers but they each shook their head. He put the plunger down and took a sip from his cup. 'No, it's the *love* of money, not money itself.'

'What do you mean?' asked Darling

'You know, the letter from Paul to Timothy? I can't remember the whole thing but it's something like ... people who want to get rich fall into temptation and harmful desires. *For the love of money is a root of all kinds of evil.* So it's not having money that's the problem, it's the lust for money.'

'Really?' said Walker. 'That makes me feel better. Who knows, one day I might be rich, but I don't want to go to hell over it. I don't love it. Don't even know when I'm being paid half the time. Hate doing my tax. I'd just as soon let the government keep my money than try to squeeze out a tax deduction. Not worth the effort.'

Schäfer smiled. 'The Bible also says things about laziness.'

'You seem to know a lot about the Bible.'

'Oh, you know, Switzerland is a very religious country. We're all taught the Bible in school.'

'Really? So was I but I can't remember any of it. You must've been a good student.'

'Good enough. My father was very strict.'

Darling gave Walker an irritated look then addressed

Schäfer. 'We have just come from interviewing Pier Mathijssen in ICU. He said you were in the treatment room where he was doing experiments on patients just before he was poisoned.'

Schäfer appeared surprised. 'Pier was poisoned? Is he all right? What was he poisoned with?'

'We think someone put midazolam in his coffee.'

'But who would do that?'

'He said he asked you to look after things when he went to the bathroom.'

'Really?' Schäfer looked puzzled. 'Why would he say that?'

Darling studied Schäfer's face carefully. He couldn't tell if he was alarmed by the accusation or not. He looked more curious than anything. 'Well, did you? Were you in the room?'

'So I could pour a few ampoules into his coffee? No, I did not. Why would I do that?'

'Why would Pier lie?'

'Ah,' said Schäfer. He was silent for a moment, seemingly lost in thought. He took another sip of coffee. Walker wondered whether he was preparing a story.

Finally Schäfer spoke. 'There is another saying we have in Switzerland. Loosely translated it says "the tongue is the worst piece of meat in the world".'

'Who are you talking about? You or Pier?'

'I do not like to talk ill of another person but it seems I am driven to it.'

'Something about Pier? What is it?'

'I'm not sure that what he tells you about himself is exactly true.'

'What do you mean?'

'For one thing, I'm not entirely sure he's Dutch.'

'What do you mean? If he's not Dutch, where's he from?'

'Just some of the terms he uses. When we speak German together, he is hesitant, like it's not his first language. Dutch is very similar to German, you know. But occasionally if we get deep into conversation, his German becomes almost perfect, as if he's forgotten to hide it. And sometimes he uses phrases that are very German. Those only used by someone who grew up there.'

'What like?'

Schäfer thought for a moment. 'The other day when he didn't believe something I said, he exclaimed "*Holla die Waldfee!*" It's something some Germans say when they're astonished. It literally translates to "Whoa, the wood fairy". Australians would say, Holy crap! That phrase is very German. I have never heard it used outside the southern parts of Germany. And there are other things he says.'

'So what if he's German?'

'Nothing, I suppose. But if he is saying things about me, I'd be careful about believing him.'

'You still haven't convinced me that you weren't in the room when Pier was not there.'

'That's true. But as it happens, I was doing a clinic at the time with Dr Piper.'

'We can check with her.'

'Be my guest. And while you're at it, there is another thing about Pier. Something I've not yet told anyone.'

'What?'

'Do you know he was in Brisbane last month? Just before the solicitor's death?'

'How do you know that?'

'I saw his plane tickets. He left them in his top drawer in the office which I share with him. I was looking for a stapler. Two tickets – one was from Sydney to Brisbane, the other a return flight a few days later.'

'Your word against his again. You say he was in Brisbane at that time. When we interviewed him recently he says he wasn't.'

'But that is something that can be checked. The airlines have records.'

They left Schäfer in the tearoom and went searching for Madeline Piper. They found her at her desk in the radiation oncology department. Her office walls were bare except for a corkboard which was covered with sheets of paper – a handwritten to-do list, a typed table of phone numbers, and a large photo of Madeline in hiking gear standing near a rocky outcrop with what looked like English moors in the background. She looked very happy. Walker wondered who had taken the photo.

Bianca led the questioning. 'We're checking the whereabouts of Peter Schäfer this morning,' she said.

'Does this have something to do with Pier Mathijssen?'

'Have you heard what's happened to him?'

'News travels fast around here.'

'Peter Schäfer says he was in clinic with you,' said Bianca.

'Yes, he was,' said Madeline. 'It was a quiet clinic for a change.'

'Were you with him the whole time?'

'Yes. Except, I went off for fifteen minutes or so to get us coffee. Since it was quiet, I decided to treat everyone to cappuccinos.'

'So he was by himself for fifteen minutes?'

'Maybe twenty minutes. There was a line at the coffee cart.'

'Thank you, Dr Piper. What's the name of the nurse in your clinic this morning?' Bianca wrote it down and smiled. 'We'll let you know if we need any more information.'

Tessie, the nurse, was a short Filipino woman who was still tidying up in the clinic area, getting ready for the next clinic. She seemed excited with the police attention.

'Peter, yes, he was here. Do you think he poisoned Pier?' She frowned. 'I'm not sure he could have. At most, he was gone from the clinic for five minutes to use the bathroom. Even if he took the back stairs he could not have got there and back in time.'

'Please, just answer our questions, Tessie, if you don't mind,' said Bianca.

Tessie ignored her. 'I guess he could have put something in

his coffee before the clinic started. Something slow release. Or maybe he coated the empty cup with something.'

'Who said anything about coffee?'

'Maybe it was some sort of powerful poison that is invisible to the naked eye. Curare or something like that.'

'Tessie, we would just like you to confirm that Peter Schäfer was not absent from the clinic for more than five minutes.'

'Yes, yes, that is correct. Dr Piper went for coffee but Peter stayed in the clinic.'

'Are you sure of that?'

'Hundred per cent.'

Darling interrupted. 'Did you go for a break yourself?'

'Me? Of course. I had my tea break. Since Dr Piper was not here, I had a break too.'

'How long?'

'About fifteen minutes.'

'And was Peter here by himself? Was there anyone else helping you?'

'No one else. Peter was here the whole time.'

'How can you be sure?'

'He was here when I got back.'

'So you were gone for fifteen minutes. Then Peter Schäfer could have been gone for fifteen minutes too.'

Tessie smiled. 'Yes, that's right. Just like I said.'

Bianca closed her notepad. 'Thank you very much for your help, Tessie.'

As they were leaving, Darling hung back and indicated Walker should as well. He called to Bianca. 'I'll meet you in the car, Bianca.'

Darling turned to Walker. 'Royce Wills is coming around to see you tonight to interview you about your father.'

'Tonight? What would I know? I was a kid at the time.'

'That's what he thinks too, which is why he's not inviting you down to the station.'

'I'm going out to dinner.'

Darling smiled. 'Great. Who with?'

'One of the doctors from the hospital.'

'Dr Piper?'

'Maybe. Why would you say her?'

Darling shrugged. 'She looks your type. Anyway, it's none of my business. Will you be home at six? They won't take long.'

CHAPTER FOURTEEN

SENIOR DETECTIVE SERGEANT Royce Wills had put on a bit of weight since Walker had last seen him but he still wore the same thick-rimmed glasses and his ears stuck out from his head just as much. With him was another familiar figure, just as tall as Wills but with more muscle than fat. They had come as promised at 6 pm, and they stood in the hallway of Walker's terrace.

'Constable Jones,' said Walker. 'Very nice to see you again. I was wondering what had happened to you after our Detective Darling moved to central office.' He glanced at Wills then back again. 'You've moved too, by the looks of things.'

'Cold case squad,' said Jones. 'It's a step up,' he added, although he didn't look happy about it.

Walker turned back to Wills. 'So this is about my father.'

'This is more to advise you than anything,' Wills said officiously. 'I doubt you can really add anything to the case.'

'I was four or five at the time.'

Wills glanced down at his notepad. 'Five.'

'Good to know. What can you tell me?'

'Please take a seat,' said Wills, gesturing towards the lounge room. When Walker obliged, Wills flicked a finger towards his offsider. 'Jones.'

Constable Jones fixed his eyes on the far wall then began to recite the story without the use of notes. 'On the seventeenth of August 1960, John Leremy was stabbed in High Lane, Millers Point. He was pronounced dead at the scene. The murderer or murderers were not identified at the time and the murder until now, remained unsolved.'

Walker crossed his arms and sunk his head into his chest. He didn't want to look at Jones or especially Wills.

Jones continued. 'A known associate of Leremy, Ralph Collinson, was investigated for the murder but had a solid alibi. He was at his own engagement party at the Glebe Town Hall in front of a hundred witnesses, including some of the local detectives.'

'Who's Ralph Collinson?' asked Walker.

Wills intervened. 'Ralph "The Ripper" Collinson ran a few illegal gambling houses in Newtown back then. In his spare time, Leremy was a standover man for Collinson.'

'Spare time?'

'Leremy's main job was as a dockside worker,' said Wills. 'He worked with your father.'

'Never heard of him,' said Walker.

'I don't expect you to,' said Wills. 'Your father is now dead and you were only five at the time.' He flicked his hand at Jones to continue.

'We have recent information that on the night of the murder, Leremy was having a heated argument in the Captain Cook Hotel. The murder took place later in the lane behind the pub.'

Walker had already heard this from Wendy, but he decided to play dumb. 'So? Who was he arguing with?'

'Your father.'

'Who says?'

'A witness,' said Wills. 'Another one of Collinson's standover men who has graced our jails with his presence for the last ten years.'

'Did he see the murder?'

Jones shook his head. 'No, but he witnessed the argument between Leremy and your father.'

'What about?' Walker had heard the answer from Wendy too but wanted Jones to corroborate.

Jones paused, as if he didn't want to continue.

'Your mother,' said Wills. 'The witness said they had a stand-up barney about your mum in the pub in front of everyone. Shouting. Your father threatened Leremy.'

'What? About my mother? What did she have to do with this Leremy?'

This time, even Wills paused. He turned away and indicated to Jones to continue.

'Chris, they said Leremy was having an affair with your mum. That your dad warned him to keep away, or else.'

'Ha!' exclaimed Walker. He'd been thinking hard about this since Wendy had first told him. 'She had cancer, for goodness sake. She died soon after that. I very much doubt that a woman dying from cancer would be running around having an affair. I know, I'm a cancer doctor.'

Wills' head flicked back to Walker. 'Who says she died from cancer?'

'What?' Walker was flummoxed. 'My father said. Everyone said.' He paused. 'It would be on her death certificate.'

'Do you have it?'

'Me? No. I never thought to get it. Why should I?'

Jones's voice was kind. 'There's no record of a Jane Walker dying in Sydney in the 1960s.'

Walker stood up. 'What do you mean? Are you saying she didn't die?'

'We're still searching,' said Jones. 'All the Jane Walkers who died in New South Wales have been accounted for and none of them were your mother.'

'What are you saying?'

Wills jumped in. 'She disappeared after Leremy was stabbed. She knew something.'

Walker sat back down, dumbfounded.

'Mr Walker,' Wills continued, 'we have to ask you this question. Have you been in contact with your mother at any time since then?'

Walker raised his head but his eyes would not focus. 'What? No. Are you saying she's alive? That's ridiculous, she would have contacted me.'

'Mr Walker,' intoned Wills, 'if that is true, if your mother has never contacted you, then we also need to consider another possibility for your mother's disappearance.'

'Uh?' None of this made sense.

'That your father also murdered your mother.' Wills paused, letting the words sink in. 'Then disposed of her body.'

Wills gestured to Jones, who pulled a document out of his coat pocket and handed it to Walker.

'What's this?'

'It's a warrant, Chris,' said Jones.

'To do what?'

'To dig up your backyard,' said Wills. 'We're going to look for your mother's body.'

CHAPTER FIFTEEN

WALKER HAD ASKED Madeline again for dinner that night and she readily accepted, even though it was short notice. Either she was interested in him, he thought, or she had nothing else to do. Given that she was newly arrived, it could be either.

Walker slumped down in the lounge and thought about what Wills had said. Could his father have killed his mother? It just didn't seem right. He couldn't imagine his father doing that. But then, he didn't really know his mother. He only had vague recollections of her – her face, her perfume. Maybe she did have an affair. Would that be enough to drive his father to murder? What if Flea had had an affair? Would he have been able to take her life? He didn't think so.

But what about what Wills had said about not finding a record of her death? That would go along with her being killed and her body dumped somewhere no one could find. Or that she was still alive! If that was true then it meant that she had abandoned him. Could a mother do that to her only child?

'That's ridiculous,' he said and stood abruptly. He didn't want to think about it. Madeline would be here soon. He felt like cancelling. But he had to eat and had no way of getting in contact with her. She hadn't yet had the phone connected at her flat.

She arrived soon after the police had left, dressed in the

same outfit she'd worn at work, clearly not out to make an impression. Walker decided to keep it simple and have dinner at the local. After what Wills had said he didn't have the energy for anything else.

They took a seat at a table in a small room off the main bar of the Hero. It was a Wednesday, so there was no music and the room was cramped. Their table was hard against the sandstone so they had to sit adjacent to each other, which Walker didn't mind. He found it easier to have a conversation that way. He ordered them steaks at the bar and took their drinks back to the table.

'What do you think about Pier?' he asked after sitting down. 'Do you really think someone would try to poison him?'

She shrugged. 'Don't know. I don't know much about him.'

'The police think it was Peter Schäfer.'

'I don't see how. Or why.'

She didn't seem very interested. Walker felt flat after the interview with Wills so he didn't feel like talking either. He took a sip of his beer and stared out the window.

'Are you okay, Chris?' she asked. 'You're not your usual self.'

'And what's my usual self?' he scoffed, then immediately felt bad. 'Sorry, Madeline. I've had the police around asking about my father and I'm all out of sorts.' He told her about his conversation with Royce Wills. 'And to top it off, he made up some cock-and-bull story about my father killing my mother. They're coming to dig up my backyard tomorrow, looking for her body.'

Instead of telling him how ridiculous that sounded, she asked, 'Do you think he could have?'

Walker's initial reaction was to snap back at her but he stopped himself. Could his father *really* have killed his mother? He was too young at the time to know what his mother was like. And his father had been so distant after she died, so he hadn't really known his father either. He turned to face her. 'To tell the truth, I just don't know.'

She reached out and grabbed his hand. 'We'll just have to see what the police find. But don't worry, I'll be here for you. If you want.'

He squeezed her hand. 'Thank you. I'd like that.' This was the first time she'd expressed any affection towards him. Maybe she was softening to him?

Their steaks arrived and they began eating. Walker glanced up to see a man walking towards them. He was staring at Madeline, smiling. She looked up. Walker noticed her body tense.

'Shaun, what are you doing here?' She clearly wasn't happy to see him.

'Maddie,' he exclaimed. Walker felt the surprise was fake. 'Of all the people to bump into.'

She said nothing at first. She looked away from him and stared at the opposite wall, her face unreadable. The man just stood there smiling, looking pleased with himself.

Finally, she stirred. 'This is Shaun Callen,' she said to Walker. She didn't add any other information.

He was shorter than Walker with wiry orange hair and a face full of freckles, a snappy dresser in a tight suit and pointy black shoes.

Shaun offered his hand and Walker took it. The grasp was overly tight and he placed his other hand over Walker's and held on. 'And you are?'

'Christopher. Pleased to meet you.'

'Christopher.' Shane rolled the name around as if it was a novelty. He let go of Walker's hand after giving a final stiff squeeze. 'Do you mind if I call you Chris?' He stood between them, a hand on the back of each of their chairs, and looked down on them. Walker had to twist his neck to see his face.

'Why are you here?' Madeline asked, her voice tight. She refused to raise her face and stared at the tabletop.

Shaun looked around the pub. 'Here? Well, I've heard it's a lovely place to get a drink.'

'You know what I mean. What are you doing in Sydney?'

'Oh, didn't you know? I've moved here. I've got a great job at a top law firm in the city. Blake Dawson Waldron. You'd be interested. I'm working in medical litigation. Right up my alley. Something I can get my teeth into.'

'Oh?' Madeline seemed uninterested.

'Yes. I've seen first-hand how you medical people stuff things up without a care for anyone. Now I can do something about it. Protect the people. I can't believe what you lot think you can get away with. Gone are the days when you can bury your mistakes.' He laughed at his own joke. 'We need people like me to find you out and make you pay through the nose.'

'Yes, I can see that would suit you perfectly.'

Shaun went on as if she'd agreed with him. 'I'm working on a case at the moment. A stuff-shirt ophthalmologist from Macquarie Street named Christopher Roger. He sent a poor woman blind. We're going to sue him big time. It'll come before the High Court next year. We'll get the bastard good and proper.'

'How lovely for you.' Madeline still refused to look at him. She cut a piece of steak and took a bite.

Shaun slapped the back of Walker's chair. 'What do you do, Chris? Are you a doc like this one?'

Walker glanced at Madeline uncertainly. 'Yes. A medical oncologist.'

'Cancer too, huh? Bloody useless if you ask me. Once you've got cancer you're a goner. You lot just torture the poor bastards until they die. You should leave them alone. Can't see how anyone could pay you for it. I'd love to get one of you under my microscope.' He smiled. 'Who knows, Chris, it might just be you one day.'

Walker let out an empty laugh. 'Maybe.'

Shaun laughed back. 'Hey, the guy I'm suing has the same first name as you, Chris. Maybe it's an omen?'

Neither Walker nor Madeline answered. Walker wondered whether he should get up and punch him in the nose. No one in the pub would do anything. He'd punch his face in then shove him onto the street. He'd done it before. Then he'd pull off one of his stupid pointy shoes and shove it up his—

Shaun cut into Walker's thoughts. 'Oh Maddie, I heard your mother died. That's very sad. I always liked your mother. And I know she liked me. She often said so. I have to warn you, I'm looking at her will at the moment. Given our relationship,' he gave Walker a meaningful look, 'it could be argued that some of that money should be mine.'

Finally, she looked up. 'But that's ridiculous, we weren't married.'

'As good as,' he said with a smile. 'Before the law. The law sees a de facto relationship the same as being married.'

'De facto relationship! Is that what you call it? You weren't there half the time. Out running after other women mostly. And when you were there, you wanted to rule over me like some sort of king.'

He put on a patient face. 'We lived together, Maddie. We had a domestic relationship. I even followed you to Manchester. The courts would look very favourably on that. Infidelity doesn't come into it. I wanted to look after you. You're a difficult person to live with. Who can blame me for finding solace outside of the home when you chose to withdraw your affection?'

'You followed me to Manchester to keep an eye on me. You couldn't bear me to have a life of my own. You're just a controlling little—'

Shaun put his hands up. 'Whoa, Maddie. Don't say anything that will just make it worse. You've got to keep on my good side. You know, don't poke the bear.' He smirked. 'There's your mother's money riding on it. Now then, since that's all clear, I think I'll leave you two to enjoy the rest of your evening.'

He turned and began to move away but then turned back, as if he'd had a sudden thought. 'Oh yes, there's another thing. Through the case, I've met this lovely lawyer from Parramatta. Absolute stunner.' He smiled at Walker. 'I think you might know her, Chris. Cassandra Hollow?' He winked. 'Very affectionate girl. We're getting on like a house on fire.' Still beaming, he turned and marched away.

'What a total fuckwit,' said Walker.

Madeline said nothing. She looked numbly at the wall and chewed on her steak mechanically.

When he realised she wasn't going to talk, Walker said, 'I thought you said you were single?'

'What?' She seemed irritated. 'You know I am.'

'So, who is he then?'

'Who do you think?' She didn't seem to want to explain, didn't seem to care about Walker's feelings.

'Obviously an old boyfriend?'

She gave an annoyed sigh. 'I met him at uni. We lived together for a little while. Took me a while to realise he was a total control freak. Moved to Manchester to get away from him but the bastard turned up there.'

'Is he one of the reasons you've come to Sydney?'

Her face was unreadable. 'One of them.'

'How long were you together?'

'Together? I'd hardly call it that. A year or two, I guess.' Now she looked at Walker. 'Who's Cassandra Hollow?'

It was Walker's turn to look away. 'We went out for a while.'

'When?'

'A few months ago.' He went on quickly. 'I haven't seen her since I met you.'

She screwed up her face. 'What's that got to do with anything? Why don't you see her now?'

Walker didn't know what to say. They grew apart? She was too clingy? He wasn't really interested in her? But he knew they were all lies. He still liked her. And she was never clingy. He chewed his steak thoughtfully. Why wasn't he still seeing her?

Madeline seemed to have lost interest. 'I wonder why he's here.' She looked at Walker keenly. 'You should be careful for Cassandra. You should warn her off him.'

'Warn her? She's big girl. I'm sure she can look after herself.'

'You don't know what he's like. He's cunning and malicious. He wants to control. He'll hurt her ... in more ways than one.'

'Is he violent? Did he hit you?'

Her jaw tightened but she didn't answer at first. She swallowed. 'Once. You must warn your friend.'

'I wouldn't call her my—'

'Whoever she is to you,' she hissed, 'warn her.'

CHAPTER SIXTEEN

THEY STARTED DIGGING up Walker's backyard the next day. Police arrived at first light in trucks and cars and started to unload their equipment through the back gate under the watchful eye of the large ginger cat who gazed down on them disdainfully from the roof of the shed.

Walker looked down from a rear window, a cup of coffee in hand, as they marked out the area they planned to dig in white chalk on the brick cobblestone. David Jones was there dressed in blue overalls. Walker noticed the cat had lost interest and had started to lick its back leg. 'That's how I feel too, Archie. Wasting their time.' He hoped he was right. What if they dug up some bones? His mother's. Could his father have done that? He didn't know what to believe.

After he dressed for work, he went downstairs and opened the back door. They already had a square of bricks pulled up and stacked neatly against the fence. An officer with Forensic Services emblazoned on her back had started working with a hand pick that looked like an archaeological tool, carefully digging through the clay soil. Another was sieving any earth loosened by the first onto a blue sheet. Walker couldn't see anything but dirt.

'I'll be off, Constable Jones. I think you're wasting your time. Please be sure to put everything back neatly when you've finished.' He turned away knowing they would be there for days. If they found anything, he didn't want to be there when they did.

Walker went straight to the ward to see a new patient who had been admitted overnight through the Emergency Room. Pier Mathijssen seemed to have recovered from his attempted poisoning but Tania Forcett had insisted he take the day off, so Walker saw the patient with Benjamin Casey and Élodie Segal.

'Febrile neutropenia,' reported Ben, as they stood around the patient's bed. 'Neutrophils zero on last night's count. They started IV antibiotics immediately.'

The patient was a young man of about thirty who was watching a cricket match on a bedside television. He switched it off when they arrived.

'Hi, Graham,' said Walker. 'You did the right thing coming in when you developed a fever. We've got on top of the infection early and your fever's settling already.'

'Can I go home? I feel well enough.' His gaze took in the three other patients in the room who were older and frail. 'It gets me down seeing these other poor souls. The guy next to me was moaning all night.'

'Not for another few days. If we stop the antibiotics now, the infection will come back. Your white cells are still really low. It's pretty intensive chemotherapy we're giving you.'

'You can say that again,' Graham said morosely. 'I'm not sure I can stand much more of this.' He turned the TV back on as they walked away.

'Primitive neuroectodermal tumour of the kidney,' said Walker when they gathered in the corridor. 'They removed the kidney two months ago but he still has a mass of nodes in the abdomen.'

Élodie peered back into the room where the young man lay. She seemed like she might cry. 'Will he die?'

'Not if we can help it,' said Walker. 'He's having intensive chemo and there's a chance of cure. He doesn't have that much cancer.'

'Oh,' said Élodie, her voice almost inaudible. 'I hope he is cured. I didn't think young people could get cancer.'

Walker threw a troubled look at Ben, who rolled his eyes.

Walker turned his attention back to the French medical student. 'Well, it's a rare cancer. Perhaps you should read up about it.'

'Oh, I will. I'll get the name off Ben later.'

'We need to watch out for his mental state,' said Walker to Ben. 'He seems much more down than usual. Can we get him his own room? And get the social worker to see him.'

'The single rooms have all got patients who are dying at the moment. But I'll check with Jenny.'

Madeline and Peter Schäfer came up to them. 'Have you finished? Can we borrow Ben?'

'Be my guest,' said Walker, bowing and waving his arm. 'He's all yours.'

'What's wrong with you, Élodie?' said Madeline. 'You look upset.'

'That poor young man with cancer,' she said, pointing into the room. She looked to be on the verge of tears again.

'Oh?' said Madeline, giving Walker a questioning glance.

'Peripheral neuroectodermal tumour,' he stated.

'Oh yes,' said Madeline. 'We treated a few of those in Brisbane. Nasty. But very sensitive to chemotherapy. Rare though.'

Élodie's demeanour changed abruptly. 'You lived in Brisbane?'

Madeline smiled proudly. 'All my life. And before you say anything, we're not all rednecks and our politicians aren't all corrupt.'

Élodie appeared confused.

Walker jumped in. 'But all your coppers are, according to Mr Fitzgerald.' He laughed. 'And probably *most* of your politicians.' When he noticed that Élodie didn't appear to follow, he added, 'There's been an inquiry.'

'Oh,' said Élodie without interest. She turned back to Madeline. 'Where in Brisbane did you live?'

'At my mother's house in New Farm. It's near the city.'

'On the river?'

'No way. Mum was a successful businesswoman but didn't make that sort of money. Close to it though, just a few streets back to be safe from the floods. New Farm's a bit of a dump but it's changing. People are moving back in and starting to fix up the old houses.'

'And close to the medical school.'

'Yes, it was. Sounds like you know Brisbane?'

'Oh, not really. I've only been there once.'

'Holiday?'

'Sightseeing. Just for a few days before I came to Sydney. Looked like a nice city from what I saw of it. Quiet.'

'You can say that again. Nothing compared to Manchester. Are you from Paris? I'd love to go there.'

Élodie smiled. 'Yes, it's beautiful. I hope you visit one day.' She turned to Schäfer. 'What about you, Peter? Have you been to Brisbane?'

'No, never.' He frowned. 'You seem very interested in who has been to Brisbane.'

Élodie seemed abashed. 'Do I? I'm sorry. I'm just interested in what people have seen. I thought I might get some sightseeing tips.'

'You going back to Brisbane?' asked Peter.

'No plans,' said Élodie. 'But you never know.'

Afterwards, Walker and Madeline left the ward together. He couldn't help but think about Élodie. She didn't seem like other medical students. For a start, her medical knowledge seemed to be lacking for a final-year student.

'Maybe they do things differently in France,' said Madeline when he mentioned it to her.

'Maybe. She doesn't seem that keen.'

'Give her a break. She's not sitting for an exam. She's just here for the experience.'

'Maybe you're right. But I'm going to check with Tania anyway.'

Walker and Madeline parted on the first floor and went in opposite directions. A short time later, Walker found Tania Forcett in her office and he took a seat next to her desk.

'Did Barry Darling investigate the break-in?' asked Walker.

'Constable Bianca came and asked questions, said they'd look into it. I haven't heard anything yet. Security has changed the locks though.'

'Good. I wanted to see you about our French medical student.'

'What of her?'

'She doesn't seem very knowledgeable.'

'What do you mean?'

'According to Pier, she doesn't know a lot of basic stuff. Did you hear about that Queensland doctor, who wasn't even a doctor, practising as a surgeon for the last five years? Has Élodie been checked out properly?'

Tania frowned. 'She's not operating on anyone, is she? I mean she's not putting cannulas in. Or chest drains.'

'No. That's another thing. She doesn't seem to be interested in doing anything like that. She's had a lot of chances. Isn't she supposed to be a doctor next year in France?'

Tania stood and opened the top drawer of a locked filing cabinet using a key from her pocket. She pulled out a folder and flipped through it. It had 'Élodie Segal' written on the cover. Walker could tell by the writing it was the same manila folder that had fallen down behind the desk when Tania's office had been broken into.

Tania pulled out two sheets of paper and put them on the desk for Walker to see. One was some sort of certificate in French. The other was an official-looking letter written in English from the Académie de Paris. He skimmed through the letter.

'Looks okay, I guess.'

'Perhaps you're being too hard on her, Chris. The training may be very different in France. They might do all their practical work as interns.'

'I suppose so.'

'She's not putting any patients at risk, is she?'

'No way. She's mostly hanging around on ward rounds. I've never seen her talking to patients much. I'm not sure what she does all day.'

'I'm sure she's mostly here on a holiday. Can you blame her for trying to see some of the sights while she's here? She'll be gone soon.'

'I guess you're right. It's an elective, after all.'

The phone rang and Tania picked it up. The call sounded like another doctor asking about one of her patients. She had put the folder down on the desk, still open. Walker could see the first document on the top. It was an Australian visa. It looked official enough, in the name of Patrice Élodie Segal.

He started to feel bad complaining about her. As Tania said, she was here for a break from university. He probably should have insisted she take time off and see more of Sydney. Western Meadows was not in the most salubrious part of the city, after all. And there didn't seem to be any information in her folder that was worth stealing.

Tania finished her call and he stood up.

'That all seems in order. She's only here for another month, so it's no big deal. I guess I was getting a bit worried since Pier was making a big thing of it. He spends more time with her. He was insistent that I check out her credentials with you.' Walker put up both hands. 'I've done that now so everyone should be happy. I'll tell Pier to rest easy.'

CHAPTER SEVENTEEN

WALKER GOT HOME after dark and was surprised to see police trucks still parked on the street. He went down the side lane to the back of his house. A huge mound of dirt had been dumped on the edge of the lane, partially covered by a tarpaulin. A bright light could be seen over the fence emanating from his backyard and he could hear the hum of a portable generator.

The back gate was open and through it he could see a ring of blue-clothed men looking down into a hole. Walker's heart dropped. They had found his mother's body!

Reluctantly, he edged through the gate and squeezed between the line of officers who ignored him.

In the bottom of the hole was a woman on her hands and knees, a torch in one hand, her face close to the ground, intently examining something. Walker couldn't see what she was looking at. No one spoke.

Walker raised his head to look across the circle. David Jones didn't acknowledge him. He was frowning down at whatever the woman was working on.

Finally, she sat back and looked up. 'Yes, it's definite.'

'Are you sure?' asked Jones.

'Positive.' She stood up and brushed off her clothes. 'This

site will need to be closed. We'll get the experts in first thing tomorrow.'

Walker's eyes drifted back down to the bottom. He didn't want to look but he knew he had to. But all he could see was what looked like a rough sandstone rock. There were no bones.

Walker moved beside Jones, who was still staring down. 'What is it? What did you find?'

Jones finally turned to Walker, still frowning. 'Bloody foundations.'

'What?'

'Bloody First Fleet. Probably a convict's home or shop. The archaeologists will have to take over. I'm sorry, Chris, but this will slow things down. They'll be here for ages.'

'But you didn't find any bones?'

'No.'

'But that means there's no body. Do you know what that means? If you've dug down to the First Fleet then my mother's not going to be down there.'

'Well, we haven't done the whole yard.' Jones pointed to the shed that housed a laundry and outside toilet. 'We haven't done under there yet.'

'Who's going to bury a body in a dunny?'

Jones shrugged. 'We have to be thorough.'

Walker turned away and blew out a relieved breath. He didn't care whether they were here until Christmas – his mother wasn't down there.

The next day, Pier was back on the ward after having a few days off to recover.

'Feeling better?'

'I'm fine. I was actually feeling perfect after a few hours but Dr Forcett insisted I take time off.'

Walker hesitated before he went on. 'Do you really think someone tried to kill you?'

'I can't say. I don't know who would try or why. Thankfully, whoever it was didn't try very hard. Anyway, I'm back now.'

'Okay, as long as you feel well enough. I checked into Élodie Segal. I sat down with Tania. All her documents were in order – visa, letters from Paris.'

'Are you sure? They're easily forged.'

'How would you know that?'

'It's just something I've heard. Was there a passport?'

Walker nodded. 'All official. She's here for an elective so I suggest we go easy on her. It's just another month.'

'Well, why doesn't she take some time off and sightsee. She's at the hospital all the time. Lives in the students' quarters. I don't think she's even been in to see the Opera House.'

'How would you know that? Are you keeping tabs on her?'

Pier turned away abruptly. 'That's a ridiculous suggestion.'

Walker wondered whether Jenny was wrong. Maybe Pier wasn't gay. He couldn't see it himself. 'Don't worry, Pier, I wouldn't hold it against you. She's quite attractive.'

Pier gave a perplexed frown but then laughed when he took Walker's meaning. 'I can assure you, I have no romantic interest in her.'

Walker paused. He still wasn't sure. Maybe he should ask? Instead, he said, 'What about you? Are you seeing the Sydney sights? Why don't you come into the city and have drinks with Madeline and me?'

'Madeline? Are you seeing her?'

Walker screwed his lips tightly. 'Well, to be honest, I don't know. I've given her more than enough hints. She appears to like me. But she doesn't seem to want to take it any further.'

Pier considered his words for a moment before answering. 'Yes, I agree, that's strange. She's not gay. So maybe she's not attracted to you.'

'Gay? Why would she be gay?'

Pier gave him a look as if he thought him strange. 'Do you have trouble with people being homosexual?'

'No,' he said, too quickly. 'Not at all.'

'Good, because your department head is gay.'

Walker nodded. 'Yes, so Jenny said. So, maybe Élodie is gay also. That would explain it.'

'Élodie's not gay. And what would it explain?'

'Her not wanting to go out with you.'

Pier gave Walker a look of intense incredulity. Then he gave a gleeful laugh.

'What? said Walker. 'Okay, maybe I don't get gay relationships!'

Pier kept laughing gently. 'That's okay, Dr Walker. Maybe you should ask Jenny about it.'

'Don't tell me she's gay.'

Pier continued to chuckle. 'You have no idea.'

'Speak of the devils, here they come now,' said Walker, indicating Jenny and Élodie who were walking towards them. 'We were just talking about you two,' he said when they reached him.

'Oh?' said Jenny suspiciously. 'Knowing you, Chris, I won't embarrass you and ask what you were speaking about.'

'That's probably for the best,' said Pier, still smirking.

There was a shout from along the corridor and they all turned in that direction. A nurse stood outside one of the patient rooms, blood dripping from her face. Together, they rushed to her.

In the bathroom attached to the room stood a naked man – the young man who had been admitted the other day. Blood was sprayed on the wall, floor and ceiling. Graham held one hand in the other to show his wrist, which he'd slashed. He extended his hand so bright blood pumped from the severed arteries like a water pistol.

'Get back,' he growled. 'I don't want to hurt anyone. Just let me be.'

Pier stepped towards him but Graham directed the blood at him and drenched his face. Pier cried out, covering his eyes and twisting away. Jenny pulled him out of the room, leaving Élodie and Walker to confront the man.

They paused. 'Why are you doing this?' asked Walker.

'What do you think? This cancer. You won't be able to fix it. I don't want to die a miserable death like those other poor bastards.'

'We're trying to cure you,' said Walker.

The blood was oozing down his hand and dripping onto the floor in a steady stream. 'You can't do that. Everyone knows it.' He pointed at Élodie. 'She was crying about it yesterday.'

Graham appeared to be getting weaker. He stumbled and Walker lunged at him but he raised his hand and sprayed blood onto Walker's face, causing him to pull back and squeeze his eyes shut.

There was a cry and Walker heard a chair fall to the ground. When he opened his eyes, Graham was on his knees and Élodie stood behind him. She held his bleeding hand between hers, stifling the flow, and at the same time had his arm bent back, immobilising him. 'Jenny, throw me a towel,' she called.

Moments later, despite her small frame, she had Graham on the ground, a knee in his back so he couldn't move and was winding the towel around his wrist, stopping the flow. Two security guards arrived and they managed to get him back to his bed, where Jenny bandaged his wrist tightly. Pier and Walker helped to restrain him, their faces and shirts covered with blood. Élodie seemed unmarked except for bloodied hands.

'Nicely done, Élodie,' said Walker, stepping away to allow the nurses and Ben to sort Graham out. 'Where'd you learn that?'

She smiled. 'I may not know about pulmonary embolism but I do know a few other things.'

Walker smiled back. 'You'll have to show me that trick one day.'

CHAPTER EIGHTEEN

BRUCE ROWNTREE WAS waiting at his front door when Walker pulled up outside on Lower Fort Street. Walker stepped out of the car, mindful of the blood that covered him. He'd managed to wash it off his face and hands but the blood had soaked into the fabric of his white shirt. It was going to be hard to get the stains out.

But Rowntree seemed oblivious. He held up a large brown envelope. 'I've got something for you here, Kit. Thought I should come straight around and show it to you.'

'Hang on,' said Walker, 'I'll let us in.'

He opened the door and walked through to the kitchen then turned to face Rowntree. He pointed at the blood. 'Aren't you going to ask?'

'Nah, looks like some doctor's shit. You probably come home like that every day.' He tapped the envelope. 'What I've got here is more important than a bit of blood.'

Walker shrugged his shoulders and sat down at the table. 'Okay, give me a look then.'

Rowntree sat down and pushed the envelope across the tabletop. 'What I have here, Kit, is highly confidential. I can let you look at it but you can't keep it. And you can't tell anyone that you've seen it.'

'What is it? Do I really want to be involved?'

'I've come into the possession of a transcript of an interview with an undisclosed witness who had been in the pub the night your dad had an altercation. A certain dirty copper, who shall remain nameless, made a copy of the transcript from the police records for Ralph Collinson. But Collinson is now in jail, so said copper gave me the transcript in exchange for a favour.'

'What favour?'

'Don't you worry about that. That's my business. I shouldn't even give this to you. So, whatever you do, don't go giving this to Wendy or any other copper. Collinson's in jail but that doesn't mean he's harmless. He's still got lots of friends outside.'

Rowntree handed Walker the envelope and he pulled the wad of papers out onto the table. He began to read.

This interview was held at Long Bay Jail, Matraville, on 16 June 1990. 'Redacted name' is being interviewed by Senior Detective Sergeant Royce Wills.

Police: Can you tell me what happened in the Captain Cook pub on the evening of the seventeenth of February 1960, specifically the conversation you overheard between Lester Walker and John Leremy.

Witness: Conversation. It was more like a shouting match.

Police: Can you recall what was said?

Witness: Walker and Leremy were sitting together having a beer.

Police: At a table or the bar?

Witness: A table. A small one. They were opposite each other. They were there when I came in having a quiet beer together. You know, like friends. They worked on the docks together.

Police: Then you heard an argument?

Witness: Yeah. Leremy said in a loud voice, as if he wanted everyone in the pub to hear, 'I don't know how your wife can stand you. Good-looking woman like her. Don't know why she's hanging around a loser like you.'

Police: And Walker? What did he say?

Witness: Walker said something like, 'You stay away from her. If you go anywhere near her, I'll gut you like a fish'.

Police: He said that? Gut you like a fish?

Witness: Yeah. Then Leremy goes, 'Oh really, you puny little fly.

I squash men like you every day. Just face it, you'll never satisfy a woman like your wife. She needs a real man. Someone who can roger her silly so she's begging for more. I remember those words. I thought it was a bit over the top even for a pub like the Cook. Then Walker says, 'Someone like you, Two-Face?'

Police: Two-Face?

Witness: Two-Face Leremy. That's what he was called. Then Leremy said, 'Yeah, like me. I might go round there now. Let her feel what it's like to have a real man. You can watch if you like. You might learn something.'

Police: Did that make Walker angry?

Witness: Too right it did. He was ropable. Thought he was about to smash him in the mouth. But then Walker became all quiet. Then he said, 'No wonder Collinson thinks you're a dickhead.'

Leremy didn't like that but it seemed to shut him up. He started talking close to Walker so I couldn't hear, although I could hear Collinson mentioned a few times.

Police: What happened then?

Witness: Walker got up and left.

Police: Did he come back?

Witness: Not when I was there.

Police: And when did you leave?

Witness: After ten.

Police: And what did John Leremy do?

Witness: He sat there for a while drinking his beer. The next time I looked over he was gone.

Police: Which door did he take?

Witness: I think the back. I was sitting near the front door and I didn't see him go that way.

Police: Is there anything else you would like to tell us?

Witness: Don't think so. That's everything I can remember.

Walker turned over the last page and sat back in his chair. 'What do you know about this Two-Face Leremy? What did he have to do with my father?'

'John Leremy did work with your dad on the wharves,' said

Rowntree. 'But his main source of income was being a goon for Collinson. Collinson ran a bunch of betting shops in Newtown. Roger Neville was another one of the goons who's ended up in Long Bay. Neville The Nose, they called him. I reckon he's the snitch in the transcript. They got him for murder at last in 1980. He must have had a falling out with Collinson back then otherwise he'd have made sure the cops backed off. Collinson was in bed with the cops. You know, mutual back-scratching society.'

'What do you mean?'

Rowntree let out a sigh. 'My, my, Kit, you're so naive. Don't you know how these things work? Collinson fed info to two crooked cops – Ned Stoner and Owen Olsen – about what was going down in other parts of the city so they could make arrests and get promotions. In return, Stoner and Olsen would neutralise his enemies and protect his business.'

'So what made this Nose fellow make up a story about my father?'

'He's up for parole. Looking for brownie points. If he gives them info that leads to an arrest, they might let him out.'

'So who killed Leremy then?'

'That I don't know. Have my suspicions. Two-Face Leremy was a greedy bastard by nature. Normally, he would've been under Collinson's protection. The only person who would allow Leremy to be killed would be Collinson himself. If Leremy had passed on dirt to Collinson's enemies, that would be enough. Collinson would think nothing of stabbing him in the back. Literally.'

'So, Collinson then?'

'Except for his alibi. He was at his own engagement party at the Glebe Town Hall in front of a hundred witnesses, including Stoner and Olsen. They testified that he was at the party the whole night. No way he could have got from Glebe to the Captain Cook without someone noticing.'

'Or lying about it.'

'Precisely. It's a well-known fact that Collinson disappeared from the party for over an hour but no one's saying anything. Anyway, this is far above our pay grade. Leave that to the cops to investigate. The main thing is to clear your father's name.' He pointed to the paper on the table. 'At least we're now on a level playing field. We know what the coppers have got.'

CHAPTER NINETEEN

BACK AT THE Parramatta Police Station, Darling and Bianca were again going over the case. Darling was flicking through a copy of the Bible, trying to cross-reference the verses Reverend Wesley had given them with the contents of the letter found in Krantz's pocket. He was reading around the passages to see if there were any other clues. So far, he'd drawn a blank. He was concentrating on the part of the letter that said *Vengeance is mine, for the day of your calamity is at hand.* He couldn't get it to match the words in the Bible.

He called out to his colleague who was seated at a desk nearby going through the mail. 'Bianca, you've had a religious upbringing – where am I going wrong? I've gone to that Deuteronomy passage the reverend pointed us to but they don't match.' He traced his finger along a line in the Bible that sat on the desk. 'Here it says, *It is mine to avenge; I will repay. In due time their foot will slip; their day of disaster is near and their doom rushes upon them.*' He lifted his head. 'It doesn't say anything about vengeance.'

'What version of Bible is it?'

'What? There are versions?'

'Look on the cover, it'll tell you.'

He flipped to the front. 'New International Version.'

'The reverend would have read from the King James Version, which is what the Anglicans use, if I'm not mistaken. We used The Good News Bible at school. That would have different wording again.'

'How many bloody versions are there?'

'Hundreds, probably, especially when you take in the other languages. The original Old Testament was in old Hebrew and the New Testament in Greek, so they're all translations.'

Darling threw the book down on his desk in disgust. 'How are we supposed to make any sense out of this?'

'In fact, that sounds like a clue, sir. If the writer used the King James Version, then he was probably of the Protestant faith. Although, I suppose they could have copied it from whatever Bible they had handy.'

'I think you may be onto something there, Bianca. He was looking for the word "vengeance". They must have known what they were looking for and must have heard it read like that sometime in their life. So they might have been raised as a Protestant.' He opened the Bible again. 'It's a small clue but at least it's something.'

'Sir,' said Bianca, holding up an A3-sized piece of paper, 'look at this from the Brisbane police. It makes interesting reading. It was in the Brisbane *Courier-Mail* six months ago.'

Bianca handed him a photocopy of a newspaper article.

He read out the headline. '"Herr heir leaves fortune to feathered friends".' He glanced at Bianca. 'Catchy title. So what?'

'Keep reading.'

Darling began to read the article aloud. 'The Currumbin Bird Sanctuary got an early surprise Christmas present this year from an unlikely source. A local resident and longtime friend of the sanctuary, Markus Schneider, has left his fortune to the Gold Coast's most famous bird park after he died from natural causes two months ago.' Darling looked up again. 'What's this got to do with us, Bianca?'

She clicked her tongue irritably. 'Just keep reading.'

'The sanctuary released a statement saying that the two million dollars will go a long way to improve conditions and facilities. "Markus really loved our birds," said the Currumbin CEO.' Darling looked up. 'I'll say. Two million dollars for a bunch of birds. The headline should have read "Birdbrain splashes fortune on birds", if you ask me.' He chuckled at his own cleverness. When Bianca failed to join in, he returned to the article. 'But in a twist that is more in keeping with a TV soapie than real life, the source of Markus Schneider's fortune is even more interesting than the donation. Local probate lawyer ...' Darling slowed and gave Bianca a meaningful look before continuing, 'Solomon Krantz, reported that Markus had inherited a substantial sum from his brother, Gustaf Schneider, who had been tragically murdered in Munich Germany two years ago. To make matters even more curious, Gustaf's only child had been cut out of his will and all the money had gone to Markus. Paul Schneider has since disappeared.'

Darling continued reading. '"I was surprised that the will was not challenged," said Mr Krantz, "but I heard nothing from the son, so I proceeded with the wishes of my client."' Darling folded the sheet. 'Well, I'll be damned.'

'What do you think it means?' asked Bianca.

'Don't know. Is it just coincidence that a few months later, Krantz was murdered?'

'The son? Could it be Paul Schneider who killed Krantz?'

'Maybe. But what would he gain from it?'

'Revenge?'

'I guess. But if he was the murdering type, he'd get more satisfaction from murdering his uncle Markus.'

'Maybe he did.'

Darling raised the paper. 'It said he died of natural causes.' He paused for a moment. 'Good work, Bianca. How did you go comparing Krantz's clients with the hotel list?'

'There's no match. None of Krantz's client in the last two

years match any of the hotel guests.'

'Not even partially? Not even the surname?'

'No.'

'Can I have a look?'

Bianca handed him a sheet of paper and he ran his eye down the list of names. 'Who are all these people?'

'All locals wanting the usual solicitor stuff. Wills, estates, legal letters, a bit of conveyancing.'

'We'll need to contact them and see if there are any links with any of the hotel guests. We should concentrate on the most recent cases first.'

'I'll get onto it,' said Bianca.

'Get yourself up to Brisbane as soon as you can. Go to his office, talk to his secretary. See what you can find.'

'Can't we ask the local police to do that? It's going to be a lot of work. I'll have to check all his files.'

Darling twisted a ring on his finger. 'You know the old jungle saying,' he intoned. 'The Phantom never refuses a challenge.'

Bianca returned his beaming smile with a baffled look. 'Excuse me, sir? The Phantom … what?'

Darling lost his smile and shook his head despondently. 'Never mind, Bianca. I'd rather you do it. You must have heard about their Police Commissioner, Terry Lewis?'

She nodded. 'Caught up in the Fitzgerald Inquiry for corruption and forgery. I hear he got fourteen years.'

'I figure the local cops are going to be in a spin. They may not give the attention to the case that it deserves.'

'Okay, I'll book my ticket.'

Darling got up and walked to the corkboard. 'What do we know about any possible Brisbane connections?'

Bianca joined him. 'We know a number of the Western Meadows team were either from Brisbane or had been there recently.' She read from a list tacked to the board. 'According to our initial interviews we have three people from Western Meadows who said they'd been to Brisbane in the last six months—Madeline Piper, Élodie Segal and Pier Mathijssen.'

'What's their connection with Brisbane?'

'Madeline Piper is a doctor and has lived in Brisbane all her life. There is no known connection with Krantz.'

'Her mother was a businesswoman. Could Krantz have been doing some work for her?'

'Good question,' said Bianca. She scribbled in her notepad. 'I'll follow up on that.' She looked back to the board. 'Next we have Élodie Segal. She's a French medical student who claims she was visiting Brisbane as a tourist. Again, there's no obvious connection with Krantz.'

'And Pier Mathijssen was also in Brisbane,' said Darling. 'He also claims he was sightseeing. I think we need to interview him again about what he was doing there.'

'And Élodie Segal?'

'Yes, of course,' agreed Darling. 'We need to cover every possibility. I'll look into that personally.'

CHAPTER TWENTY

MADELINE HAD INSISTED on meeting Walker at the Hero rather than going to his place first. At five to seven he'd left home hoping to get there first but as soon as he entered the door of the old pub, he spied her at the bar. She was talking to James, the barman. James was laughing, his prominent Adam's apple dancing up and down his neck at something that she'd said. James never laughed. Walker struggled to remember ever seeing that laconic string-bean break into anything more than a smile in the past. But then again, he'd also thought he was the silent type then found out later, through Cassie, that was because Walker had never thought to start a conversation with him.

Following the direction of James's stare, Madeline turned towards him as he approached, a joyous smile on her face. 'Good evening, Chris. Jim and I were just having a good old talk about you.'

Jim! James hated to be called Jim. Walker gave a weak smile. 'All good, I hope.'

Madeline shared a look with Jim then turned back. 'No, I wouldn't say that.'

Walker let out a laugh but there was nothing in it. He glared at the barman. 'Telling stories out of school, are we, James?'

James placed a schooner of pilsner on the bar for Walker.

He'd lost his smile. Before he moved away to tend to another patron, he said, 'It was a pleasure meeting you, Madeline. I hope to see you in here again.'

'What were you two talking about?' asked Walker after James had left.

She looked over her glass as she took a sip of her white wine. 'Oh, you know, this and that.'

He smiled uncomfortably. 'That's not fair, hearing about my personal affairs behind my back.'

'Who said it was personal?'

'Anything interesting is personal. Everything else is fluff.'

Madeline smiled. 'You know, you're right. Jim was telling me about you and your friend Wendy and what you got up to when you were kids.'

Walker was relieved. He thought it might have been about Flea. Or at least Cassandra. 'Oh, I'm sure he exaggerated. We were just normal kids.'

'Not too much parental guidance from what I heard. I would have loved to have grown up like that. My mum kept a tight rein on me.'

'You make it sound as if we were neglected.'

'I didn't mean that. Sounds like you had more freedom than me though.'

Walker gulped his beer. 'I guess so.' He realised he was being too sensitive again. He didn't want the evening to end up like the last one. 'We did get in trouble with the police a few times.'

'Really? What for?'

'Car stealing. Petty theft.'

'Wow! Drugs?'

'No, we never did drugs.'

'Not even when you were teenagers?'

'No, Flea's folks were druggies. She was dead against anything to do with drugs. Not even weed.' Walker hesitated. He could kick himself. Here he was babbling on about his dead wife.

'Flea … that would be Felicity, your wife? The one who died in New Guinea.'

'You know about her?'

Madeline put her hand on his. 'Jim and I talked for quite a while. He knows a lot about you.'

Walker clamped his jaw tight. 'He shouldn't have. It's not his business.'

'Chris, if we're going to be friends, we have to find out about each other, both the good and the bad.'

'Flea wasn't bad.'

'I didn't mean that. But it must have been an awful time. I can't understand how you could have come through that unscathed. Your wife murdered. Not knowing what had happened to her for years. You poor thing.'

All Walker could do was nod. A guitarist started strumming the chords of 'Reckless'. They listened to the first few lines of the verse. After the Manly ferry had arrived at Circular Quay, he turned to her. 'What about you? Any hard luck stories? Any secrets? Any long-lost relative stories?'

Madeline didn't answer immediately, and for a moment she seemed uncomfortable before she smiled. 'Nothing like that. We all have our secrets though.'

'And what's yours?'

She took a long sip before she answered. 'Well, for one, I didn't have a father. Never met him. All I've got of his is his surname.'

Walker already knew that but he decided not to push. 'Same as me. I didn't have a mother.' He realised he was starting over the same conversation they had had at the Fortune of War on their first date. Maybe this would end better?

However, for some reason this time it seemed to upset her. She squeezed his hand. 'But you had her for a little while. You said you were five when she left.'

'Died. She died.'

'Sorry, yes, that's what I meant. You must have some memories.'

Walker was silent while he struggled to remember. 'I was five, maybe four. Thing is, I can't remember what she looked like. Sometimes I hear her voice in my dreams. At least, I think it's her voice. But when I'm awake I can't remember. I wouldn't be able to describe her to you. I think her hair was brown.'

'You must remember how you felt about her.'

'She was my mother. She was kind to me. I loved her. I remember she was sad a lot of the time.'

For a while they sat companionably side by side sipping on their drinks and listening to the guitarist. Then Walker realised that somehow, he'd done all the talking. He'd hardly found out anything more about Madeline.

In the break between songs, he leaned towards her. 'You're very good at teasing information out of people. You should be a cop.'

She smiled. 'Comes in handy as a doctor. I'm very good at getting a medical history.'

Walker thought about his parents. Whether they had been happy together. How his father had been when his mother wasn't there anymore. He decided to ask Madeline a question. The music had started up again, so he put his mouth close to her ear. 'Was your mother sad when your dad left?'

She turned so her mouth was close. 'I don't know. I always remember her as vivacious and happy. Hardworking. My mum said that my father left before I was born. She might have been sad but my memories of her are all lively. She laughed a lot.'

After the band had finished, Madeline said she needed to leave due to an early brachytherapy list in the morning. They left together. Walker helped her down the stairs from the pub and didn't let go of her hand when she reached the footpath. She seemed content to walk holding hands with him. The route to the train went past his house and Walker paused at his front gate.

He held both her hands. 'You don't have to go home, you know,' he said to her.

Madeline smiled, bent her head to his and kissed him on the cheek. 'I don't think that's very sensible, Chris. But you can be a gentleman and walk me to the station?'

They walked to Circular Quay in silence. When they reached the gate, Madeline turned to him and again gave him a peck on the cheek. 'Thanks for a lovely evening, Chris. I'll see you tomorrow.'

Walker watched her until she disappeared from view up the stairs to the platform.

CHAPTER TWENTY-ONE

AT WILLS' REQUEST, Darling agreed to introduce him to some of the residents of Lower Fort Street so he could interview them about Lester Walker. The first port of call was Chris Walker's neighbour, Janet Bidwell.

Jones knocked and the door was opened by a lady wearing a tie-dyed kaftan. She was past middle-age with a long face and a huge mane of hair that was beaded and tied with ribbons.

Darling greeted her. 'Janet, thanks for agreeing to meet. These are the two officers I told you about, Senior Detective Sergeant Royce Wills and Constable David Jones. I'm just observing, so I won't be asking any questions.'

Jones and Wills showed their badges and asked whether they could come inside. Her loungeroom was a riot of coloured rugs, large floral paintings, candles and plants. A glass pyramid sat on a low rattan table in the middle of the room and Janet indicated for them take a seat. She plopped herself onto a wicker rocking chair.

Royce Wills took an armchair and Archie immediately jumped onto a cabinet next to him at face height a short distance away. Archie locked a stare on Wills, full of utter disdain. Wills appeared disconcerted by the large cat's interest and leaned away.

'Is the cat bothering you, officer?' asked Janet.

Wills gave a half-nod. 'Not my favourite animal.'

'Okay then,' said Janet. She remained seated.

Darling had to stifle a smile.

Jones began. 'Mrs Bidwell, we're inquiring about the whereabouts of Jane Walker and we're hoping you could help us.'

Janet put her hand to her mouth. 'Jane! Oh dear, that was a long time ago.'

'Do you remember when you last saw her?'

'Oh, let me see … that would be in the early sixties.'

'Were you living here then?'

'Oh yes, I was born here. In this actual house. Yes, I knew Jane and Lester. Their son, Chris, still lives next door. Wendy here used to live across the road.'

Wills gave a fake smile. 'Wendy.' He glanced at Darling then back to Janet. 'Very nice. Do you know what happened to Jane Walker?'

'She died.'

'Do you know that for a fact?' asked Wills.

'Why would anyone lie about that? She was here and then she became very unwell and went to hospital. A few weeks later she died, poor thing.'

'No funeral?'

'I heard she was buried in her home town. She was a country girl – Armidale, I think.'

'What did her husband say she died from?'

'Cancer.' She paused. 'I'm not really sure though, love. Doctors didn't explain a lot in those days. Best that you ask her son, Chris. He'd know.'

'Would it surprise you that there is no record of her death?'

'Wouldn't surprise me at all. Sloppy records in those days. Probably got the name mixed up in the hospital.'

'How did Lester Walker seem afterwards?' asked Jones.

'Shattered, as you'd expect. He was never the same afterwards.' She shook her head. 'Terrible for someone so young to die. And with a little child and all.'

Wills leaned forward. 'Mrs Bidwell, we are led to believe that Jane Williams did not die from cancer or any other natural cause. We're investigating her possible murder.'

She raised a hand to her mouth. 'Oh dear. Murder. Is that why you're digging up Chris's backyard? You looking for a body?'

'That's classified.'

'You found anything? I doubt it, otherwise the newspapers would be all over it. I see the archaeologists have stuck their noses into it. I could have warned you. If you ever go digging up around here, make sure you do it a night when the archaeologists are nowhere in sight. Convict bits and pieces are everywhere, just a few inches under. Chris'll never be rid of them, you know.'

Wills snapped his notebook shut. Archie had moved closer to him and the shaggy cat's pupils had turned large and dark. Wills glanced at the powerful claws and backed further away. 'Is there anything else you can tell us about Jane and Lester Walker? Did they fight?'

'Who's married and doesn't fight? Course they fought. But they made up afterwards. Having said that, Jane never looked particularly happy. Lester drank a lot. Spent hours at work then most nights at the pub. Maybe she got sick of him and pissed off?'

'Where to?'

'How would I know? Armidale?'

'Do you think that might have happened?'

'Wouldn't be the first woman who ran out on her man around here. Place is full of them. You'd be hard-pressed to find a proper family in these parts. I don't know any, except for the Barleys up in Windmill Street. But that's probably 'cause he's off travelling most of the time.'

Archie stood and stared intently at Will's closest ear.

Wills lurched to his feet. 'Thank you, Mrs Bidwell, you've been most helpful.' Jones joined him. 'Please contact us if you have any other information.'

She showed them to the door and Darling hung back after the two had left.

'He's a right dick, Wendy,' she said, staring up the road after them. 'Bloody coppers. Always sticking their grubby noses where they don't belong.'

'I'm a copper, Janet.'

She looked him up and down. 'Yes, you are, but at least you're from around here.' She looked back towards the officers who were getting into their car. 'The nerve of them coming around here and insinuating that Lester killed poor Jane. He'd never do that. Luckily Bruce Rowntree told me the bloody coppers would probably come knocking. Good man, Bruce. Sticks up for his own.'

'What do you really think happened to Jane Walker, Janet?'

'Died of cancer. And I know that Lester wouldn't have knocked her off. But I heard the gossip about her having an affair. She was a good-looking woman. Sexy. Around then, she had this lime-green miniskirt, just like Twiggy but even before she was modelling them. Not real short, but short enough to show her legs.'

'Do you think she could have had an affair with Leremy?'

'Maybe. I don't think she was the type but she used to get a lot of attention. And Lester wasn't the best husband. Always at the pub or working.'

'If Jane had an affair with Leremy, it's possible that Lester could have been driven to murder.'

Janet scrunched up her mouth. 'Maybe. He just didn't seem like a killer.'

'It's not the first time that jealousy has caused an otherwise gentle man to commit murder.'

'I guess so, Wendy.' She still looked unsure. 'I'll have to leave that to you coppers.'

He stepped through the door. 'Thanks again for your help, Janet. I better be going.'

'I hear you've got yourself a house in Glebe. And you've got yourself a nice girl.'

'Who told you that?'

She tapped the side of her nose and grinned. 'I have my sources too.'

'Bye, Janet.'

'Bye, Wendy.' As Darling walked away, she called after him. 'And Wendy, make friends again with Kit, for God's sake.'

Darling turned back to her. 'Oh, we have. Maybe not the way we were but we're friends again.'

CHAPTER TWENTY-TWO

CONSTABLE DAVID JONES stood in front of a large board at the police headquarters in Central Street, idly wondering which colour marker pen to use. Wills called the thing a whiteboard and considered it to be very modern. It was held upright by a heavy metal frame that could be moved on wheels, although it kept getting stuck in the carpet, threatening to topple the whole bloody contraption. Jones didn't like it. You could never wipe the writing off properly, so you ended up writing over someone else's partially erased scribble. And it was hard to stick anything to it. The magnetic strips that held sheets of paper in place were always falling off, so people resorted to sticky tape – which, again, was never pulled off completely. The whole thing ended up being a bloody sticky mess. Jones liked the corkboard. It was easy and neat and it left a nice orderly story so one could think about the problem, not about how to keep a photo in place for more than five minutes at a stretch. This *thing* just muddled your mind like alphabet soup. But Wills insisted on it. Wills was the first to introduce it to head office and wanted it used it at every opportunity. He wanted to make a name for himself and this would be his signature investigative method.

Wills leaned back on his desk facing Jones, arms crossed over his chest, his eyes closed as if meditating. 'Okay, Jones, let me show you how to use this rig. It will help sort things out in no time.'

'Right you are, sir. What should I write first?'

'The victim. Jane Walker.' Jones started writing. 'No, Jones, erase that. Just write JW, it will save on space.' Jones looked back to see that Wills had one eye open, which he now closed. 'Next, list the suspects. Lester Williams – LW, Two-Face Leremy—'

'Is that TFL or JL for John Leremy?'

'Make it JL. Then there's …' Wills paused, thinking.

'Should we add Ralph Collinson, sir?'

'Collinson? He had an alibi, provided by two of our own officers. Why would we add him?'

Jones paused, his pen hovering over the white surface. 'Sir, don't you think it's odd that police officers attended the wedding of one of Sydney's most notorious criminals?'

Wills jumped up. 'Keep your voice down, Jones. Be careful what sort of theories you bandy around within earshot of the others. Could end you up in hot water.'

'We're in police headquarters, sir.'

'Exactly. You never know who's listening.' He leaned back again. 'Let's proceed.'

'Shall I put RC up anyway?'

'Go ahead. But see the usefulness of initials? It will mean nothing to the casual eye. You've learned something already.'

Jones stepped back and reviewed the board. 'It's not much of a list of suspects.'

'Put up Roger "The Nose" Neville.'

'The jail snitch, sir? The one who claims he heard LW fighting with JL? Would that be RN or RTNN?'

'Are you making fun of me, Jones?'

'No, sir. I find this all very elucidating.'

'Now here comes the best bit. Using a different colour pen, draw a circle around each person and connect them to another person who has a direct link with them.'

'Sir?'

'Draw a circle around JW in orange and link her with LW, then LW in green linked to JN. Then in blue, link JN to both RN and RC.'

Jones did as directed then stood back. To him, it just looked like a jumble of coloured lines. And he couldn't remember who any of the initials stood for. He stared for a moment longer before glancing back at Wills.

Wills was scratching his cheek and wore a slightly dazed look. 'Perhaps we'll leave that for the moment, Jones. I think this system needs further refinement to get the most out of it. Let's review what we have in a different way. What are the facts?'

'We have a dead body in a lane, John Leremy. Stabbed through the heart.'

'Good, yes,' said Wills. 'We have many people witnessing Lester Walker and John Leremy having an argument in the Captain Cook Hotel on the night the body was found. The argument was about Walker's wife.'

'We have Jane Walker disappearing a few months later.'

'Correct, but there is no record of her death. Lester Walker claims she had cancer but we cannot find any evidence of that. We have more than one person saying that Jane Walker was an attractive woman.'

'Sexy, many said.'

'Yes,' agreed Wills. 'Like a model. And that Lester and Jane Walker did not seem particularly happy.' He thought for a moment before continuing. 'We have evidence from Roger Neville—'

Jones looked up at the board. 'RN.'

'Yes, Jones, let's forgo the initials for the moment. Roger Neville said that Lester Walker's wife was having an affair with Leremy.'

'Could Jane Walker have just run off?'

'That's possible. But unlikely. She hasn't turned up anywhere after all this time. And she has a son. You know what women are like with their boys. If she were still alive, she would have turned up to see Chris Walker after her husband died.'

'So what are you thinking, sir?'

'I think Lester Walker killed Leremy and then killed his wife and disposed of the body.'

'Where? We've dug up Walker's backyard but there was nothing.'

'Just think, Jones. What was Lester Walker's job?'

'Wharfie.'

'Yes, he was a wharfie. If you were a wharfie and a murderer, what's the most likely place you would dispose of a body?

Jones though for a moment. 'Off the wharf?'

Wills nodded knowingly. 'Exactly. The harbour. He had access to the wharves. He could have killed her, popped her body in the boot of his car then threw it in the water, weighed down somehow.'

'Sounds possible,' agreed Jones.

Wills rubbed his hands together. 'If we find her body, that will be the link. It will solve two murders in one fell swoop.'

'What now?'

'I'm going to talk to our sailor buddies down at Pyrmont. I think we'll find the evidence we need at the bottom of the harbour.'

'Pyrmont?'

'The Water Police.'

CHAPTER TWENTY-THREE

IT WAS GETTING towards the end of the day and Walker didn't have anything to do for once. Or at least, he didn't have anything he *had* to do or felt like doing. There was always something – letters to write, papers to review, blood tests to sign. He thought he would ask Madeline out for a coffee. He had to settle once and for all whether he had any chance with her.

He headed down to the radiation oncology department and saw Madeline and Pier standing together some way along an empty corridor. As he walked towards them, he noticed they seemed to be arguing. Madeline was backed against the wall and Pier was close to her, gesticulating. Just before Walker reached them, Pier turned to look at him. He was scowling. He leaned in close to Madeline and said something, then spun away and walked in the opposite direction.

'Everything okay?' asked Walker when he reached her. She seemed agitated and her hair had fallen forward to partially obscure her eyes.

'He's full of himself,' said Madeline. 'Thinks he's god's gift to medicine.'

'Wow! Where did that come from?' said Walker. 'I agree he's a bit aloof sometimes but I've not seen that in him. What's going on?'

'You don't know him like I do.'

'Really? How do you know him?'

Madeline paused as if she didn't want to add any more.

Then she sighed. 'I worked with him in Manchester.'

'Oh?' Walker looked after the retreating figure. 'I knew Pier was in Manchester but didn't know you were there together.'

'We only overlapped by a few months. We were working on similar studies.'

'Long enough for you to form a strong opinion though.'

Madeline pulled the hair back from her forehead and pushed away from the wall. 'I'm sure I'm making too much of it.' She smiled. 'You know how pushy these Dutch can be. Sometimes it gets to me.'

'What were you fighting about just now?'

'Fighting? I think that's too strong. Let's say we were having a robust discussion. It was about a paper we co-wrote. It was nothing.' She looked in the direction Pier had taken. 'I just found him a bit annoying.'

'Okay then,' said Walker. 'Want a coffee?'

'Yes, please. Besides, there's something I want to ask you.'

'Oh?'

'A favour.'

'Interesting. What sort of favour?'

'A big favour. Wait until we've got our coffees. I'll take you somewhere nice. Let's go to Parramatta.'

Half an hour later, Madeline and Walker strolled along George Street in Parramatta looking for a coffee shop and found one between a second-hand bookstore and a real estate agent. They took one of the tables on the footpath and ordered their beverages.

'So, what's this big favour?' asked Walker.

'The owner of the flat I'm renting wants to move back in. They're coming back from overseas next week.'

'Oh?' said Walker slowly.

'But,' she added with raised finger, 'the agent has offered me another flat. Great rate, great position, so I want to take it.'

'Fantastic. So what's the favour? You want me to help you move? Of course I will.'

'No, not that, but I'll take you up on that offer later. No, the problem is, the new flat is not available for a month.'

'Oh,' said Walker again. He tapped his fingers together thoughtfully, elbows on table. 'So, you need somewhere to live in the meantime.'

Madeline put on her most charming smile. 'Just for a month.'

'And you want me to put you up?'

She raised her shoulders sweetly. 'I'm small. I hardly take up any room. I don't have any furniture. And I'm tidy.'

'You sound like a pet.'

'I could be. You could think of me as a pet. Like you're minding me for someone.'

'Can you cook?'

'Yes, I can,' she said eagerly. 'Not very well and I don't have much of a repertoire. But I can use a microwave and I can boil water.'

Walker laughed. 'Wow, sounds very tempting. A pet that can't cook.'

'I'm good company. Maybe I'll stop you scowling and brooding all the time.'

Walker smiled and nodded. 'That you are.' He leaned back in his chair and folded his arms over his chest, pretending to consider the situation. 'Mmm. I might do it – on one condition.'

'Name it.'

'I can call you Maddie.'

'No,' she said immediately. 'You can take me in *and* call me Madeline.'

Walker scratched his chin as if he was considering her proposal. 'You drive a hard bargain.' Then he sat forward abruptly and offered his hand. 'It's a deal.'

Walker looked up and saw a familiar face coming towards them along the street. Cassandra Hollow. He promptly drew his hand back and dropped his head, burying his face in the menu.

'Chris.' She stopped at their table. Cassie looked stunning, as usual, wearing a short black dress that showed off her legs and figure while at the same time looking professional.

Walker sat up straight, as if he'd only just seen her. 'Oh hi, Cassie. I haven't seen you for a while.'

'Just popping out for lunch.' She glanced at his coffee mate.

'This is Madeline,' said Walker. 'Madeline, this is Cassandra. Madeline and I work together at the hospital.'

Cassie frowned. 'Oh, you're a doctor?'

'Yes. Radiation oncologist.'

'Hard job. I know how it affects Chris.' Her eyes flicked to Walker and away again. 'I don't know how you do it.'

'It's hard sometimes but we help a lot of people. Are you the Cassandra who knows Shaun Callen?'

She seemed tense. 'Yes, I know Shaun. We're working on a case together. Different law firms but we interact.'

Madeline offered her one of the seats at their table. 'Please, if you've got time.'

'I don't want to interrupt …'

Madeline laughed. 'You're not interrupting anything. We're just having coffee. I actually wanted to speak to you.'

Cassie reluctantly took a seat, still frowning. 'Oh? What could you possibly want to talk to me about? Do you need legal advice?'

'No, it's about Shaun. I used to go out with him.'

Now Cassie wore a poker face. 'Funny. He hasn't mentioned you. We've been seeing quite a bit of each other. We're both unattached.'

Walker had the impression that Cassie was refusing to look at him. She had even pivoted her body away from him.

'Chris tells me you two used to be an item.'

'An item? I'm not sure what that means.'

'You know, boyfriend and girlfriend.'

'All right,' she snapped. 'I know what you mean. It's just I thought it would be uncomfortable to talk about it.'

'Why?' Madeline looked from Walker to Cassie. 'Do you still have something for each other?'

'That's something you'd have to ask Chris. Anyway, what did you want to ask me? I'm sure it's not about my old flames.'

'I thought I should warn you. Shaun – he's a nasty piece of business.'

'I haven't seen that. He's been a perfect gentleman with me.'

'It starts off like that. He's very confident, very charming. But then he wants to control you.'

'Maybe it's all in the interpretation. Feelings of being controlled for one person might feel like care and affection to another.' She flicked a glance at Walker.

'Believe me, the only person Shaun Callen cares about is himself.'

'Well, I'm sure you're welcome to your opinion. But I'm very happy to form my own, if you don't mind.'

'I'm just warning you to watch out.'

Cassie stood up. 'Well, he's not in your life anymore. He wants to be with me.' She glared at Madeline then Walker. 'You two can be happy without us interfering. I'll ask you to show us the same courtesy.' With that, she strode away, high heels clipping on the footpath.

'What a strange thing to say,' said Madeline, peering after her.

'What do you mean?'

'She was speaking about us as if we were a couple. Where did she get that idea?'

Walker leaned forward and dropped his voice. 'Well, Madeline, that was one thing I wanted to talk about.'

'Mmm?'

She appeared so innocent, but surely she couldn't be that unaware.

'Us,' he said.

'What about us?'

'Well, you know. We see each other a lot. We enjoy each other's company.'

She smiled. 'Yes, we do, don't we? We get along well. It's nice.'

'But you don't seem to want more than that.'

'More?'

'You know, something a bit more romantic.'

She leaned back in her chair and let out a laugh. 'Us? Like that?' She grimaced. 'I don't think so, Chris.'

'But why not?'

She examined him carefully for a few moments. Her smile faded. 'I just don't see you like that, I'm sorry.'

'You were with Shaun.'

'So?'

'Are you saying he's more attractive than me?'

'Not at all. You're much better looking. But you have to feel something for someone. You know ...' she wriggled in her seat, 'lust.'

'And you don't have that for me, at all?'

She grimaced again and shrugged her shoulders. 'Sorry.'

'So what do women see in Shaun? What did you see in him?'

'Oh, at first he's clever and witty. He has a sort of animal magnetism. Very confident. And he's very good in bed.'

'Oh, thanks. Did you have to tell me that?'

'You asked.'

'You could hold some things back.'

'Whatever for?'

Walker felt rotten. 'So you used to do it a lot, did you?'

She nodded candidly. 'Early on. All the time.'

He crossed his arms over his chest and looked away. *Why him and not me? He's a ranga with freckles, for goodness sake.*

Walker turned his attention back to her. 'Well, I guess that's that then.'

She reached out her hand. Reluctantly, he took hold of it. Her hand was warm.

'Chris, I really, really like you. I feel close to you. But just not like that. Can't that be enough?'

He let out a deep breath. 'I guess,' he mumbled.

CHAPTER TWENTY-FOUR

THAT NIGHT, WALKER had gone home despondent. It was clear Madeline only wanted to be friends, but he just wasn't sure he could be. He knew what would happen. He'd go out with her as 'friends' and spend the whole evening fantasising about sleeping with her.

'Why does she have to be so attractive?' he asked Archie, who was sitting near the back door in the kitchen. The cat looked up at him. He looked so wise and thoughtful, for a moment Walker thought he might answer. But then Archie spied a bug on the wall and jumped at it. Missed!

'This is not going to work, Archie. I'm going to tell her that we can't be friends.' This time Archie ignored him.

There was a tap on the front door. Walker's heart raced. Maybe it was Madeline!

Bruce Rowntree was at the door.

'Nice to see you too, Kit,' said Rowntree when he saw Walker's expression.

He turned into the lounge room. 'What do you want, Bruce?' he grumbled over his shoulder.

'It's about the cops. And your dad. They're going to start looking in the harbour.'

'What for?'

'What do you think?'

Walker thought for a moment then swore under his breath. 'My mother's body?'

'Bingo.'

Rowntree flopped down on the lounge and lit a fag. Walker couldn't be bothered to stop him.

'The cops have got nothing on your father,' said Bruce. 'They've dug up your backyard, they've interviewed every old friend and acquaintance of your mum and dad and they still have nothing. All they've got is that they can't find evidence your mum died of cancer.'

'But neither can they find her. Which is why they think my dad murdered her and hid her body.'

'Why? Why would he kill her? And where? Where would he dump her?'

Walker shook his head mutely.

Rowntree pointed his fag at Walker and blew out a puff of smoke. 'I'll tell you where. The docks. One of the wharves.'

'Do you think?'

'Of course I don't think so, but I know how the coppers work. Everyone knows there's enough dead bodies at the bottom of the harbour to feed the fish for the next century. Why do you think there's so many sharks?'

'So, are you agreeing with them? Do you think my father killed my mother and threw her body into the harbour?'

Rowntree waved his hands in despair. 'Course not, you fuckwit. Haven't you been listening to me? That's what the coppers will think. That's where they're going to search next.'

'Do you know that for a fact?'

Rowntree tapped the side of his nose. 'I have my sources.'

'When?'

'Tomorrow. And we need to be there.'

'Why?'

'Don't be so naive, you prick. You know just as well as me what they get up to. Just as likely to plant a few bones down there to frame someone as not. That dickhead Wills has got it in for your father. I've heard he lost face when Wendy shat all over him in the last case and he wants to claw back out of the shithole he's found himself in. Get in the good books with the powers that be. And he'd see it as an opportunity to stitch up the father of one of Wendy's friends in the process.' He pointed his fag at him. 'You. Two birds with one stone!'

'Where are they looking?'

'Wharf nine. That's where your dad worked before roll-on roll-off started at Darling Harbour. If he was going to dump a body, he'd do it there.'

Walker didn't know what to think. What if his father *had* killed his mother? He couldn't believe it but he was only a kid at the time. He didn't think he wanted to be there if the police actually found a body. Or body parts. He didn't want to see bits of his mother dredged off the bottom of the harbour and dumped onto the deck of a boat. But Rowntree was right. The police couldn't be trusted. Everyone knew the force was rotten to the core. The Fitzgerald Inquiry had proved that beyond a doubt in Queensland and Walker had heard enough to know that the local cops were the same or worse. Wendy was probably okay. And Fred Bowles as well, but the rest of them? And he especially didn't trust Wills. He looked at Bruce Rowntree, who sat studying him, red-faced and balding, puffing on his fag, a waterfront worker union bagman who was probably more crooked than the cops.

'What's your interest in this, Bruce? You seem to be putting a lot of effort into it.'

He pulled the fag from his lips and examined it for a moment before speaking. 'I look after my union members, even after they're dead and gone. Reputation's important.'

'Is that it? You seem to have a particular interest in Wills.'

Rowntree blew out a mouth full of smoke and rubbed a thumb along his bottom lip. 'You're smart, aren't you, Kit? You've missed your calling being a useless cancer doc. You should have joined me in the union and done something with your life. If you must know, Wills has been poking his nose into the WWF. We want to amalgamate with the Foremen

Stevedores and any upset now might blow the whole deal.'

'So you don't care about my parents.'

'Of course I do. Your father was very good to me when I started with the union. And your mum too. Like I said, we look after our members, even their reputation after they're gone. If I thought for a minute that your father had knocked your mother off, I'd sit quiet and watch the coppers bugger up the investigation. But the whole thing's bullshit. Wills just wants to climb the slippery pole, and with the New South Wales Police Force, there's only one way to do that.'

'Wendy seems to be doing well for himself and he's not bent.'

'Young Wendy will only get so far. Soon he'll need to make a decision – keep a low profile and stay where he is, if he's lucky, or join the rest of the crooked bastards.'

'I didn't know you valued honesty so highly.'

'Look, Kit, I have no qualms with the coppers getting a little on the side and the crims knocking each other off from time to time. But when they want to get their greedy little mitts on my union members then the gloves are off.'

Walker sat for a moment in thought. He thanked his lucky stars he'd become a doctor. He wouldn't have lasted a year in Bruce's nasty world. 'Okay, Bruce. What do you want me to do?'

'Wharf nine, tomorrow morning. And bring your camera.'

Nine am the next day, Walker was at Wharf nine dressed in a tracksuit, gloves and a woollen hat. Sydney in July was cold. He'd lived here all his life and, like everyone else, had been brainwashed into the belief that Sydney was always bright, warm and sunny. Each year, everyone seemed surprised when June brought cold, dark days more reminiscent of the mother country. For three months, houses were draughty and miserable, and rather than fix them to be winter-appropriate, Sydneysiders shivered and complained until the warm weather returned, reaffirming their belief that they lived in a tropical paradise, the frigid months forgotten merely as an aberration.

Walker had phoned in sick that morning, not wanting to tell the secretaries the truth about his absence. It was a day full of meetings and admin and no clinics to cover, and he could always do a ward round the next day.

There were nine piers at Walsh Bay spaced about one hundred metres apart and projecting out over the harbour for about two hundred metres. Down the end where they'd gathered, the piers were in poor condition, verging on derelict. Up the other end of Hickson Road, the piers had been renovated for restaurants and a theatre. Here, the two-storey warehouse that sat between the two wharves was falling to pieces, the paint peeling from the timber cladding and the doors and windows boarded up. Walker remembered his father telling him that they were built in the early century after the original wharves had been pulled down due to the bubonic plague in 1900.

The police divers were already in the water, black heads and masks bobbing on the surface, receiving orders from the team leader who stood on the deck of a Water Police boat anchored beside the wharf. Walker was surprised they didn't have lights. It would be dark at the bottom.

'How do they see?' he asked, not expecting an answer.

'They don't,' said Bruce beside him. As usual, he was dressed only in a business shirt and crumpled suit but seemed oblivious to the icy breeze coming off the water. 'I was speaking to one of my union members last night. We look after professional divers. He said they feel along the bottom in the dark. If they find a body, they have to hug it to themselves like a big baby and bring it to the top.'

'Ghastly,' said Walker.

'It's a job. But I doubt they'll be finding a body. Body parts, if they're lucky.'

'I thought you said you don't think my mother's down there.'

'Not your mother. But I wouldn't be surprised if there are others.'

'How do you know that?'

Rowntree blew out a puff of smoke. 'Best not to ask questions, Kit. What you don't know won't hurt you.'

'Nice,' said Walker, turning back to the activity on the water. 'Gives another meaning to bottom of the harbour scheme.' Rowntree let out a short, chesty laugh.

The two divers were no longer visible and the water surface was glassy smooth since the breeze had settled. All Walker could do was watch Bruce suck on his fags. He didn't really want to talk. A green and yellow ferry went past on its way to Balmain. Further out, a container ship was making its way from White Bay to the Heads. The wash of the ferry made the police boat bob up and down but the officer on deck kept his footing. Walker saw him bend forward towards the water. An arm came up holding something, followed by the diver's head.

Walker had his Cannon T50, which he'd bought new for New Guinea but was now becoming outdated. He only had a 50mm lens so the object in the diver's grasp wasn't clearly visible. He took the shot anyway. As the officer hauled the object onboard, Walker could see it was a cricket bat, the surface slimy and discoloured.

Another hour passed and the divers continued to pull up various items, mostly junk by Walker's reckoning – bottles, pieces of lumber, old suitcases, all in various stages of decomposition. The boat had moved closer to the edge of the pier and Walker and Rowntree could have a better look at the divers' catch. The police didn't seem to mind. They even held up a few pieces for Walker to take pictures of, laughing and asking whether they were going to be the cover of tomorrow's *Sun*.

Then both divers surfaced, removed their masks and waved to the deck officer. A hushed conversation took place as the officers quickly set up a net, attaching the corners to lines that led to a winch before lowering it into the water. Walker took photos of the whole procedure. Then they waited.

About twenty minutes later, the divers gave the sign for the winching to commence. Moments later, a large light-coloured sack rose to the surface.

'What is it?' asked Walker.

'Looks like a wool bale,' said Rowntree. He pointed. 'See the writing in blue. It's the weight and grade of the wool. That's how they sold it back in the 60s.'

The winch started up again and the boat listed to the side with the weight.

'Looks heavy,' said Walker.

'I don't think it's wool. Too heavy.'

As the load cleared the water's surface, the underside of the fabric ripped and what appeared to be rocks fell into the water. Someone on the boat yelled out and the winch stopped.

'Looks like house bricks,' said Walker.

Something sagged through the gap and hung there, caught on the edge. It looked like a hard cylinder with fragments of cloth hanging from it. The grey end bobbed in and out of the water.

'What the hell is it?' gasped Rowntree.

Walker studied the bag intently before turning to him with a look of bewilderment. 'It's a radius.' When Rowntree didn't understand, he added, 'A bone. It's an arm.'

'Fuck me,' said Rowntree, flicking his fag into the water. 'They actually found a body!'

CHAPTER TWENTY-FIVE

THE NEXT DAY Walker went home via Madeline's place, picking her up on the way through. She hardly had any possessions to move – two large suitcases, a box of books, a small lamp that had a dual twisted stem like a grapevine, and a porcelain statue of a ballet dancer.

'This it?'

'I travel light. I wasn't sure how long I'd be in Sydney. Most of my stuff is back in my mother's house in Brisbane.'

Everything fit into the boot of his BMW and on the back seat, and they were soon off. Thirty minutes later they pulled up in front of Walker's place. They quickly unloaded the stuff onto the footpath and Walker went to open the door.

'You've a friend moving in, Chris?' called a voice. Janet stood on her front step nursing Archie in her arms like a big hairy baby.

'This is Madeline, Janet,' said Walker. 'A friend from work. She's a cancer doctor like me.'

'Lovely to meet you, Madeline. Nice to see Chris will have some company. He gets a bit morose if you leave him to himself.'

'I've noticed. I'll see what I can do.'

'Drop around anytime if you need anything, love.' Janet waved Chris a bit closer. 'The coppers came around a half hour ago. That Wills fellow. He said he'll be back tonight.'

A white Commodore pulled up across the street and they all turned towards it.

'Speak of the devil,' said Janet.

Walker and Madeline watched as Royce Wills and David Jones got out of their car and came across the street.

'Just in time to lend a hand, gentlemen,' said Walker. 'Constable Jones, could you grab one of those suitcases? And Detective Sergeant Wills, you can grab that box, if you don't mind.'

Wills initially looked as if he'd object but then picked up the box from the footpath, and together they moved through the front door into the lounge room where they dumped everything.

'This is Dr Madeline Piper,' said Walker. 'She'll be living with me for the next month. And before you ask, you can say anything in front of her that you would say to me.'

'Right,' said Wills, although he didn't really seem to care about Walker's confidentiality. 'We have information that I'm permitted to impart to you regarding our investigation in the vicinity of Wharf nine.'

'I thought you would,' said Walker.

'The remains recovered are that of a female between twenty-five and thirty-five years old. A full skeleton with some fabric attached to it.' He studied Walker's face carefully as he spoke. 'Your mother would have been thirty when she disappeared.'

'If you say so.' Walker knew enough about forensic pathology to understand that gender and age of a body could be determined solely from the skeleton.

'The bricks that were in the bag have been identified as the same as those in the backyard of your house.'

Walker let out a short laugh. 'And probably every other backyard in The Rocks. The houses were all built at the same time in the early nineteen hundreds after the old ones were pulled down because of the plague. I bet all the bricks come from the same brick pit.'

'Granted,' said Wills. 'But at least it indicates the murder was probably done around here.'

Walker sat down on his lounge. He didn't invite the police to sit. 'Seems pretty weak, if you ask me. The bale bag tells you the body was stuffed into the bag at the wharf. The bricks would have been put in at the same time. It doesn't say the murder was done here. Could have been done anywhere and the body brought here for dumping.'

Wills sniffed and examined his notes. Walker could tell he was annoyed. Wills tapped his notepad and looked up. 'Forensics have rehabilitated the cloth the body was wrapped in. It was a green garment. Polyester, which is why it survived for so long in the water. Polyester was big in the 60s.'

'So?'

'Jane Walker often wore a lime green dress. Many of the locals comment on it. Says she was well-known for it. Made a real fashion statement. Our source in jail says he saw her wearing it the night your father fought with Leremy.'

'But my mother didn't disappear until months later.' Then Walker realised he had said 'disappear' and not some other reason for her absence. Was he starting to believe the police?

'Still, it builds a case. Green dress, local bricks to weigh the body down.'

'It doesn't say it's my mother.'

'True. We are looking into any other reported disappearances of women of that age from the early to mid 60s. In the meantime, we'll wait for the autopsy results. Hopefully, that will be more definitive.'

Walker gave a fake smile. 'Let's wait until then, shall we? Is that all?'

'That's all,' said Wills sullenly. 'For now.'

Madeline stood at the front door with Walker, watching the policemen drive away. 'Pleasant fellow. Looks as if he's enjoying himself, informing you that your father might have killed your mother.'

'Obviously, empathy is not a key requirement to be a copper.'

Madeline closed the door and leaned back against it. A ray of the setting sun came through the back window along the hall, igniting her hair in reds and gold. Her face was in partial darkness and her woollen dress sat tight against her body. 'What shall we do now?' she asked.

Walker swallowed. 'How about the pub?'

'Perfect answer,' she said, pushing herself upright. 'Let me have a shower and I'll be ready for anything.'

Walker quickly showed her around the small terrace, placing her suitcases in her bedroom. A bathroom separated her bedroom from his and he left her to it.

Thirty minutes later, Madeline was still in the bathroom and Walker was wondering whether he should check that she was all right. He was fairly sure that Flea had never taken that long for a shower.

He climbed the stairs and paused outside the door to listen. The shower wasn't running. Just as he decided to knock, the door opened. Madeline stepped out of the bathroom, steam billowing out of the door behind her. She had a towel wrapped around her that barely covered her body.

'Oh, Chris. I hope you weren't waiting for me.'

'Um, I was … just after my toothbrush.'

'Okay, well, it's all yours.'

She went off to her bedroom and closed the door behind her, so he went into his to change.

He had his shirt half off when there was a knock at the door. Before he could say anything the door opened and Madeline came in wearing a robe, her hair wrapped in a towel. She sat down on his armchair and crossed her legs, revealing a bare upper thigh.

Walker let out a breath and finished taking off his shirt. 'Making yourself at home?'

She seemed unaffected by his discomfort. 'Yes, thanks, Chris. You've got a great shower. Nice hard stream and hot water. Thanks again for letting me stay here.'

He paused. Was she going to watch him undress? 'Do you need something?'

'Just wondering what you're wearing. I assume it's casual.'

'Anything you like. It's just the pub.'

'Okay.' She pushed herself to her feet. 'But be quick about it. I'm starving.'

They had a relaxing evening at the Hero, eating dinner at the bar, having more than a few drinks and talking about life in general. They seemed to have a lot in common – a love of science fiction, Jethro Tull and Thai food. They'd read many of the same books and as they each listed their album collections, they realised they owned many of the same LPs.

At about 11 pm they decided to call it a night. When Madeline stood, she stumbled and Walker had to catch her to stop her falling.

'Wow!' she exclaimed. 'I think I had a few too many.'

Walker realised he'd had more than his usual as well and, arm in arm, they managed to escort each other the fifty metres back to his place without mishap. They stumbled through the front door and collapsed on the lounge.

They sat close together, their bodies touching. Madeline put her head on his shoulder. 'Well, captain, we managed to get home safely. I'm not sure how I'll get up the stairs though.'

'I think we should rest here for a while,' said Walker. He showed her his palm and she gave him her hand and he gently grasped it. 'It's nice to be with someone. I miss it.'

'Mmm,' she murmured. 'I miss it too.'

He turned his head. Her face was close. He could sense her breathing. Her eyes were closed. Her lips parted. He leaned forward and gently kissed her. She returned the kiss for a moment then jerked her head back and pushed him away, slowly but firmly.

'What's the matter?'

She moved away from him. 'That was a mistake. Too much alcohol.' She let out a deep breath. 'I've told you, I don't want that sort of relationship.' Her voice was hard. 'It's not for us.'

'What do you mean? Why not?'

'I don't want to. Isn't that enough?'

'Of course. It's just that I could have sworn you wanted to.'

'It's complicated, all right? I know it must be confusing for you but I have to make it clear that we are not going to be like that.'

'Is it another man? Now or before? Has someone done something to you?'

'You could say that. Look, I can't talk about it.' She stood and straightened her skirt. She looked shaken. 'Do you want a cup of tea?' Without waiting for a reply, she headed for the kitchen. He heard the clatter of cups and kettle.

Walker wondered again about Shaun. Madeline said she'd broken up with him but now he wondered. She seemed absorbed in him and his relationship with Cassie. Walker had initially thought it was concern but was it really something different? Jealousy? Did she still have feelings for Shaun and was that blocking any interest she might have in him?

The more he thought about it, he became sure that Madeline's reluctance with him had something to do with her ex-boyfriend. And, he promised himself, he would find out what it was.

CHAPTER TWENTY-SIX

FOR THE REST of the week, Walker and Madeline kept their distance from each other, driving to and from work together but mostly keeping apart at the house, one of them watching TV while the other went out or sat in their room reading.

But by Thursday night, Walker decided they couldn't keep on that way. They'd either have to be friends or he'd have to ask her to move out. He went to find her in the lounge room.

'What are you doing tonight?' he asked.

Madeline was lying on the lounge, dressed in a T-shirt and shorts, flicking through the channels. 'Nothing. I'll probably watch some TV. *Cheers* and *Seinfeld* are on.'

'Would you like to come out?' When she frowned he waved his hand. 'Nothing like that. Just as friends. I'm meeting Wendy and Sally.'

She hesitated. 'Where to?'

'Jamison Street.'

'Argh. Not sure about a nightclub. I had enough of Tracks when I lived at Epping. But I wouldn't mind getting to know Barry. I want to find out why you call him that ridiculous name.' She glanced at her watch. 'Give me ten minutes then.'

As she left, Walker thought about Darling's nickname. Everyone in the Rocks called him that but maybe he should stop calling him Wendy, especially at work. When he thought about it, it sounded childish. And unprofessional.

Thirty minutes later, Madeline finally clipped down the stairs in high heels and the flip skirt she'd worn the first time he'd met her in the city. He couldn't help stare at her shapely legs.

'You look great,' he said, turning away to flick off the TV. He didn't want to be too effusive with his compliments.

They met Darling and Sally at the nightclub, the couple already having found a table. Darling was snappily dressed as usual in a tight shirt, mauve jacket and matching pants. Walker had only ever seen Sally in her nurse's uniform or wearing jeans and Ugg boots and he was astounded by her transformation. She wore a purple dress that showed off her cleavage and she'd done something with her blonde hair. Her genuinely warm smile topped off the look, making her one of the most attractive women in the place, in Walker's opinion. Then he remembered how he'd stolen Wendy's last girlfriend from him – Cassandra. Or at least that's what Wendy – *no, Barry*, he told himself – had thought at the time. He made a mental note not to show Sally too much attention.

Madeline and Sally seem to get on, and soon they were talking about where they were from. Walker overheard Sally say she'd grown up in Armidale.

Madeline offered to get drink and as she left, Walker leaned towards Sally. 'My mother was from Armidale,' he said loudly, over the noise.

'Really? What was her name?'

'Jane. Jane Walker.'

'What was her maiden name? You never know, I might know the family.'

Walker thought for a moment. 'Bingley,' he said frowning, then nodded with more certainty. 'Yes, Bingley.'

'I went to school with a Bingley. Michelle. Maybe they were related. Her father owned a farm near ours outside Armidale.'

'Small world.' Then Walker had a thought. 'Do you still know them?'

'Michelle and I weren't close friends. We hung around in primary, but I lost contact with her after they moved away. To Canberra, I think.'

Walker leaned closer to her so he could drop his voice. 'Do you think you could contact them again? They might have known my mother. I'm trying to find out what happened to her.'

Sally looked puzzled. 'Did you lose her?'

Walker glanced at Darling who was sitting back in his chair listening to their conversation with a frown. 'Hasn't Barry told you? The cops think my father killed her.'

Sally looked shocked. 'No. I hadn't heard.'

'That's enough, Kit,' Darling interrupted. 'We're here to enjoy ourselves, not talk about police investigations.'

Walker persisted. 'Could you check, Sally? Perhaps give your friend a call?'

Sally appeared horrified. 'I ... I don't know. I'll talk to Barry about it.'

Madeline arrived back at the table with the drinks on a tray. Her smile turned to a frown when she saw Sally's expression. 'What's happened?'

'Kit is ruining our evening by grilling Sally about his mother.'

Madeline's frown deepened. 'What could Sally possibly know about Chris's mother?'

'She knows the Bingleys from Armidale,' said Walker. 'That's where my mother's from.'

'But that's just ridiculous. Sally wouldn't know about your mother?'

'It's worth a try,' Walker said but with fading conviction.

'Nonsense.' Madeline sat down and patted Sally's arm. 'Don't listen to Chris. He's got a bee in his bonnet and can't help himself.' She turned to him, still frowning. 'Can you, Chris?'

He shrugged. Maybe it was the wrong time to talk about it but he vowed to bring it up again with Sally later. He took a long swig of the beer Madeline had given him. 'What say we go downstairs to the dance floor,' he said loudly, changing the subject. 'There's a disco tonight.'

They all agreed and quickly finished their drinks, then made their way to the stairs that led down to the dance floor.

The room was dark and in one corner the DJ gyrated behind his console to 'Groove Is In The Heart' by Deee-Lite, a rainbow of lights flashing above his head. A small crowd of people danced on the floor, a circle of friends on one side, bopping reservedly, girls dancing with girls, as well as a few couples who seemed to know what they were doing. Closer to them, a dude wearing a suit twirled, thrusting his pelvis at his partner suggestively.

'For fuck's sake,' said Walker, pointing. 'It's Shaun.'

The man spun around, waving his arms in the air as he mouthed the words of the song, eyes closed as if he was in some sort of ecstatic trance. The group stood in a line staring at him. Darling looked on in disbelief, Sally giggled and Madeline's face was screwed up with distaste.

His pelvic thrusting continued as he edged closer to his dance partner and she began to make a slow turn, as if she wanted to move away. She lifted her head and looked at them.

'Cassie!' Darling gasped.

She stopped abruptly and her mouth fell open. 'Barry! And Chris.' She looked horrified.

Shaun came up behind Cassie and clasped her around the waist, resting his chin on her shoulder. Walker couldn't help notice that he still seemed to be grinding his pelvis into her.

'Look what the cat dragged in,' Shaun squawked over the music, which was fading at the end of the track. 'Fancy meeting you lot.' His eyes flashed over Darling and Walker and fixed on Sally. 'Oh ho! I've never met you before. If I had I'd remember.' He jerked his head at Darling. 'You're not with him, I hope? I'd say you're right out of his league.'

'And I'd say you're a total fuckwit and contemplate smashing your face in,' said Darling.

Shaun raised his hands. 'Steady on. Only joking. All in good fun. Anyway, it was a compliment to your date.' He looked Darling up and down. 'At least you know how to dress. Not like Chris here. You'd think he was on the way to a football match.' He grabbed Cassandra's arm and turned her around. 'Anyway, I don't know about you losers but we're going to dance.'

He led Cassandra onto the dance floor and went back to his flamboyant moves while she made small steps from side to side, glancing back at them, wearing a worried frown.

'Well, I'm not going to let that dickhead destroy our evening,' Darling said to the others. He presented his hand to Sally, as if he were a courtier. 'Madam,' he drawled in a French accent. Sally laughed, grabbed his arm and he spun her onto the dance floor.

Walker watched them for a moment then gave Madeline an uncertain look. 'Shall we?'

'Well, I'm dancing even if you're not.' She shimmied onto the floor and began to sway with the music and Walker followed her.

Thirty minutes later, after a string of disco hits and another round of drinks, they were all in a good mood. They swapped partners mid-dance, Walker with Sally and Madeline with Darling, and soon they were gyrating around in more and more ridiculous poses that left everyone laughing. Walker had taken to surreptitiously copying Shaun's moves and wore a stupid face, leaving the others in stitches.

At the end of the song, Shaun led Cassandra over. Walker grimaced, thinking Shaun had seen him imitating him. He didn't want to have a fight. But Shaun either hadn't seen or pretended not to. Instead, he wanted to join in the dance swap, asking Sally. Sally frowned at Darling who shrugged as Shaun led her onto the floor. Darling then grabbed Madeline's hand and moved to make sure they were dancing next to Shaun and Sally, leaving Walker with Cassandra.

Walker indicated the others who were now in a tight group.

'We don't have to, Cassie. We can sit this one out.'

She shook her head, her mouth tight. 'We should dance.'

They began to dance together using small, tentative steps. Walker glanced over at the others. None were looking at them. He moved closer to Cassandra and held her in a ballroom hold and they circled slowly, keeping apart. She seemed to refuse to look at him. Her eyes were everywhere except on him. At least that gave him a chance to study her. She was as beautiful as ever, stunning really. But she seemed different, more subdued than he'd ever seen her.

'Cassie, I'm sorry I didn't contact you before.'

At last she looked at him directly. For a moment he thought she was going to cry. She bit her jaw tight and dropped her head. When she looked up, it was as if the old Cassandra was back. Direct, focused. Angry? 'Why didn't you?'

'I'm not sure. Angela left for Singapore. I'd just found out the truth about Flea's murder. I was mixed up. A bit flat.'

'I could have helped you.'

'I know. I should have—' He was stopped by a hand on his shoulder.

'You two having a deep and meaningful, are you?' Shaun's contorted face was close to his. He could smell his aftershave and sweat.

Walker stepped away from Cassandra. 'What? We weren't doing anything.' He instantly regretted it. He felt guilty. Weak. He should have stood up for her.

'Bit late for that, sport,' said Shaun with a grimace. He held out his hand and Cassandra took it. He led her possessively back to the dance floor.

Walker contemplated going after her, pushing the jerk away and telling her he still wanted her. But he realised he would just look like a fool. Which is exactly what he was. With a frustrated groan, he turned back to his friends. Sally looked upset, with Darling and Madeline crowded around her protectively.

'What's wrong?'

She had a look of distaste on her face. 'That man,' she said, pointing at Shaun.

Walker glanced at him. He was back to his overtly sexual gyrations with poor Cassandra as his victim.

'Yeah, his dancing? He thinks he's pretty hot stuff.'

'I don't care about his dancing. He asked me to sleep with him.'

'He what?' said Darling. 'Tonight?'

'No. He told me not to tell you. He said he could meet me one afternoon in the city after my morning shift.'

Darling stared at Shaun, his fists clenched, his face like a storm about to burst. Walker grabbed his arm. It felt like iron. He realised he had no chance of physically restraining him.

'Don't do anything here, Wendy,' then after a pause, 'Barry. We'll get him later. Think of your job. You're a cop. You can't beat people up in a disco.'

'I don't care,' said Darling through gritted teeth. 'The little jerk is going to pay.'

Madeline's words cut through. 'He did it on purpose.' Her voice was matter-of-fact.

Darling's head swivelled to her. 'What?'

'That's what he does. He riles people on purpose. He'd happily wear a beating from you if it got you in trouble.'

'Why? Why me?'

'Cassandra. You used to go out with her. I know what he's like. He's pissing out his territory. Warning you away from her. I've seen him do it before.'

'But that was years ago. And I'm with Sally now.'

'Doesn't matter. He doesn't think like a normal person. If he was in your position, with Sally, he'd have a go at Cassandra. He'd expect her to sleep with him. He'd force it somehow. He assumes you'd do the same. He wants to get in first, attack you through Sally. He probably expects her to take up his offer.'

Sally looked as if she would be sick. 'You're kidding. I'd rather die than be with him. What a twerp.' She grabbed Darling's other arm, so now she and Walker both held him.

He still could have broken away easily. 'But Madeline's right, Barry. There's no harm done. He's just a little prick. Come to think of it, he's probably got a little prick. I know the type. Little brain and a little prick.'

Darling turned to her and laughed. 'You're right. He's an annoying fly. We shouldn't waste our time with him.'

Sally put her arms around him and he returned the hug and gave her a kiss. He said something to her that Walker couldn't hear and she threw back her head in a shriek of laughter. He laughed along with her. Walker noticed that Shaun had stopped dancing and was looking towards them. He had the feeling that Shaun had watched their whole interaction as he'd been dancing.

Darling turned to them expansively. 'Come on. Let's go upstairs and have another drink. I'm sick of this place.'

They began to move upstairs but Madeline lagged behind and remained staring at Shaun and Cassandra. Walker went back towards her, taken by the focused look on her face. She seemed so engrossed in the other couple, she didn't notice Walker at her shoulder. When she finally became aware of him, her features metamorphosed into a bright smile and she grabbed his arm affectionately.

'Come, Chris, let's have a lovely time for what's left of the evening.'

CHAPTER TWENTY-SEVEN

IT WAS AUGUST but that Sunday it was unseasonably warm and the sun was shining, so Madeline and Walker spent the morning wandering around The Rocks markets looking through all the tourist trinkets and Australiana, taking in the sunshine. Madeline was particularly captured by a guy spraying paint from cans onto a timber panel, with the *Dark Side Of The Moon* blaring from a tape deck. Every fifteen minutes he'd complete another masterpiece, all subtly different, to the applause of a ring of appreciative onlookers.

By early afternoon they were looking for a place to eat. A band was playing at the Mercantile on George Street but the pub looked full, with all the tables taken.

'Looks like the Hero, then,' said Walker.

'A pity,' said Madeline. 'It'd be nice to try somewhere different.'

But as they turned, they heard a voice over the crowd calling out Madeline's name. It was Shaun. He was standing at a table, waving. Cassandra was with him. There were two empty chairs.

'Is this karma?' said Walker. 'Have I done something wrong in my last life?'

Madeline was staring with a look of distaste, her body tense. 'I'm not sure I can stand being anywhere near him.'

'What are the chances of us getting the last two seats in a

crowded pub on a glorious, sunny day in winter in Sydney? It's either here or take our chances back at the Hero.'

After a further pause, Madeline said, 'Okay, we'll join them but I'm not putting up with any of his rubbish.'

'What can he do in a crowded pub?'

'You'd be surprised. At least we can protect Cassandra for a little while. And I'd like to find out more about your ex-girlfriend.'

Walker felt like asking *Why?* But he held his tongue as they made their way to the table.

Shaun gave Madeline a peck on the cheek and shook Walker's hand as if they were old friends. Walker nodded to Cassandra who gave a hesitant smile in return.

Walker offered to buy a round of drinks but Shaun insisted it was his shout. As Shaun went off to get the drinks, Walker sat down opposite Cassie and Madeline sat next to her.

'I hear you've moved in together,' said Cassie.

Her voice was flat but Walker knew she was hiding her emotions. It was not like her. She was normally so ebullient, like a happy child. Lately she was more like a staid matron. He knew it was Shaun. Just her reaction in itself was enough to make him hate the man. He glanced over at the bar. Shaun looked like he was arguing with someone else waiting to be served.

'Yes,' said Madeline happily. 'Chris is putting me up until I find somewhere to live.'

'That's so generous.' Cassie gave him an acerbic smile. 'I'm sure you'll welcome Madeline with open arms.'

Walker knew she was being sarcastic. He and Cassie had spent most of the time at his place making love or recovering from it. He glanced up and down her body. She looked the same. She was wearing some sort of silky number that accentuated her curves. *What am I doing? What have I done?* It wasn't just her looks. They really had been good together. But after Angela left, he'd become unstuck. Adrift.

'Chris?' It was Madeline. 'Are you okay?'

He realised his attention had drifted off. 'Yeah. Sorry. I was thinking about something else.'

Shaun arrived back with the drinks.

'Here, Cassandra,' said Shaun. 'I got you a lovely glass of cabernet sauvignon. I know it's your favourite.'

Walker lifted his beer and took a sip. 'I always thought you liked chablis, Cassie,' he said. 'You told me you hated cab sauv. Too tart, you said.'

'Certainly the cheap stuff you were plying her with,' said Shaun. 'But since I've introduced her to the more costly vintages, she's grown to love it. Haven't you, Cassandra?'

She drew her lips into a smile and gave a short nod.

'You could be a bit more enthusiastic, darling,' said Shaun. 'That's the most expensive wine on the menu.'

She took a sip. 'Thank you, Shaun. It's beautiful.'

Shaun smiled, taking in the others at the table. 'See. It only takes little effort. And money.' He winked at Walker then returned his gaze to Cassie. 'Nothing's too good for my Cassandra.'

'So how's your court case going?' asked Walker. 'The ophthalmologist you're suing?'

'Gangbusters. We're going to nail the bastard.'

'And you, Cassie?' said Madeline. 'Are you doing a lot for the case?'

Cassie became more spirited. 'Yes, I've been doing some research—'

'Mostly background checks,' interrupted Shaun. 'Probably could get a paralegal to do it but it's good for Cassandra to see how we work. She's learning a lot. Nothing beats actually working with an expert like me. Better than book learning, hands down, every time.'

'Oh? You're very lucky, Cassie,' said Madeline. Walker heard the sarcasm. 'You must be so grateful. Doing paralegal work and all.'

Cassie grimaced. 'It's not a paralegal—'

'That's what I keep telling her,' said Shaun, cutting her off again. 'You'd think you'd show more gratitude.' He smiled at Madeline. 'Maybe it's the same with you and Chris? I'm sure you often teach him a thing or two. It irks when you go out of your way to teach someone and they just don't appreciate it.' He smiled paternally at Cassandra. 'But I shouldn't expect so much. It's one of my weaknesses, thinking everyone is as astute as I am. I must learn to be more patient.' He put a hand on her shoulder and Walker heard a soft groan.

'Have you hurt yourself, Cassie?' asked Walker.

'Oh, I wrenched my arm.' She cradled her shoulder with her hand. 'Silly of me. Tripped as I was coming down some stairs. It's not serious.'

'Looks sore. Have you had it looked—'

'Oh, she's always falling over.' Shaun gave a dismissive laugh and pretended to drink a glass. 'Can't hold her booze.' He insinuated his hand under hers on her shoulder. She winced. 'I'll just have to look after you better, won't I, darling?' He pointed at her glass of wine. 'Just be careful with that stuff.'

Madeline stood, clasping her bag.

'Going so soon?' said Shaun.

'Bathroom. I won't be a moment.'

After Madeline left, Shaun smirked at Walker. He swished the wine around in his glass, took a sip then smacked his lips. 'Want some?'

'No, thanks.' Walker wouldn't give him the pleasure.

Shaun continued to smile, but his eyes were hard. 'I think you should know that Cassandra and I are thinking of moving in together.'

Cassie opened her mouth as if to speak but then seemed to decide against it.

'Really?' said Walker. 'That's nice.'

'Yes, Cassandra and I are probably meant for each other. Madly in love.' He included Cassie in his smile, but she still said nothing. 'I hope that doesn't upset you. I know you two were an item for a short while. But now it's too late. You had your chance. Pity you let her go.'

Walker took a sip of his beer. Maybe Shaun was right. Why had he ignored her? Now this buffoon was involved, but he had the feeling that the supposed affection wasn't reciprocal.

Shaun looked in the direction taken by Madeline then stood up. 'Excuse me for a moment.' He turned back after a few steps and grinned. 'Don't talk about me behind my back, will you?'

Walker watched him disappear down the stone-walled corridor that led to the bathrooms. He turned back to Cassie. 'What do you see in him? He's a total nob.'

'That's your opinion. You don't even know him. At least he looks after me.'

'Looks after you? He humiliates you. Talks over you as if you're a child.'

'Ha! What do you care?'

'Are you really moving in with him?'

She looked less certain. 'Maybe. He has a lovely apartment in the city.' She appeared pensive. 'I could catch the train to Parramatta. It'd be nice to live in town.'

'You haven't even discussed it with him, have you? This is the first you've heard of it.'

'Don't be silly,' she said but there was no energy in her voice. She raised her eyes to his. Walker saw hurt. Distress. 'Chris, why didn't you—'

Madeline returned to the table, interrupting her. When she sat down, Walker could see something was wrong. She looked pale. 'What's the matter?'

'Nothing,' she said tightly. She gave a single shake of her head. 'I'll tell you later.'

Shaun arrived back and grasped Cassie's elbow. 'Come, darling, I think it's time to go.'

She stood unsteadily and he entwined his arm around hers. Shaun threw an empty smile towards Walker. 'Nice seeing you both. Perhaps we'll catch up another time.' With that he made for the door, Cassie close by his side.

'What was that all about?' asked Walker.

Madeline stared after them. 'He is a total bastard. That poor Cassie should get away from him.'

Walker laughed. 'I knew that. I wasn't sure you'd picked up on it.'

'He was waiting outside the bathroom door. As soon as I came out, he was all over me. He pushed me up against the wall and kissed me, put his tongue in my mouth. Shoved his hand up my skirt.'

'Fuckwit. What did you do?'

'I didn't know what to do. It happened so fast. I pushed him away. He just smiled, said something about you not being able to satisfy me. I marched away as fast as I could. I was in shock. I don't know why, I know what he's like.'

Walker got to his feet. 'I'm going after him.'

Madeline grabbed his arm and pulled him back down. 'No, leave it. I know how to deal with him. But you need to warn Cassie. She's a nice girl. She doesn't deserve a slime bag like him.'

They sat with their drinks and Walker remained silent, deep in thought.

'What's got into you?' asked Madeline. She seemed to have recovered. 'Thinking about Cassandra? Wondering why you let her go?'

Walker stared at her for a moment, both irritated and surprised by her insight. 'What? Are you a mind-reader now?'

She chuckled. 'You're an open book, Chris. It's not hard to work out what you're thinking.'

'Yeah, well, what do you think about this? I'm going up to Armidale. Stuff work. I'm taking a few days off. I'm going to find my mother's grave.' He took a swig of his beer. 'If it's there.'

'I think that's a good decision, Chris. And I'll come with you. You'll need someone to help.'

Walker was momentarily overcome. 'Really? You'll come with me?' He couldn't help himself. He leaned forward and hugged her tightly. 'Thank you. That means a lot to me.'

CHAPTER TWENTY-EIGHT

THEY SET OFF that night after quickly packing their bags when they got home from the pub. The traffic along the Pacific Highway wasn't heavy this time of year, with seemingly few people heading north from Sydney at the end of the weekend.

They drove without a break and made good time along the F3 freeway, bypassing Newcastle via Maitland before finally turning onto the Dungog Road close to 9 pm.

Dungog was a small country town that had an old-time feel about it, with many of the buildings having been built at the beginning of the century in a grand style. It was a quiet Saturday night, with only a few locals out walking along the wide main street. The first pub on the left was The Royal and Walker pulled up outside.

'A room with two single beds,' said Madeline in answer to the woman behind the reception desk.

'Our only twin room's gone, love,' said the woman. 'We've got two single rooms, a bunk room, or your choice of the double rooms.'

'We're only here for the night so it's a waste getting two rooms,' said Madeline. She turned to Walker. 'The bunks or the double?'

'I don't mind,' said Walker. He was feeling pretty tired after the drive and really didn't care which she chose.

Madeline turned back to the woman with a smile. 'We'll take the double. He looks too tired to get up to any mischief.'

The woman looked her up and down then laughed. 'Believe me, love, once he's got a gander of you in your lingerie, he'll suddenly be all energetic, you can trust me on that.'

'I don't have any lingerie,' Madeline replied with a smile.

'Even more so. I'd take him in for a few beers before you go to bed then, if you're planning to get any sleep.'

'We're just friends,' said Walker.

Now the woman looked Walker up and down, then chortled. 'Sure, love.'

They went upstairs together and threw their meagre luggage onto the bed, then went down to the dining room adjacent to the main bar. Walker ordered a steak and Madeline a hamburger, both with chips and gravy.

'You know Doug Walters was born here,' said Walker after he'd got them drinks.

'Really?' said Madeline, although she didn't appear particularly interested. 'Is he still playing cricket?'

'Not for ten years or so. Last I heard, he's a commentator for Channel Nine.'

Cricket was obviously not one of Madeline's passions, and she sat silently for some moments sipping on her drink.

'What are you hoping to find in Armidale?' she finally asked. 'Are you just going to blindly wander around cemeteries looking for your mother's grave?'

'Something like that. They can't be very big. And they must have some sort of registry.'

'Couldn't you just have phoned them?'

Walker shook his head. 'I need to see the proof myself. She's either buried there or not. I need to see it with my own eyes. If my mother is there, I'll find her grave.'

'What if she was cremated?'

'Then a commemorative plaque. If there was a funeral, there'll be some evidence of it.'

Madeline gave a lopsided smile. 'Nice to get out of Sydney anyway. All that police stuff was getting a bit much.'

'Granted, that's the other reason for coming here. If I saw Wills' stupid face one more time, I'd punch his nose in.'

Madeline's smile metamorphosed into a full grin. 'You're quite a violent chap, aren't you? Or you claim to be. You keep threatening but I've never seen you biff anyone.'

Walker returned her smile. 'Oh yeah?' He glanced around the room at the other patrons. 'Do you want me to pick a fight? Is that the sort of thing that turns you on?'

Madeline's smile faded. 'I don't need to be turned on, thank you. And no, violence doesn't do it for me.'

'Okay, Madeline, I was only joking.'

Now she was intent, serious. 'Violence in a man is definitely not a turn on. It's a sign of weakness.'

'Sounds like you've had trouble in that area. Did someone hurt you?'

'Don't worry about me. What about your friend, Cassie? I'm worried about her with Shaun.'

'Shaun? Is that it? Did he hit you when you were with him?'

'This is not about me, Chris. If you cared about Cassie, you'd look into it.'

'What's all this talk about Cassie? Who says she's my friend? What's she to me?'

'You used to date her. And I saw how you acted when she was around. You still like her but you feel guilty about something.'

Walker was dumbfounded. He realised his mouth was hanging open and he snapped it shut. 'Huh. You don't know what you're talking about. I have nothing to feel guilty about. I never hit her, if that's what you mean.'

'No, not that,' she snapped. 'You're not the type. You

obviously had a falling out over something but you still have feelings for her.'

Walker slumped back in his chair and crossed his arms. 'What would you know? You don't know anything.' He lowered his gaze to the tabletop, refusing to look at her.

'Chris, I'm just trying to help.'

'Help who? Me? You or Cassie? You're just prying.'

'Yes! Yes, I'm prying. Of course I'm prying. That's what friends do. They pry. But not out of curiosity, if that's what you think. It's to help you. And Cassie.' Then, after a pause, 'And me.'

Walker raised his eyes. Now she was looking at the tabletop. He asked softly, 'How does it help you?'

Now she looked at him. 'Us, really. Our friendship. If we're going to be friends, we have to be honest with each other.'

Walker was silent for a moment, thinking. 'Friends. Is that want you really want? Why?'

Now she smiled. She extended her hand. 'I like you. I think we make good friends. We suit each other.'

'But is that all though? Just friends? Nothing more?'

She dropped her eyes again. 'Yes, just friends. And I can't tell you why, so don't ask.'

'Is this about Shaun? Did he do something to you? So you can't …' He paused, searching for a word. 'So you can't have a physical relationship?'

Now she grasped his hand with hers. 'I told you, I can't talk about it. Please don't ask me.'

Walker sat for a long time with thoughts rushing through his mind. Had she been molested? Damaged in some way? Was there something else? Finally, he squeezed her hand in return. 'Okay, Madeline. I won't pester you. We'll just be friends.'

She gave him a dazzling smile. 'Best friends?'

He nodded slowly. 'Best friends.'

That Sunday evening, Barry Darling and Sally were curled up

on the lounge, which sat in the front room of their terrace on Bridge Street in Glebe. Sally swirled a glass of white wine while Barry nursed a bottle of beer. The hum of traffic going towards Glebe Point Road could be heard through the front windows.

'I've heard Kit and Madeline have gone to Armidale for a few days,' said Darling.

'Oh? Something about his mother?'

'Yes, he's looking for her grave.'

'He didn't really get to explain it at Jamison Street the other night. Doesn't he know where she is buried?'

'He thought she was cremated and her ashes thrown into the sea. Royce Wills has been digging around, causing all sort of bother.'

'Chris said something about his father killing his mother. Could that possibly be true?'

'It's a cold case Wills is working on. He thinks Kit's father had something to do with another murder from years ago. And he thinks he might have knocked off Kit's mother.'

'But could it be true?'

'Who knows. I doubt it. But he's convinced Kit that there's no record of her death, so Kit's gone off to find proof.'

'I guess it's possible that she's buried there,' said Sally. 'Chris said his mother was from there originally.'

'I think it's more about Wills trying to make a name for himself. And to get back at me through Kit. Wills has never forgiven me for solving the murders last year that he couldn't. He's been moved sideways and my promotion would be eating him up.'

'Can Wills hurt you directly?'

'Wouldn't put it past him, if he could work out a way.'

'Really? Do you mean physically?'

Darling took another sip. 'Maybe. I don't like to speak ill of my fellow officers but I'm not sure Wills is straight up and down.'

'Crooked?'

'I wouldn't go that far but he seems to associate with others who would match that description. If I was him, I'd watch myself. After the inquiry in Queensland, there's been talk of a similar thing here.'

'Would they find anything?'

Darling didn't answer immediately. 'Even in my short time at head office, I've seen a lot of things – bribes, drugs, money laundering. If an inquiry of some sort gets off the ground, the CIB at Kings Cross will be first in the firing line. To be honest, I'm not sure I can continue to keep my nose clean. Corruption is rife in the inner-city branches. It's accepted practice and anyone not taking part looks suspicious. Roger Rogerson was just the tip of the iceberg. I'm so glad to be back at Parramatta for a time.'

Sally sat in silence for some moments. 'Have you ever thought of moving to the country?'

'The country? Where?'

'Armidale? Tamworth?'

'Me? A city boy living in the sticks? I can't see it.'

'That's not the sticks. I grew up there, remember.' She took on a light tone. 'They are vibrant regional centres brimming with life and charm.'

'Now you sound like a travel agent.'

'But seriously Barry, I'd love you to come up to Armidale, for a weekend, at least.' She playfully elbowed him in the chest. 'Meet the folks.'

'Ah, so that's what this is all about. Parade me in front of the parents to get their tick of approval.'

'I don't need their tick of approval. You've already got mine. I want to show you off.'

'Like a new pony?'

She studied his face for a moment. 'Yes, just like a new pony.' She sighed. 'You don't have to. I'm not forcing you.'

He took her hand. 'I know. But it's a big step. Meeting potential in-laws.'

Now she couldn't hide her smile. 'Potential in-laws, is it? You're getting ahead of yourself, young man.'

He leaned back in the chair with a breezy air. 'Maybe I am, maybe I'm not.' Out of the corner of his eye, he could tell she was still beaming.

They sat quietly for a while. Darling didn't want to commit to anything now. The time had to be just right.

After a while, she asked, 'Speaking about love, what about Chris?'

Darling let out a laugh. 'So is that what we were talking about.' After she also laughed, he went on. 'I don't know about Kit and his love life. It's a train wreck. Flea, Angela, Cassie and now Madeline. How can a perfectly intelligent man continue to stuff up his life?'

'To be fair, the business with Felicity's death must have affected him. It sounded horrible. Anyone would be affected by that.'

Darling sat for a moment, lost in thought – how he'd got caught up with Flea and Kit. Her death. How he blamed him. What Kit might have done when he was semi-conscious in that hut in the New Guinea Highlands. He pushed the thoughts away. They were ancient history. 'Angela was a disaster. It was too complicated falling for a work colleague who was under suspicion for murder. Cassandra? I hate to say it but they seem a good match. I used to be angry that he had stolen her from me. But he never did. We were never properly together.' He looked at Sally. 'Not like you and me.'

'And Madeline?'

He slowly shook his head. 'I just don't know. She's obviously not interested in him. He has to let it go. It's starting to get embarrassing.'

'You've both got a twisted past.'

'Twisted?'

'Complicated. Look how you both grew up.' She turned her body towards him and lightened her voice. 'Which brings me back to our first topic.'

Darling frowned. 'Which was?'

'Whether you're a city boy or a country boy.'

He laughed. 'That was never a topic.'

'Yes, it was. Whether you could live in Armidale or not. You say you're a city boy but how do you know you're not a country boy?'

'What do you mean?'

She made an exaggerated face. 'Sorry to bring it up, Barry, but you were an orphan. How do you know that your parents weren't farmers?'

He let out an uncertain laugh. 'What are you talking about?'

'Look at you. You're Mediterranean.'

'Am I now?'

'Obviously. And where do all the Mediterranean immigrants come from?'

'I don't know.'

'A farm back in the home country.'

'You don't know that.'

'You don't know that it's not the case, either. Both your mum and dad could well be country folk. I can tell by looking at you, you have it in your blood.'

'Ha!' Then he became thoughtful. 'Maybe you're right. I could be a farm boy.'

Sally leaned back in the lounge and nodded as if she had won the argument. Again, they sat in companiable silence until Sally spoke.

'Why is Chris calling you Barry all of a sudden?' she asked. 'He's making a point of it. Have you two had a falling out again?'

'Not that I know of. I noticed it too. I'm not sure what's going on.' He took a sip, thoughtfully. 'Maybe I should start calling him Chris?'

'Why? What's wrong with Kit? And what's wrong with him calling you Wendy? There's a history to it and the nicknames connect you.'

'Some people think it's childish.'

'Don't worry about *some people*, Barry. Worry about your friends and family. And most importantly,' she added with a cheeky smile, 'you worry about me.'

He leaned forward and gave her a gentle kiss. 'And why should I worry about you? Thinking of committing some sort of crime?'

She kissed him back. 'Yes, a very bad crime. You might have to arrest me.'

He put his arms around her. 'Arrest you? And what would I do with you then?'

'Depends on how bad my crime is. But you might have to be very firm with me.'

'Mmm. I think I could manage that.' He eased her back onto the lounge.

'Show me.'

CHAPTER TWENTY-NINE

THELMA BIANCA LANDED at Brisbane domestic terminal on an Ansett flight on Monday at 9 am and took a taxi directly to Milton, a riverside suburb on the edge of the CBD. Krantz's office was above an Italian restaurant in a two-storey complex that appeared to be recently constructed. Thelma dragged her overnight bag up the stairs and found the office. At a desk in the front room she met Mary Alpone, Krantz's secretary, a thin older woman with a blue rinse. A bank of four-drawer cabinets sat along one wall and Mary was busy sorting through the contents of one of them. Leaves of paper were strewn on the floor and a cardboard box sat open on her desk half-full of documents in manila folders.

Mary glared at her over the rim of her cat's-eye glasses when Thelma came through the door. 'You must be Detective Bianca,' she said without a smile. 'I've been expecting you. I told you on the phone that I'm not sure how I can help you. It's a long way to come for a wasted trip. I've already discussed this with the Brisbane police.' She spoke with a clipped, officious tone.

'Tidying up?' Thelma remarked, glancing again at the pile on the floor. 'I hope you're not destroying anything I might need to examine.'

'All of this is confidential,' Mary said sternly. 'You will not be examining any of it.'

Thelma smiled and handed her a folded sheet of paper. 'This is a warrant issued by the Brisbane police yesterday. I will be examining anything I wish.' She ran her eyes along the wall of filing cabinets. 'All of it, in fact. Any assistance you can give me will be much appreciated.'

Mary snatched the paper from her and quickly read it then harrumphed.

Thelma's grin widened. 'And if you help me, I'll get out of your hair faster.'

Mary pursed her lips before speaking. 'What do you want to see?'

Madeline and Walker left Dungog early Monday after a large breakfast, heading north for the final leg of their journey. Walker had spent a restless night lying beside Madeline who, after a quick shower, had hopped into bed wearing a comfortable tracksuit. Within moments she was snoring.

He laid in a daze for hours, his thoughts flicking between Madeline and Cassandra. He relived moments he'd spent with Cassie, her lovemaking passionate and uninhibited. Once during the night, Cassie was straddling him, brushing her breasts against his chest, moaning with pleasure, but when he looked up, it was Madeline groaning, as if in agony. He'd woken in a sweat. Madeline was turned away from him, the covers pulled up to her chin, fast asleep.

Another time, he dreamed of Shaun and Madeline. They were in bed together and Madeline was crying out in pain but Walker couldn't quite see how he was hurting her. Shaun had something in his hand and Madeline fought to push him away, moaning and pleading. Walker tried to pull at Shaun's arm but each time his hand was batted away as if he was a powerless child.

Madeline was quiet beside him in the car as she looked out at the lush farmlands whizzing by. There were few cars on the narrow back road and Walker was taking his time. He didn't feel like talking. Fragments of the dreams kept recycling through his mind but he felt like he couldn't mention any of them to her. He just hoped he'd forget them. Madeline seemed to sense his disquiet and reached out and squeezed his hand, then went back to observing the passing vista.

They reached Armidale after 10 am and drove directly to the cemetery on the south side of town, a large grassed area dissected by a number of narrow roads.

'Can't see an office,' said Madeline. 'Where do we start?'

On the right was a wooden sign that said *Church of England*. 'Here, I guess,' said Walker.

'Are you sure she was that?'

'That's the church we went to when I was a kid. The Garrison church up the street is Anglican.'

Madeline got out of the car and stretched after the four-hour drive. She looked along the multiple rows of headstones. 'How are we going about this? It's going to take forever.'

'We'll each take a row. Look for surnames of Walker or Bingley. We can start in the middle and work our way out.'

It was a beautiful winter's day – cold, but no wind and pleasant in the sun. Walker ambled along the rows reading the headstones, trying to make sense of the system. He was hoping they'd be structured chronologically, which would have made it easy, but they seemed to be jumbled together in no obvious order. Sometimes a family was clustered together, but he also found people of the same surname two or more rows apart.

Initially, he read the headstones in full, checking the name and year of death and any other information. But after the second row, he looked up to see that Madeline had already finished five or so rows. At this rate it would take him hours, so he switched to focusing on the surname only.

That afternoon, Thelma opened the final cabinet drawer with a deep sigh. She had skimmed each case to get an idea of the work Krantz did, documenting the name of each client, their occupation, the work requested and the amount paid. She couldn't find anything that pointed to unethical or criminal behaviour – no apparent criminals, no high-risk clients or jobs, and no obvious over- or under-billing. She was beginning to think Mary was right, that this was all a waste of time. But it was essential work. If Krantz had been murdered for anything to do with his professional practice, the evidence would be here somewhere.

Mary had left Thelma to herself for most of the day but now she returned bearing a takeaway coffee and a cake from downstairs. 'You must be hungry.'

'That's very kind of you. I'm starving.'

She ran her eyes over the notes on the desk that Thelma had taken. 'Find anything?'

Thelma covered the sheet with a folder. 'Not much. Thanks again for the coffee.'

'Perhaps I was a bit rude to you earlier. Mr Krantz's death has really thrown me. I've been his secretary for over twenty years. It's all such a shock.'

'Do you know why he went to Sydney?'

Mary's face remained blank. 'He told me it was for a holiday, but I think more likely it was to do with one of his cases. But it wasn't clear that any of them had to do with a person from Sydney.'

'Which cases was he working on just before he died?' Thelma had already got the list of names but she was hoping Mary could add something.

'The usual. He was doing conveyancing work for some properties, all here in Brisbane. He was sorting out the will of one of our old clients who had died, all straightforward as far as I could see. And he was doing a number of new wills for other clients. He was preparing a brief for a barrister to represent a client who was suing an engineering firm for some work done on his building out at Brisbane Technology Park.'

'It would be very helpful if you pull the folders on all of those for me, please, Mary. I've already skimmed them but I think I should go over those with a fine-tooth comb.'

Ten minutes later, Mary had assembled a dozen manila folders into a neat pile. 'What of the other case that I read about in the paper? The fellow who left all his money to the bird sanctuary.'

Mary straightened and pushed her glasses back. 'Oh yes, that. What a strange case. Markus Schneider. He had no living heirs.'

'If the newspaper report was accurate, he got his money from his brother who was murdered in Munich a few years ago.'

'That is my understanding. There was supposed to be a son but he disappeared. Mr Krantz expected him to turn up out of the blue, given the amount of money.'

'And did he?'

'No. But we did have one inquiry. A young man who said he was a friend of the son. He was trying to track him down and hoped that he'd made contact.'

'Did you get a name?'

Mary pointed to a pile of boxes in the corner. 'It might be in one of those, ready for shredding. Just appointment notes. I probably would have written his name somewhere.'

'Do you remember what he looked like?'

'It had been raining. He wore a long coat and a hat. All I can remember is that he was tall and had a foreign accent.'

'What did he want to know?'

'Whether the son had turned up. When the answer was no, he left. I told him the son wasn't in the will anyway. He also wanted to know whether there were any other family members in the will.'

'And were there? Who was he interested in?'

'No. A sister of Markus and Gustaf, from memory. I couldn't help him.'

Thelma glanced at the stack of boxes. There was nothing to suggest that Schneider's death had anything to do with Krantz's death. The incident was over six months ago. She picked up the folders that Mary had recovered and bounced them in her hands. 'A bit of light reading for tonight. I'll take these with me to the hotel.'

'Where're you staying?'

Thelma let out a laugh. 'It's a bit embarrassing but I booked a room at the Mayfair Crest Hotel on Roma Street.'

Mary also laughed. 'Ah, the place where our corrupt police chief met his underworld cronies. They'd exchange brown paper bags containing thousands of dollars at the lounge bar, apparently.'

'A guilty pleasure,' said Thelma. 'I'm partial to a bit of criminal tourism. I might not get another chance.'

Waving goodbye, Thelma tucked the stack of folders under her arm and grabbed the handle of her overnight bag and managed to drag it down to the street where she hailed a taxi to the hotel.

Two hours later, Walker went back where they had started searching the cemetery. Madeline was already waiting for him.

'Nothing,' she said when he reached her.

'Me neither. Not one in either name. I would have thought there'd be a Walker at least, since it's a common name.'

'There were a lot of Williams and Pearsons but no Walkers,' agreed Madeline.

'I saw a number of Bennets but no Bingleys,' said Walker.

'Do you think she was buried in another denomination? Catholic maybe?'

He looked across the narrow road to the other rows of tombstones. 'I guess it's possible. Maybe she was born a Catholic. I don't really know.'

Madeline sighed. 'There's only one thing to do then. We'll have to cover the whole area.'

'That'll take the rest of the day,' said Walker.

'She's your mother. And I only want to make this trip once. Let's do it properly.'

They started again further along and realised there was a

Presbyterian section adjacent to the Church of England.

'I thought they were the same,' said Walker. 'Luckily we checked further. I bet she's buried here.'

'I think the Presbyterians are the Scottish version of the same thing.'

'Pretty sure my mother was not Scottish, but we'd better check anyway.'

An hour later, they'd still drawn a blank, so they moved on to the Methodists and Baptists and even walked quickly through the Jewish section.

'I'm starving,' said Walker when they finally regrouped next to the car parked under a tree.

'Me too. We've only got the Catholic section to go.'

'Looks pretty big,' Walker said despondently, gazing over rows of headstones that seemed to stretch for more than a hundred metres on the opposite side of the road.

'Let's just get it over and done with, then we can eat.'

Now they walked quickly along the rows. Walker had trouble concentrating on the names. He thought he was maybe hypoglycaemic. A few times he had to retrace his steps and re-read the headstones.

Finally, they finished and met near the only building visible – a large chapel set in the middle of the Catholic area.

Walker blew out a deep breath when Madeline said she'd found nothing. 'Well, that's that then. She's not here.'

'Pity there's no one to ask. You think they'd have a registry of some sort.' She looked at the door of the chapel. 'Seems like it's locked up.'

'They're probably only open for funerals.'

As they watched, the door opened and a man dressed in a black cassock came out. Madeline waved and called out to him. 'Father, I wonder if you might help us?'

The priest turned towards them and waited silently until they reached him.

'Father,' said Madeline, 'we're looking for the grave of a Jane Bingley. Do you think you can help?'

The priest frowned in thought. 'Bingley. The Bingleys are not buried here. And they're not Catholic. They all lived up at Guyra. There's a cemetery there.'

'Where's Guyra?' asked Walker.

'Thirty minutes north along the main road. I'm from there, so I know. But the Bingleys have mostly died off or moved away. I'm not sure there's anyone from the family left, but you can always try.'

'My mother died in 1960,' said Walker.

'Oh, she could have been buried there then. It was bit before my time. The cemetery's not large so it won't take long to search.'

After thanking the priest, they decided to drive straight to Guyra and get lunch there.

CHAPTER THIRTY

GUYRA WAS A small town on the New England Highway set in lush farmlands. They saw the sign to the cemetery on the way in but kept driving to the main town, both eager for sustenance.

They stopped at the first milk bar, ordered a hamburger with the lot and a chocolate milkshake each, then sat at a small table near the counter.

The chef, a fellow beyond middle age with a large belly, talked to them as he cooked their meal. 'On your way up north, then? Better be careful. We're forecast snow this evening. The roads will be slippery.'

'No,' said Walker. 'As a matter of fact, we're here to check your cemetery. I'm searching for my mother's grave. Jane Bingley.'

'Jane Bingley?' The chef flipped a patty then paused and scratched his ear. 'The name rings a bell. But the Bingleys have all left. Gone to Queanbeyan, most of them. When did she die?'

'1960.'

'Jane Bingley. I think I went to school with a Jane Bingley. She was a few years ahead of me. I remember her being quite a looker. All the boys were goo-goo over her. But she went to the big smoke as soon as she left school.'

'That sounds like my mother.'

'You said she died in 1960? That's a great shame. She was a

lovely girl, and not just to look at. She was a gentle soul. It's a pity she died so young. What from?'

'Cancer,' said Walker with a glance at Madeline. He didn't want to explain the whole story.

'And you said she was buried here? I think I would have remembered her funeral. No one gets buried around here without everyone knowing about it. Especially someone like Jane Bingley.'

'Well, we're not sure she was buried here. I was only five at the time and my father's died since.'

'Sorry to hear that.' He turned away from the stove and looked at them carefully. 'So she just had the two of you then?'

'Two of us?' Walker made a face at Madeline but she gave no reaction. 'No, just me,' he replied. 'Madeline is a friend who's helping me look.'

The chef examined them again then shrugged his shoulder and returned to his cooking.

Twenty minutes later Walker leaned back in his chair and rubbed his belly, finally satiated. 'I guess we should get going. From what the cook said though, I don't think we're going to find anything.'

Madeline had little to say over lunch. She looked out the window. 'It's going to snow tonight,' she said. 'After we've had a look at the cemetery, I suggest we stay in town rather than try to make it back to Armidale.'

In the car, Madeline remained silent and just gazed blankly at the passing scene. As promised, the cemetery was small with a few sections for different denominations. The Anglican area was the largest, but even so, it took less than an hour. There were a lot of Bingleys but none of them named Jane, and none buried in the 1960s. Incidentally, there were also about a dozen gravestones for people named Walker but again, none of them matched.

It was late afternoon by the time they finished and getting dark. Storm clouds had settled overhead.

'It's freezing,' said Madeline, rubbing her shoulders and

frowning up at the roiling clouds. 'And I'm exhausted. Let's find somewhere warm to stay.'

'You okay?' said Walker. 'You've barely said a word since lunch.'

'Like I said, I'm tired.' She sounded annoyed. 'Let's just get to the hotel.'

Madeline again said nothing on the trip back to town and Walker wondered what he'd done to upset her. He wasn't looking forward to spending another night in the same room. He'd had enough of this friendship stuff that she kept going on about without further explanation.

It started snowing just as they reached the hotel, a soft spitting sludge. 'I think we need a good night's sleep tonight,' said Walker. 'We're both exhausted and it's a long drive back to Sydney tomorrow. I suggest we get two single rooms.'

'Suits me,' Madeline snapped as she stepped out of the car. Then she called back over her shoulder, 'I'm eating in the room.'

Thelma's room at the Mayfair Crest Hotel was basic and in need of an upgrade but at least it was clean. After a shower, she ordered a steak to be delivered to her room then grabbed a beer from the fridge and sat on the bed with the folders. By the time dinner had arrived she'd gone through half of the pile – nothing interesting, just conveyancing and new wills. She wanted to leave the engineering lawsuit until last, thinking that sounded the juiciest.

She cut up her steak and ate her food with the fork, flicking through the other case, the will of a woman who had recently died.

Then a name jumped out of the page – the executor of the will. Madeline Piper. Thelma flicked to the front page looking for the dead woman's name. Jean Holly.

No wonder she'd found no match between Krantz's client list and the guest list of the Katoomba hotel. Madeline and her mother had different last names.

CHAPTER THIRTY-ONE

IT WAS A long and silent trip back to Sydney on the Tuesday, taking over eight hours with only a short break at the Oak Dairy bar at Freemans Waterhole.

'This'll be bypassed when the F3 extension opens in a few months,' said Walker at the break, pointing to the old building that surrounded them. They sat at a table on a narrow veranda in the cold.

He'd expected Madeline to ignore him but instead she put down her hamburger.

'Chris, I have to apologise. I realise I've been short with you but I want you to know that it's nothing you've said or done.'

'I hadn't noticed.'

She ignored his trite comment. 'I think it was all this searching for your mother's grave. With my mother dying a few months ago, it just got to me. Brought back memories, I suppose.' She held out her hand. 'I'm sorry. I've been selfish. At least I know how my mother died – you have no idea. I forget what effect that must have on you.'

He looked down at her hand but didn't hold it. 'Are you sure that's all it is? It seems more than that.'

'No, I'm certain that's what it is. There's nothing else.'

But it didn't feel right to Walker. He felt there was more to it but he couldn't fathom what it might be. 'Okay then.' He shrugged then grabbed her hand. 'I guess you're forgiven.'

She smiled and gave his hand a squeeze. 'That's it then.

We're all made up and friends again.'

'Sure,' he said.

But she still barely said a word for the rest of the trip back to The Rocks.

Walker woke up late on the Tuesday morning after another bad night's sleep. He could hear movement downstairs, so he stomped down in bare feet and dressing-gown, his legs and back stiff. Madeline was in the kitchen already dressed for work and looked as if she'd just finished breakfast.

'Tea?' she asked.

Before he could answer, there was knock on the front door.

It was Royce Wills and David Jones. 'Sorry to disturb you so early,' said Wills, 'but I thought you'd like to know that there's been some progress on the case.'

Walker showed them into the lounge room and Madeline joined them.

Wills closed his eyes and appeared to be weighing multiple facts carefully within his capacious mind.

He cleared his throat. 'The forensics have so far been very elucidating. First, the material of the wool bale gives us a date. It was made of polypropylene which did not come into use until about 1960. The particular type was transitioned to another type in late 1960.'

He smiled as if it was he who'd ascertained the facts. He took on a grave air. 'Next, the remains are that of a woman. It is mostly bones, so we can't tell who she was by her features.' Walker felt like interrupting. Wills had already told him this. He decided it would be all over faster if he just let Wills say his piece.

'But we are searching dental records,' Wills continued. 'If she'd been to a dentist in Sydney, we'll be able to ID her.'

He grabbed three fingers together as if he was counting the facts. 'The cloth is being reconstituted and we think we'll be able to get something there. Polyester last for decades, under water.'

Looking from face to face, he grasped his fourth finger and paused for effect. His face again was grim, like a priest taking a confession. 'One more thing. Foetal remains were found.' Again, he looked from face to face. 'Other bones.'

'What?'

'She was pregnant. Probably less than twenty weeks but more than twelve.'

Madeline cut in. 'Are you sure? Pregnant? And someone murdered her?'

'That's right,' said Wills with a look of satisfaction.

'So what are you saying?' said Walker.

Now his tone was sombre. 'Mr Walker, I think you must prepare yourself for the possibility that your father did murder your mother. And that she was carrying the child of John Leremy, with whom she had had an affair. And which was the motive for the murder.' Wills poorly suppressed his smugness.

Jones stared at the ground, looking uncomfortable.

Wills gave up the pretence. He looked pleased with himself. 'I told you I'd crack this case. Thirty years old, do you believe it?' Then he put on a face which he probably thought was empathetic. 'I realise this must be a shock to you, Mr Walker, but it is best that the truth comes out. You must know that there was never any thought of a claim of guilt against you. We have no cause to bring any charges.'

'That's nice,' said Madeline sarcastically, 'given he was five at the time.'

Wills grinned, missing Madeline's scorn. 'Quite. No fault at all.'

'But you haven't proven that the body is my mother's,' said Walker.

'That's true. But it's only a matter of time. We have the dentists onto it. They are quite definitive.'

Walker looked Wills up and down. The jerk seemed to barely contain his joy. He wondered whether he could get away with punching his nose in. Then he remembered what Madeline had said to him in Dungog. All talk and no action –

or words to that effect. Maybe he should prove her wrong. But before he could do anything, Madeline was showing Wills and Jones to the front door.

'Thank you, Detective Sergeant. So kind of you to share this unproven and preliminary information with us.' She opened the door. 'We look forward to seeing you again only when you have some sort of proof. And by the way, it's Dr Walker to you, not Mr.'

Wills stepped through the door followed by Jones and Madeline slammed it after them.

'Fuckwit!' she hissed at the closed door. She turned back to Walker. 'Don't worry about him, Chris. Go upstairs and have a nice hot shower while I make you some breakfast. We can be late for work.'

CHAPTER THIRTY-TWO

IT WAS A cold winter's night and Walker didn't feel like staying home, after having arrived with Madeline an hour before. She was slumped on the lounge in the corner, flicking through the *Journal of Clinical Oncology*. As far as Walker could tell, she wasn't focusing on any of the articles, probably just reading the titles and abstract conclusions.

'You want to go to the pub for dinner, Madeline?'

'Sure,' she said immediately, throwing the journal on the floor next to her. 'Let me get my bag.'

She disappeared upstairs and reappeared a few minutes later wearing fresh lipstick with a bag over her shoulder. He couldn't be sure but she might have put on a different dress and she also wore a thin pink woollen jumper. Whatever she'd done, she looked fresh and pretty and ready for a night out.

Walker glanced down at his jeans and flannel shirt wondering whether he should change as well. But he decided against it. They were just going to the local and Madeline had made it clear that she wasn't interested in him for any sort of physical relationship. Yet again he wondered why she was so insistent on hanging around him at all. The free rent didn't seem to be enough by itself.

As they walked the short distance to the Hero of Waterloo, the sky began spitting and a cold wind blew around them, making the pub even more welcoming when they finally closed the door behind them.

The pub was half full and they took a seat together at one end of the bar. Being a weeknight, there was no live music and the air was full of lively conversations reverberating off the stone walls. Walker bought them each a drink – a chardonnay and a pilsner – and Madeline offered to pay for the steaks, which he accepted. Just as he finished his last mouthful, Walker saw Bruce Rowntree coming towards them from one of the back rooms. As usual, his rumpled suit and hair made it seem like he'd just got out of bed.

'Kit,' said Rowntree, raising his chin in greeting when he reached them. He glanced at Madeline with raised eyebrows. 'Interrupting something?'

'No, Bruce,' said Walker. 'This is one of my colleagues from Western Meadows, Madeline Piper. She's living with me at the moment.'

Rowntree nodded knowingly as he looked her up and down. 'Nice.'

'She's been kicked out of her rental. Staying with me until she finds a place.'

Rowntree smiled. 'You don't need to explain anything to me, Kit. We're all adults here.' His grin widened as he took in Madeline. 'In an old house in Paris covered with vines, lived twelve little girls, in two straight lines.'

'Yep, that's me, all right.' She smirked. 'And I never get sick of people reciting that line.'

Rowntree laughed. 'Good one, love. I liked that story. My mum used to read it to me.' He offered his hand for her to shake. 'Bruce Rowntree.' He jabbed his thumb at Walker. 'Mind if I borrow this one for a mo?'

Madeline waved her hands. 'Be my guest. Take all night if you want. I'll sit here quietly with my chardy.'

'Grab me a beer, will you, Kit?' said Rowntree as he moved away. 'I'll get a table out back.'

Walker joined him in the next room at a small table near the closed side door. A pool of water had collected on the floor from the rain that had come in when patrons entered and exited. Walker could hear the rain pounding on the door and the windowpane was an opaque river. From his position, he had a view through into the main parlour. Madeline sat at the bar, half-obscured by the wall.

'Anyway, Kit, I gotta talk to you about Wills,' said Rowntree. 'He's causing problems with the union. Threatening to dig up old news. Things that could harm us.'

'And what's that got to do with me?'

'Not with you *per se*. With your dad.'

'Are you going to tell me that he did kill my mother?'

'Fuck off, Kit. You know and I know that's total bullshit.' He pointed with his fag to emphasise his words. 'Wills is just a dirty copper like the rest of them. But he'll get his comeuppance soon. Fitzgerald is whacking his fist down the filthy drain that is the Queensland Police Force and he's pulling out all sorts of black turds. He's even got his fingers up the arse of old Joh Bjelke-Petersen. No one will escape. And you know what, it's going to be the same here. Give it a few years and I wouldn't be surprised if we didn't have our own Royal Commission. The NSW police are rotten to the core. They need to be lanced like a festering boil. Get rid of the all the crap and scum who've infected the place. People say the union's rotten but just kick the putrid bag that's the New South Wales Police Force and see what oozes out.'

'But what's this got to do with me?' asked Walker. He glanced over towards Madeline. She'd turned away and seemed to be in conversation with someone, although he couldn't see who it was, even when he leaned to the side. She was frowning as she listened to whoever it was.

Rowntree looked back over his shoulder. 'Don't worry, Kit, she'll be there when you get back. I won't keep you for long.'

'Oh, doesn't matter. We're not together or anything. She's free to talk to anyone she wants.'

'Sure,' said Rowntree. 'She's just living with you because

she's a doctor on a good income and can't find a place to rent in all of Sydney.'

'Fuck off, Bruce. It's not like that.'

He raised his hands in defence. 'What you do in the privacy of your own home and in between your own sheets is your business alone, young Kit.'

'Bruce, I'll ask you again – what do you want?'

'Your dad was mixed up with the dirty coppers, Kit.'

'What?'

'Leremy was a goon for Collinson. But so was your dad.'

Walker sat in shock for a moment. 'Are you saying my dad was dirty?'

'It's not like that, Kit. Everyone was in on it. If you weren't you'd end up at the bottom of the harbour. Really. That's one of the reasons I got out of the docks and into the union. Believe it or not, it was cleaner being in the WWF. Working on the docks, you got caught up with all sorts of things. Drug-smuggling, counterfeit money, and that. And the coppers oversaw it all.'

'Are you kidding me? My father was a drug smuggler?'

Rowntree flapped his hand at him. 'No, nothing like that. Just turning a blind eye. But your dad also made a bit of extra cash on the side working as a bouncer in Collinson's gambling joints in Newtown. That's how he knew Leremy. And your mum. Leremy would come around to your dad's for a drink. But your mum was too good-looking, sexy, you know, and Leremy took a liking to her.'

'Are you saying my father did kill Leremy?'

'No way. And even if he did, he'd be within his rights. Leremy was a lech. He wanted your mum. Your dad had every right to bump him off. But anyway, he didn't.'

Walker looked out into the main room again, not sure what to think. Madeline was staring at the wall behind the bar. She seemed to be swaying on her stool and her eyes were half-closed. *How many drinks had she had?* He couldn't remember her ever getting drunk before.

'I thought I'd better let you know about your dad, in case it comes out. Wills wouldn't give a shit about besmirching your father's name. And he's got his greasy paws on the union, so that's a mistake. There's only one way that'll turn out, and it won't be good for Wills.'

Walker gulped the rest of his beer. 'Okay, Bruce. Thanks for letting me know. I'm not sure it makes me feel better.'

'I'm telling you this not to make you feel better, Kit, but to make you prepared.'

Walker nodded and looked up towards the main bar. Madeline was gone. Her empty wineglass sat on the bar.

'I'll see you later, Bruce. I've got to go.' When he moved into the main room, Madeline was nowhere to be seen. He addressed the lanky barman. 'James, have you seen Madeline?'

James pointed to the main door. 'Gone, Kit. I think she got sick of waiting for you. Looked pretty tired.'

CHAPTER THIRTY-THREE

WALKER SHOVED OPEN the pub door and was immediately hit by a barrage of rain. At a yell from one of the patrons, he pulled the door shut behind him. The road was a slick stream and a pool of water swirled around the drain across the road. A car went past spraying an arching jet onto the footpath and he jumped back but still got his lower legs soaked. He glanced down Windmill Street away from the pub. One of the homeless was crouched in a doorway of a terrace, trying to get out of the rain, otherwise the street was clear. He ran as fast as he could through the deluge and soon got home but was already soaked to the skin. The house was in darkness. He shoved his head through the door and called out her name. Nothing.

He looked back into the storm. Large drops bounced on the bitumen in the streetlights and the street gutters were surging rivers. Thin waterfalls flowed off every terrace as the downpipes were overwhelmed. He wondered what he should do. Madeline would surely be home soon. There was no way she could get lost in the fifty metres between the pub and the house. He paused uncertainly, looking up and down the street, one hand on the open door.

She probably went to the bathroom in the pub. She'll be home in a sec.

But James said she left the pub. He wouldn't make a mistake. The barman knew where everyone was in his pub at any given moment.

Walker hurried back up the street towards the pub. He couldn't get any more wet than he already was, so there was no sense rushing and risking a fall. Just as he put his hand on the pub door, he glanced down Windmill Street. The homeless guy hadn't moved, hadn't even tried to get out of the rain. He appeared to be slumped near the front gate of the terrace. Walker approached him, his feet squelching in his shoes.

It was Madeline. She looked unconscious. He bent down and felt a pulse in her neck. Her heart was still beating. She was breathing.

'Need some help?' said a voice over his shoulder. A face full of freckles topped in curly orange hair peered down at him.

'What are you doing here, Shaun?'

'What's happened to Madeline?'

Walker looked back down at her. 'I don't know.' He pulled her into a sitting position and her head slumped forward. She gave a grunt then started to mumble but none of her words were comprehensible.

'Help me get her back home,' said Walker.

Shaun came beside him and together they heaved her to her feet. She seemed to take the weight but Walker knew she'd fall if he let her go. Holding her between them, and with Madeline walking unsteadily, they made it down the street and through the front door of his terrace. At Walker's insistence, they managed to get her upstairs into her bedroom and lay her on the bed.

Walker stood and turned to Shaun. 'I'll take it from here.'

He stared down at Madeline, a curious look on his face. 'You sure? I can help.'

'No. You can let yourself out. I'll look after her.'

Shaun huffed. 'Suit yourself. Looks like she's had one too many if you ask me.'

Walker stood between Shaun and Madeline, obscuring his

examination of her. 'I didn't ask you. Like I said, I can take it from here. See yourself out.'

He listened for the footsteps going down the stairs and the front door closing before he turned back to Madeline. She was sopping wet and her hands were freezing, her face pale. He shook her shoulders. 'Madeline.'

Her eyes opened briefly and she grunted. At least she was still breathing. He did a quick neurological examination. Her face and arm movements appeared symmetrical and the tone of her limbs seemed normal. He couldn't see any sign of a head injury. If he hadn't been with her at the pub, he would swear she'd got herself smashed. But there was no way she could have drunk enough in that short time. Someone must have slipped something into her drink. And he knew who that someone would be. Shaun turning up the pub was more than a coincidence.

He didn't think he'd need to take her to the hospital but she would have to be watched closely. And he couldn't leave her in these soaking clothes. He blew out a lung full. 'Only one thing to do, Madeline.'

He quickly took off her boots and socks. Sitting her up, he slipped the thin woollen jumper over her head. When he let her go, she slumped back onto the bed like a sack of potatoes.

'I'm going to have to take off your dress, Madeline, okay?'

When she made no reply, he rolled her onto her side and unzipped the dress at the back. After a moment's hesitation, he tried to heave it down over her hips but it got stuck. She was wearing a black bra. The top of her breasts looked wet and pale and her nipples stood out. He had more success pulling the dress over her head. Now she lay diagonally across the bed wearing only a bra and panties.

'Shit,' he said. She was completely unconscious. Helpless. Lifting her body to his chest, he unclipped her bra and slipped it off. He gently lay her back down on the bed and examined her naked body for a moment. She wasn't exactly thin but there was no fat and her muscles were well defined, as if she went to the gym. There was a mole next to her umbilicus. He picked up her towel hung on the back of her door and patted her dry as best he could. Her skin felt ice cold. Her panties were soaked. He slipped his fingers around the sides and gazed into her face. She was breathing deeply, still unconscious. With a grunt he covered her body with a thick doona then reached up and slipped the panties off. They were soaked through and stuck to her thighs as he dragged them off.

Her hands were still deathly cold. He lay beside her and turned her onto her side, hugging her through the doona and rubbing her back, desperately trying to warm her.

'This is no good, Madeline. I have to warm you somehow.' He remembered a movie he'd seen when he was a boy, a Western, where a buxom actress had warmed an unconscious cowboy by crawling naked into bed with him.

He stood up. 'Well, I'm no cowboy.'

Ten minutes later, he had an electric heater in the corner and had placed two hot water bottles wrapped in towels under her doona. He went into his room and got his own doona and put that on her as well.

Then he pulled his old red armchair into her room and sat in it, observing her intently. Her breathing looked steady enough. He leaned forward and slipped his hand beneath the doona and felt her arm. It didn't feel like a block of ice anymore. He leaned back in his chair. Outside, the rain lashed against the window. All he could do was wait.

Walker woke with sunlight streaming onto his face. He was slumped over the arm of the chair and his neck felt like he'd been hit. Groaning and rubbing his neck, he sat forward. Madeline looked to be asleep, her breaths steady and deep. She looked healthy – her hair seemed dry and her face had some colour. The room felt hot. The electric heater was still on and he rose to switch it off.

He went downstairs to the kitchen and made two mugs of tea. As he waited for the teabag to steep, he stared out the window into the backyard. The hole the police and archaeologists had dug was full of water and the extracted dirt was a muddy pile on the pavers. Archie stood on top of the pile of dirt looking down into the water. Walker tapped on the window and the cat solemnly turned his head towards him then away again without a hint of recognition.

When he got back to her room, Madeline was awake. She hadn't moved but her eyes were open.

'What happened to me?' she croaked.

'I think you were drugged in the pub. Someone spiked your drink.'

She frowned, struggling to think. 'You mean a Mickey Finn? Why would anyone do that?'

'Usually so they can take sexual advantage. There've been reports lately.' Walker handed her the teacup and she sat upright with the blankets gathered up to her chin. She leaned forward to take a sip, revealing her bare back.

'Tell me,' Walker said, 'what was Shaun Callen doing at the pub?'

'Shaun?' She squeezed her eyes shut then opened them again. 'I didn't see him.'

'I saw you talking to someone at the bar. You sure it wasn't Shaun? I couldn't tell from where I was sitting but I could see you were having a conversation with someone beside you.'

She frowned and shook her head. 'Nope, not Shaun. That was …' She hesitated before going on. 'Some guy trying to crack onto me, but I told him I wasn't interested.'

'Can you remember what he looked like? We need to tell the police. He'll try it again.'

Instead of answering, she looked down at the pile of clothes next to her bed. Walker had left them where they'd dropped and they were still wet. Her bra and scrunched-up panties sat on the top. He shifted uncomfortably. She would have to know that she didn't undress herself.

'How'd I get so wet?'

'You were collapsed on the street in the rain. You almost froze to death.'

She fished around under the doonas then pulled out one of the hot-water bottles. 'I presume you did this for me.' She glanced at the armchair. 'And sat here all night looking over me. Thank you for that. I owe you one. I guess I could have died.'

'I'm sorry it happened at all. I should have kept a closer eye on you.'

She gave a sleepy smile. 'I'm not a child. You don't have to look after me.' But Walker thought she looked pleased. Then she became thoughtful. 'But why did you mention Shaun?'

'He helped me get you back to the house. You were out of it. I don't think I could have done it by myself.'

Her face now was unreadable. 'Did he help you here? In the bedroom?'

'No, I sent him packing as soon as we had you up the stairs.'

'Was it only you that undressed me? Saw me naked?'

'Only me.'

She nodded slowly, thoughtful. 'Good.' Then another smile and she reached out her hand and gave his a firm squeeze. 'Thank you.'

'You sure you didn't see him in the pub? I wouldn't put it past him to spike your drink.'

'Me neither. But why would he? He has the lovely Cassandra.'

'Revenge?'

She raised her head stiffly and held his eyes. 'For what?'

'Don't know. Maybe he still wants you.'

She relaxed and rested her head back on the pillow. 'Ha! He wants every woman. Until he gets them. Then he just wants to belittle them. Like he tried to do to me at the Mercantile. Him trying to stick his tongue down my throat was not about sex. He wanted to show his power over me.'

'Is that what he did to you in the past?'

She closed her eyes. 'Maybe. But I don't think he could be bothered trying to drug me for sex. What for? He's already had me. I'm old meat as far as he's concerned.'

'Nice guy. Remind me to punch his nose next time I see him.'

She let out a short laugh. 'I've heard that before from a lot of people.' She frowned, her eyes still closed. 'Funny how no one ever seems to do it.'

CHAPTER THIRTY-FOUR

WALKER WAITED ON the ward with Pier and Jenny for Ben Casey to turn up so they could start the ward round. Élodie Segal stood with them wearing a short white coat, the pockets stuffed with papers. It looked like she'd been making notes and studying. Now Walker felt bad about giving her a hard time on the last round. She was probably in Australia for a holiday, not to get a grilling from a grouchy superior. What did he really care whether she was properly trained? She wasn't going to be practising in Australia. She was a problem for the French.

'Where's Ben?' he asked.

'Coming,' said Jenny. 'He was checking on one of our outliers.'

'How's he going?' Walker asked Pier.

'Steady, dependable.'

'Good.'

'And what about you, Pier? Have you settled into the Australian way of doing things?'

'I think so. Medicine is much the same all over the world, I think.'

'I promised to show you a good Aussie pub. What are you doing tonight? I'll take you out for drinks at my local.'

'Sounds good. What time?'

They agreed to meet at the Hero of Waterloo at 7 pm.

'And you, Jenny, you're also welcome.' Then he added

quickly. 'As well as your husband.'

'What? On a weeknight? All the way into the city? I have to be up at five. Thanks but no thanks.'

Then Walker realised Élodie was listening. He hesitated to ask her knowing how it would look – an older supervisor asking a beautiful young woman to the pub. But then he realised Pier would also be there. 'And what about you, Élodie? Have you been to any of the city pubs?'

She shook her head. 'Thanks anyway. I'm meeting someone.'

Walker felt relieved. 'Another time then.'

Finally, Ben turned up and they began the round. The first patient was an older man who had been admitted the previous evening.

'This is Mr Banti, aged sixty-four. He started chemo for small cell lung cancer one week ago. He has a background history of alcoholic cirrhosis and portal hypertension. He came in with haematemesis.'

Walker introduced himself and the rest of the team. Banti was a thin man with distended blood vessels on his face and bruising on his arms. He had an IV in one arm and a bag of fluid hung on a pole beside the bed. He looked like he was about to be sick and merely lifted his hand in greeting.

Walker asked of Ben, 'Why under us?'

'Gastro said they wouldn't take him since he's on chemo. They said they wouldn't do anything about the bleeding, given the lung cancer.'

'Élodie, what do you think Mr Banti may be bleeding from?' It was a straightforward question that any student should be able to answer. Walker wanted to ask her something she could answer to bolster her confidence.

The French medical student looked like a deer caught in headlights. 'Me?'

'Yes. Is there anything else you would like to know?'

When she remained silent, Walker thought he'd give her a clue. 'About the nature of the blood?'

She made a face. Ben and Pier looked at the ground uncomfortably.

Walker turned to the patient. 'Mr Banti, what colour was the stuff you vomited up last night?'

The man screwed up his lips as if he'd swallowed something sour. 'Black.'

Walker turned back to Élodie. 'We call that coffee grounds. Does that give you a hint?'

'A stomach ulcer?' said Élodie with an uncertain look.

'Could be. But he has cirrhosis and therefore might have …'

When she failed to answer, Walker turned to the intern. 'Ben?'

'He'll have portal hypertension from his alcoholic cirrhosis. He's probably bleeding from oesophageal varices.'

'Oh, of course,' said Élodie. 'I was about to say that.'

Walker moved to the side of the bed and put a hand on the patient's shoulder. 'How are you feeling now, Mr Banti? You seem uncomfortable.'

The patient groaned then leaned towards Walker and proceeded to vomit a large amount of black and red fluid over his shirt. It smelled of blood. Walker tried to jump back but it was too late. His shirt and pants were saturated.

With another groan, the patient flopped onto his back. Walker felt his pulse. 'Jenny, we need a blood pressure reading.'

But she was already out of the room and returned a moment later wheeling a sphygmomanometer. She put the cuff around the patient's arm and pumped it up and listened at the elbow with her stethoscope.

'Eighty,' she said.

'Ben,' said Walker. 'Does he have blood crossmatched?'

'It should be on the way,' answered Ben. 'I already ordered two units this morning.'

'Good. Increase the fluid rate,' he said. 'Jenny, could we have some more normal saline?'

The patient rolled to his side and again vomited a large

amount of blood onto the pillow. This time it looked more red than black.

'That's fresh,' said Walker. 'Jenny, please run to the gastro ward. We need a Sengstaken-Blakemore tube – they should have one. Ben, see if you can get the gastroenterologist on-call and tell them what's happening then call ICU.'

Pier took another blood pressure reading. 'Sixty,' he said grimly.

Walker called to another nurse who stood nearby. 'Call blood bank, tell them we need the blood now, and we'll need more. Pier, you'll have to speak to them to crossmatch another four units. Or get O negative if they can't do it immediately.'

Jenny returned carrying a long cardboard box. 'None of gastro team are on the ward. They're all in endoscopy.' She thrust the box at Walker. 'Can you use one of these?'

He opened it and pulled out a red plastic tube that branched into three more tubes. The other end had two deflated balloons. 'I've done it before, here and in New Guinea. I always seemed to get the bleeders on night duty. I need some lignocaine gel and a lot of that KY gunk.' The other nurse brought it to him.

Walker leaned over the patient. 'Mr Banti, I'm going to have to put a tube down your throat into the stomach to stop the bleeding.' His eyes were closed, but he groaned and nodded. 'It will help a lot if you try to swallow the tube. I'll go slowly.

'I'm going to squirt some of this gel into your nose to numb it.' Walker grabbed the tube and filled one side of the patient's nose with the clear gel. He picked up the tube and held the balloon end at the tip of the patient's nose then traced its route against his skin down the throat and chest to where he estimated the stomach to be, marking the spot on the tube with Texta. He covered the length of the tube with the KY gel, concentrating on the expanded end with the balloons.

Walker put his hand behind the patient's head and grabbed the tube with his right hand. 'Here we go, Mr Banti. I'm going to put this into your nose. Remember to try to swallow when you feel it in your throat. I'll go slowly,' he repeated.

Élodie had put on a plastic gown and now stood on the other side of the patient, paying no regard to the blood everywhere on her side. 'We'll help you, Mr Banti,' she said in a calm voice. 'Don't worry. We will get you through this.'

Walker slid the tube through the patient's nose and pushed gently. There was some obstruction so he firmly increased the pressure and the tube advanced. 'Now swallow, please.'

Banti tried his best. Walker knew many would not tolerate this procedure – it could be done under a general anaesthetic but they didn't have the time. Slowly, he advanced the tube, pausing to allow Banti to cope with the large tube in his throat while Élodie continued to pat his shoulder, offering encouraging words. With more coaxing, swallowing by Mr Banti and gentle pushing, Walker estimated the tube was in the stomach, as indicated by his Texta mark which was now level with Banti's lips. He put a syringe on one of the three tube ends and aspirated. Blackish-red blood came up. He then carefully pumped air down another tube end, inflating the balloon in the stomach. He pulled on the tube. It didn't budge.

During all of this, the blood had arrived and Jenny set up the transfusion using a blood warmer, allowing the blood to go into the veins as fast as possible.

'The stomach balloon is up. We can leave the oesophageal balloon deflated unless there's more bleeding.'

He tied a flat cotton line to the end of the tube and threaded it through an IV stand that Jenny had set up at the end of the bed, then hung a small bag of fluid to the cotton line, causing steady pressure to be applied to the stomach balloon, hopefully compressing the bleeding blood vessels in the lower oesophagus.

Just as they started the second blood unit, the gastro and ICU teams arrived.

'The blood pressure's up to ninety systolic,' said Jenny.

Walker, still covered in blood, stepped away and addressed the other teams. 'Over to you. I'm going home for a wash.'

CHAPTER THIRTY-FIVE

WALKER LEFT THE bedside and wiped his head and shirt with a towel. Élodie came up beside him.

'Thank you for your help, Élodie,' he said. 'I think you really calmed him. It's hard to swallow a tube that size at the same time as feeling like you want to vomit.'

She pulled off the plastic gown and threw it into a bin. 'I may not know a lot about medicine but I know when someone needs help.'

'Most students can't tolerate that much blood. It often takes a few years to become desensitised.'

She shrugged. 'Blood doesn't bother me.' She glanced towards the patient who was in the process of being wheeled away to ICU. 'If you don't mind, I'll follow him to intensive care. I'd like to see what they do there.'

Élodie grabbed her white coat, which she'd thrown over the back of a chair, and walked away. A sheet of paper fell from the coat onto the floor and Walker called out to her, but she'd already turned the corner out of the room. It was probably just a cheat sheet that all medical students carried to help work out diagnoses, but he realised it might have confidential patient details listed. Sighing, he picked it up and unfolded the paper.

It was a list of names, which Walker assumed were patients that someone had given her to examine or take a history from for practice. He was about to pocket it when he noticed one name – Markus Schneider. It rang a bell. He'd heard it recently and not in the context of the hospital.

'That looks like a list of the solicitor's clients,' said a voice. It was Pier, who stood behind him, looking at the paper over his shoulder.

Walker folded it. 'How do you know?'

'Markus Schneider. It was in the newspapers. Krantz handled his will. He left a lot of money to a bird sanctuary.'

'It has nothing to do with us,' said Walker.

'That's right,' agreed Pier. 'So why does Élodie have it?'

'I don't know,' Walker said slowly. 'I'll ask Barry Darling.' He glanced at Pier, who appeared to be troubled. 'I agree, it certainly seems strange.'

'I think there's more to Élodie Segal than she lets on.'

Walker merely grunted and walked away. He needed to get home and have a shower. This was the second time in a week that he'd have to go home covered in blood.

As he made his way to the car, he thought about Élodie. She was a poor medical student by anyone's standards and again he wondered about her credentials. But the documents from the French authorities looked official. Maybe they were fake? But why would she pretend to be a medical student? And what did she have to do with Solomon Krantz?

Walker pulled up outside his house to see a balding figure in a suit waiting for him. 'What does Bruce want now?' he mumbled to himself.

Again, Rowntree failed to comment on the blood that covered the front of his shirt and pants. 'Wills wants to see you,' he said when Walker reached him.

'He'll have to wait,' he said grumpily. 'I'm having a shower then I'm going to the pub.'

'Where's Madeline?' said Rowntree, looking over at the car.

'Damn!' said Walker. 'I don't believe it. I forgot all about her. It was probably all this,' he added, indicating his blood-stained shirt.

'Don't they give you surgical clothes when you operate on

people?' asked Rowntree. 'You lot need a fuckin' union.'

Walker sighed in frustration. 'I'm not a bloody surgeon, Bruce.'

'You can say that again. Don't they teach you how to operate on people properly at university? I'm beginning to wonder where all the taxpayers' money is going on training you lot.'

Walker sighed again then opened his front door. 'I'm going to the pub straight after,' he warned as he went up the stairs for a shower.

'Great,' called out Rowntree. 'I could do with a beer.'

As he was finishing his shower, Walker heard a knock on the bathroom door. Madeline's voice came floating through. 'It's me, Chris. Just letting you know I made it home. I got the train. It took no time. I'll have a shower after you.'

He quickly put a towel around his waist and opened the door. She pushed in, wearing nothing but a thin silk robe.

'Madeline, I'm so sorry for not waiting for you.'

'Not to worry.' She certainly didn't seem piqued. She turned the shower on and grabbed the edges of the robe, as if she was about to disrobe. She paused. 'Are you going to watch me?'

'Certainly not,' Walker stuttered. He backed out through the door.

'Well, close it behind you.'

He closed the door and stood up against it. 'Before I forget to tell you, I've asked Pier to come to the pub with us tonight.'

There was a pause before she called out over the running water, 'What did you do that for?' She sounded annoyed.

'I promised to show him a proper Aussie pub.'

'Can't you do that on your own time?'

Walker wondered what she meant by that. Was this her time?

'Anyway, he said he'll meet us there at seven.' Troubled, he went to his room and got dressed.

Thirty minutes later, Madeline joined Walker and Rowntree in the lounge room wearing boots, jeans and a tight woollen sweater.

'You look nice, love,' said Rowntree. He stood up. 'Let's get moving. I'd kill for a VB.'

'You go ahead, Bruce,' said Walker. 'I've got to tell Madeline something.'

'I'll find us a table.'

After he left, Walker pulled out the paper that Élodie had dropped. 'What do you think of this?' he asked, handing it to her.

Madeline frowned as she read the list. She seemed to examine each name carefully. Finally, she thrust it back at him. 'It's just a list of names. What is it?'

'Probably nothing. Élodie dropped it at the hospital.'

Madeline seemed surprised. 'Élodie? Why would she have a list with those names?'

'I thought you didn't recognise them?'

She paused. 'No, you're right, I don't know them. But I know they're not patient names. I know all the ward patients. That's something else.' She shrugged. 'Anyway, it's got nothing to do with me.'

Walker folded the paper and slipped it into his pocket. He noticed that Madeline's eyes followed his hand.

CHAPTER THIRTY-SIX

THE HERO WAS full and noisy. A trio was on the small stage playing a rendition of Madonna's 'Like a Prayer', the bearded singer-guitarist moaning out the words in a rough baritone, accompanied by a woman on a synthesiser and another on bass guitar.

They found Pier standing near the main door, watching the band. He hadn't got himself a drink yet so Walker figured he must have just arrived. Madeline greeted him stiffly and Pier returned a cold smile. '

'Let's get a drink,' said Walker.

They had to squeeze through the crowd to get to the end of the bar where they clustered while Walker tried to catch James's eye. A group of young women were dancing energetically on the small dance floor in front of the raised platform. One of the girls wore a wedding veil and all were garbed in short, revealing dresses. They sounded drunk.

Walker leaned towards Madeline and spoke into her ear. 'Take Pier and go find Bruce out the back. I'll bring the drinks.' She nodded and they moved away. Finally, he got James's attention and ordered three beers and a wine.

'You and Maddie entertaining a guest, Kit?' asked James as

he poured the beers.

'Yes, a colleague from work. Thought we'd show him a real city pub. He's from Holland.'

'Amsterdam,' said James. 'So yes, you could say Holland rather than the Netherlands.'

'How do you know he's Dutch? There's no way you could have guessed that.'

'He's been in before. Just the other night. He was talking to Maddie when you were out back with Bruce Rowntree.'

'Pier? I don't think so. I think you've mixed him up with someone else. Madeline said it was a stranger who tried to crack on to her.'

James shook his head as he put the last beer on the bar. 'I exchanged a few words with him in Dutch. Trying to keep up my languages. Definitely the same bloke.' He scrunched his face. 'Meyer, I think. No, it was Mathijssen. I remember because I went to school with a guy of the same name. Although we pronounced it differently back then.'

Walker grabbed the drinks and turned to leave, but then he turned back. 'James,' he said, 'Madeline doesn't like to be called Maddie.'

The lanky barman raised his eyebrows. 'Maybe by you. She said she prefers me to call her Maddie. Just like I prefer my friends to call me Jim.'

'Jim?' He paused dumbfounded. 'I've always thought you preferred James. I've been coming here for twenty years.'

James – or Jim, Walker wasn't sure what to call him now – smirked. 'Exactly. Says a lot, Kit.' He started to serve the next customer.

As soon as Walker reached the table with their drinks, he began interrogating Pier. 'You were here the night Madeline had a Mickey Finn put in her drink.'

Walker expected Pier to deny it but instead the tall Dutchman said, 'Yes, so I heard.' He turned to Madeline. 'I never asked you, did you recover from it okay?'

'Yes, thank you,' said Madeline flatly.

'Did you do it?' pressed Walker. 'Did you put something in her drink?'

'Okay, Chris,' interrupted Madeline. 'That's all behind us. I don't think we need to involve Pier.'

Bruce Rowntree looked keenly from person the person, a sneaky smile on his lips. 'A Mickey Finn. It's years since I've heard of one of those being used.' He addressed Pier. 'What were you trying to do, get into her pants?'

'Please, Bruce,' scoffed Madeline. 'For one thing, Pier is gay.'

'Really?' said Rowntree. 'Yes, I hear a lot of the Dutch are.'

'Don't be ridiculous, Bruce,' snapped Walker, but then hesitated, wondering whether it was true. They seemed pretty progressive. He turned his attention back to Pier. 'Why would you spike Madeline's drink?'

Pier looked affronted. 'I don't know what you're—'

'It's really none of your business, Chris,' interrupted Madeline. 'This is between Pier and me. It does not concern you.'

'What do you mean?'

'And this is the reason you should check with me when you start inviting people to the pub,' she said in a miffed tone. 'These sort of embarrassing situations could easily be avoided.'

'Embarrassing! You could have died,' said Walker.

'Pish,' she said, flapping her hand nonchalantly. 'I'm perfectly fine.'

'I'm the one who sat up all night watching you to make sure you were breathing,' said Walker.

She leaned over and grabbed his hand. 'And I thank you for that, Chris. You're a good friend.'

'Nice,' said Rowntree, looking again at all parties, clearly pleased with the way the evening was turning out.

There was silence as they examined each other. Walker was gobsmacked. Pier and Madeline calmly sipped on their drinks, obviously not intending to discuss the topic any further.

'Should we then talk about Élodie's note?' said Pier.

'There's more?' said Rowntree. He took a gulp of his beer then glanced down at the nearly empty glass. 'I might need another of these in a sec, Chris.'

'How do you know about that?' Madeline demanded.

'I was there when she dropped it,' said Pier. 'What is a medical student doing with a list of clients of a murdered man?'

'Where would she get it from?' said Walker.

'From the lawyer's office, obviously,' said Madeline.

'When would she have gone there?' asked Pier.

'She told me she'd been to Brisbane,' said Madeline.

'She must have visited Krantz's office when she was there,' said Pier.

'But why?' Walker asked. 'What has she got to do with it?'

'I don't know but I think it's important to find out. I don't trust her. I don't think she is who she says she is. You should look at her file in Dr Fawcett's office—' Pier stopped abruptly, as if he realised he had said too much.

'How do you know that Dr Fawcett keeps files on staff?' said Madeline. 'I wouldn't have known that if not for the break-in. And you weren't there.'

'Or were you?' said Walker.

Pier took a gulp of his beer and dropped his head, refusing to speak.

Walker pointed his finger at the Dutchman. 'It was you. You broke into Tania Fawcett's office looking for information on Élodie.'

It seemed that Pier would deny the accusation but then he lifted his head defiantly. 'What of it? What are you going to do? I didn't steal anything.'

'Break and enter for a start,' said Walker.

'Ha! You can't prove anything.'

'And I did see her file,' added Walker. 'Tania let me look. There was nothing suspicious in it. I told you.'

Pier let out a short laugh. 'You wouldn't know what to look for. Any documents were probably a forgery.'

'So you can tell a real document from a fake? Why is that?'

Pier took another sip of beer and refused to speak.

They sat in silence again, each lost in thought. Rowntree finished his drink and held up the glass to indicate it was empty. Walker ignored him.

Eventually Walker said, 'This is getting us nowhere. I'm going to take this list to Barry Darling and see what he can find out.'

'So let me get this straight,' announced Rowntree, with a satisfied look. 'Our gay Dutch friend here slipped Madeline a Mickey Finn but she doesn't want to take it any further. Then we have a French medical student who's skulking around with a secret list obtained from a dead man. The gay guy broke into someone's office to look for evidence on the French chick and apparently has the skills to detect forged documents. And we have poor Kit here, doing his level best to crack onto young Madeline but she doesn't want a bar of him. This Western Meadows sounds like an interesting place to work. Is there something I've missed?'

'Only my ex-boyfriend – who's a total nob-head – is now going out with Chris's old girlfriend,' said Madeline. 'I'm worried about her.'

'The beautiful Cassandra?' Rowntree gave Walker a puzzled look. 'How'd you let her get away, Kit?'

'We weren't …' He sighed and gave up. He didn't have the energy. Why *did* he let her get away?

'Oh, what do we have here?' spruiked Rowntree, pointing towards the main door. 'If it's not Senior Detective Sergeant Royce Wills. I wonder what crap he's going to throw at us now. Must be desperate to come here.'

Wills, decked out in full uniform with cap under arm, didn't look happy. He gave an uncomfortable look around the pub. 'I thought I'd find you here, Dr Walker, when I realised you were not at home.' He emphasised the 'doctor'. 'Didn't Mr Rowntree tell you I'd be around?'

Rowntree gave a wide smile. 'I certainly did. But we had something better to do.'

Wills gave Rowntree a dirty look then came close to Walker but remained standing beside the table.

He dropped his voice. 'We have the results of the dental examination.'

'And?' said Walker.

'Professor Chris Griffiths from Western Meadows Dental School has looked at the material. It's quite definitive, I'm afraid.'

Walker dropped his head and Madeline grasped his hand. Then Walker looked up again. 'Yes?'

'The body is that of Sophie Haria, a prostitute who disappeared in 1962.'

'A prostitute? Not my mother?'

'We think it was probably a girlfriend of one of the drug bosses from the time. Who knows why but she was obviously bumped off, maybe because she was pregnant and didn't want an abortion. Or for some other reason, who knows? Anyway, it's not Jane Walker.'

'So where is my mother's body?'

'That we don't know. And quite frankly, I don't care. We can't mount a case against your father based solely on the hearsay of a criminal who is currently in jail. The department will assign no further resources to search for your mother's body. This cold case will just have to stay like that – as cold as the bottom of the harbour where your mother's body probably still lies.'

'Well, fuck you too, you stupid copper,' said Bruce. 'And get your mitts off the WWF as well, if you know what's good for you.'

'Is that a threat?'

'It's a prophecy, you dick. A prophecy that your career is swirling down the shithole just as fast as this case.'

'You can't talk to me like that, Rowntree. I'll have you up for verbal assault of a police officer.'

'Get off the grass, Wills, there's no such thing. You lot are soon gonna get what you all deserve. The Queensland inquiry will be nothing compared to an integrity commission here, which you and I both know is coming.'

'An inquiry will be a waste of time. They'll find nothing.'

'You think so? You think you can hide the decades of shit you've all been up to? The lawyers are going to find out. They'll have a field day. We all know you lot are just an old boys club climbing over each other's backs to get your filthy snouts in the same trough. You're like a bunch of tossers standing in a ring with your hands in the pockets of the fellow in front, wanking him off while trying to stop the fucker behind rogering you up the arse. That's all coming out and worse. And I'll be first in line to tell them what I know. You won't last a few months, Wills. Best start looking for another job now.'

Wills looked as if he would explode. He took a step towards Rowntree and lowered his voice. 'I'll get you for this,' he hissed.

Rowntree pushed his face towards Wills so their noses almost touched, then smiled. 'Fuck off, Royce.'

Still seething, Wills gave Rowntree another killer look before he turned on his heel and left the pub.

'Elegantly put, Bruce,' Madeline said appreciatively. 'I doubt you've made yourself a friend there.'

'Wills is no friend,' said Rowntree, as he watched the policeman disappear. 'But he's probably not even a dirty copper. He's too stupid to be dirty.'

Madeline addressed Walker. 'Come, Chris, let's get home. I'll cook us some dinner?'

He was surprised. 'You, cooking? What?'

'I've found these great new things in Coles. Two-minute noodles.'

CHAPTER THIRTY-SEVEN

WALKER HAD FINISHED for the day and was in his office signing off his letters when he got a call. It was Cassandra. She said that Angela Chee had left a box of medical records at their flat and she hadn't found it until after Angela was in Singapore. She said they looked confidential and wanted Walker to take them back to the hospital.

Walker felt like telling her it had nothing to do with him. He could put her through to security and organise them to pick it up. Then he realised that wouldn't work. For a start, Angela would be in a lot of trouble since medical records were not to be taken out of the hospital. And he realised Cassie would get the third degree from the security officers and they probably wouldn't come and pick them up anyway. There was no way Cassie could return them herself without looking suspicious. On the other hand, Walker could easily dump them with the secretaries in radiation oncology and eventually they'd find their way back to medical records with no one the wiser. At any one time, there were piles of medical records sitting in doctors' offices and clinical areas all over the hospital. It was almost impossible to keep track of them.

'Okay, Cassie, I'll come around tonight on the way home. Are you there now?'

He went and told Madeline about the detour he'd have to make.

'Good for you,' she said. 'I'll leave you to it and catch the train. I find it quite relaxing, actually. Besides, I think you two have a bit of talking to do.'

Walker claimed he didn't know what she meant but as he drove off, he realised he was glad he was seeing Cassie alone.

Thirty minutes later, he arrived at Cassandra's building. But walking up the stairs to the unit brought back the memory of when Angela had been poisoned here by the Malaysian medical student, Fuk Yee-Hah. He'd injected her with a muscle paralysing agent before fleeing. Walker had resuscitated Angela, saving her life. He hesitated at the door now before knocking. It seemed so long ago.

Cassie answered the door wearing an understated white dress that covered her body but accentuated her curves. She'd brushed her long blonde hair forward over one eye. Even when she tried to hide it, her natural beauty shone through.

'You've changed your hair,' said Walker.

'Mm. Something different. Come in.' She turned away and went to the bench to make a cup of coffee, pouring boiled water from the jug. 'Do you want one?'

Walker looked around the unit. Nothing had changed since Angela had left. The simple furniture and Asian-influenced decorations seemed the same. It felt as if Angela would come out of the bedroom to welcome him at any moment. He couldn't see anything that looked like a box of medical records. He realised they were probably in Angela's old room. He wondered whether he could ask Cassie to bring them out. He didn't want to go in there.

'I'd better not stay long,' he murmured. It all felt so uncomfortable.

She glanced back at him. 'Why? You got a date? How's Madeline?'

'No, I'm doing nothing. She's good. But I don't see her that much' he added quickly. Why did he feel guilty? Madeline and he had done nothing.

'What's the hurry then?'

'I guess you're right. I suppose I can have a cup of coffee.'

She brought him a mug and sat on the lounge. It had become dark outside and she hadn't switched on the lamps, so her face was in darkness. Walker sat stiffly at the other end of the lounge and took a sip of his coffee. Cassie wasn't her normal self. She seemed unsure. Then he realised what it was. She was unhappy. Sorrowful. Was it Shaun? Or was it him?

He knew what a jerk he'd been. He'd spent all this time worrying about himself and had never thought how his actions would affect her. They had been together, a couple, not just two people having sex for fun.

'Cassie, I'm sorry I didn't phone you or come around.' When she remained silent, he continued. 'After Angela left for Singapore, I was all mixed up. And finding out about Flea …' That he may have been fed human flesh to sustain his life. *Not Flea's, please God, not Flea's.* He pushed the thought away. 'I guess I just didn't want any sort of a relationship for a while.'

She was still facing away, stirring her mug. 'Hasn't stopped you seeing Madeline.'

'That's different. We work together. And I'm not *seeing* her.'

'Every time I bump into you lately, you're with her. You've always got your heads together, talking.'

'Yeah, but we're not doing anything. You know, nothing romantic.'

She finally turned. 'Not from want of trying on your part, I bet.'

Walker realised she was right. If Madeline had shown the least bit of interest, he'd be in, boots and all. But she hadn't. And he had the feeling she never would. He knew he'd made a mistake with Cassie. He moved closer to her and looked into her eyes. She dropped her head and turned away. But not before he saw it.

'Cassie, how did you get that?' There was a bruise around her left eye and on her cheek. She'd obviously applied makeup over it to try to hide it.

'It's nothing.'

'Looks like someone punched you. Did Shaun do it?'

'I fell. I knocked myself on the coffee table. Silly, really. I tripped.'

He held her shoulders and gently turned her. 'That looks really painful. Have you had an X-ray?'

She shook her head. 'I said it's nothing. Don't make such a big thing of it.' She turned her head away to hide the bruise from him.

Walker held her face in his hands and gently turned it towards him again as he probed her maxilla and orbit with his thumb. 'Is that sore? I don't think you broke anything but I still think you should have an X-ray.'

She pushed his hands away. 'I told you, forget it. I haven't broken anything.' She sounded irritated.

He held up his hands. 'Fine. I can understand you don't want me to examine you, but at least see your GP.'

'Leave me alone, Chris. You don't have the right to have an opinion about me anymore.'

'Cassie, I know Shaun did this. You should go to the police.' When she didn't reply, he said, 'Do you know he assaulted Madeline?'

'Assaulted?'

Walker was surprised that she didn't appear shocked. More curious than anything, interested.

'Did he hit her?' she asked.

'No.' He paused. He didn't want to talk about his suspicions regarding what might have gone on before, in Brisbane. 'He rammed his tongue down her throat and put his hand up her skirt at the pub the other day.'

She looked disappointed. 'Oh. What did she do about it?'

'She pushed him away.'

'And then? Did he do anything?'

'Cassie, why are you asking me these questions? Your boyfriend is trying to have it off with other women. Doesn't that upset you?'

'Of course,' she said, but Walker didn't think she looked upset. 'But he didn't hit her?'

'Isn't that bad enough?'

'Yes, it is.' Her voice was flat, emotionless. 'He shouldn't have done that. You know he probably just did it to annoy you.'

'Me? What have I got to do with it?'

'It riles him that you were with me. He hates it. Keeps asking me questions, comparing us. Wants to make sure I like him better than I liked you. I think he tried it on with Madeline again, hoping she'd bite. It would make him feel good that he had one up on you.'

'What are you talking about? I told you, Madeline and I are not involved like that. But the fact that he sexually assaulted a friend of mine bothers me. I don't understand you, Cassie. You don't seem to care.'

'Of course I do. I like Madeline. He shouldn't have done that. It's degrading. But Madeline stood up to him. She's strong. So, no harm done.'

Walker examined her in silence for a moment. This wasn't the Cassie he knew. She seemed subdued. Cowed. 'Cassie,' he began softly, 'Shaun has been violent towards you. That's how you got that bruise.'

'Of course not. I told you. I bumped into a door.'

'You said you tripped and fell on a coffee table.'

'Did I? I've been bumping myself a lot lately.'

'And your shoulder? Did he do that too?'

'There's nothing wrong with my shoulder.'

'In the pub. You had a sore shoulder. He did that to you, I know it.'

Now she became heated. 'What do you care, Chris? You

could have had me. We were together, but then you ignored me, didn't answer any of my calls. Wouldn't even answer the door when I went to your house. You humiliated me. What do you care if someone else is humiliating me?'

'So you're saying he *is* hitting you.'

Cassie slumped onto the lounge and burst into tears, sobbing noisily, holding her hands against her face.

Walker watched her for a moment, unsure of what to do. He wasn't certain what was allowed after everything he'd done. Slowly, he moved beside her and gently put an arm on her shoulder.

CHAPTER THIRTY-EIGHT

SHAUN PULLED HIS coat up around his neck to keep out the cold and rain as he took the stairs up to the platform at Parramatta station, hoping the train was on time. It was drizzling and he'd forgotten to bring an umbrella. The rain and chill wind reminded him of Manchester. How many more months would this accursed winter last?

He had a meeting in the city in an hour. At least the train went to Wynyard so he wouldn't have to change. He walked to the end of the platform so he'd be closest to the other exit. There was no one else on this part of the station. It was mid-afternoon and the atrocious weather kept everyone away, except the very hardy.

He thought of Cassie. She wasn't hardy. He'd just finished a meeting at the Parramatta office and she'd been involved. He wondered what he was going to do with her. Early on, she'd been great to sleep with, but lately she'd become less than energetic. True, he'd knocked her around a bit, but that'd been her fault. She was asking for it. And he had other girlfriends who seemed to get off on that sort of rough stuff. She was starting to remind him of Madeline. Too headstrong, and that didn't suit a woman. Cassie had probably learned that in law school – the dog-eat-dog mentality. But she should know that that was only for men. He knew he couldn't say it publicly but women just didn't make good lawyers. Not litigation and criminal lawyers, at least. You needed balls for that. Real balls, not the fake ones women lawyers bunged on. You needed to be able to strong-arm your enemy, go for the jugular. Women should stick to conveyancing or probate. Or maybe family law.

Admittedly, she was good at what she did, but she was acting under his direction. She was an excellent investigator and had found out things that even he had missed. But when he'd just left her, she seemed different. In one way, subdued. But he thought he also sensed resistance. She refused to kiss him and her face looked … what? Hard. Yes, that was it, she looked tough. Strong, a bit like when he first met her. He took in a breath and blew it out forcefully. *Don't tell me she's going to cause trouble?* He wondered what had caused the change. He'd expected her to go out with him last night but she said she was busy. Doing what? He realised he should have asked her in the office but there were too many people watching. Oh well, it looked like he'd have to be firmer with her. He allowed himself a small smile. It'd be fun. For him, at least.

He glanced up to see the train coming towards the station. There were a few people clustered in the middle of the platform where there was shelter. He was irritated to see a couple of people walking towards his end, obviously with the same idea as him. There would be fewer passengers in the front carriage. One of them stopped where the third carriage would probably come to a halt, but the other person kept coming, a man in a long leather coat with the hood pulled up. His head was down to keep his face out of the rain. Shaun looked at the train approaching to estimate where the door would open. There was no way he was going to let the fellow get on the train before him.

With a sense of irritation, Shaun realised he'd come too far along the platform. The other fellow would be closer to the door. The train was almost here. He gritted his teeth and walked the few paces to the platform edge to insinuate himself between the man and the door. No one would beat him, not at anything.

The front of the train was almost level. He could see the driver.

He felt a hand on his back. He was falling. There was no time to cry out. His shoulder hit the rocky ground between the track then something hit his head.

CHAPTER THIRTY-NINE

IT WAS THE end of the working day and Madeline poked her head into Walker's office. He'd spent the afternoon on a talk about testis cancer he had to give the following week to the medical trainees.

'Are you coming home tonight or seeing Cassandra?' she asked.

Walker tried to look dumb. 'What do you mean?'

'After what happened to Shaun, I think she may need a bit of solace.'

Shaun's accident had been in the news all day. MAN SHOVED IN FRONT OF TRAIN, BLOOD ON THE TRACKS, PARRAMATTA TRAIN TERROR read the headlines. Shaun Callen was named and known to be a lawyer, and theories ranged from revenge for poor legal advice to a pointless attack by a homeless man, to Shaun being a Russian undercover agent who'd been taken out by ASIO operatives.

'Why do you think I'm the one to give her solace?'

'Maybe not solace,' she said with a cheeky smile. 'Maybe whatever you gave her the night before last then.'

Walker looked down at the overhead transparencies he had been crafting for the talk. 'I don't know what you mean.'

'Come on, Chris. I know you spent the night with

Cassandra, you don't have to be shy about it. I know you two have a history. It would be nice to see you get back together. It'd be nice to see you with someone, *anyone,* for that matter.'

Walker mindlessly coloured in a segment of a pie chart he'd drawn. 'I suppose she might need a friend. It was quite horrible what happened to Shaun.'

'Horrible? Yes, but understandable. That bastard had it coming.'

He looked up at her. 'Do you really think so?'

'Yes, I do. He was an awful person who was terrible to everyone he came into contact with. Finally it caught up with him.'

Walker stood up. 'Maybe I *will* see Cassie. She doesn't have anyone. And I bet the newspapers will track her down. They could make her life hell.'

'That's the spirit. I'll catch the train again. I can look after myself. I'll go to the pub for dinner. Come, I'll walk you to your car.'

They left together and made their way towards the doctors' carpark at the rear of the hospital. They turned a corner to the airbridge that led to the pathology building. At the far end, two people stood together.

'Is that Élodie and Peter Schäfer?' said Madeline, puzzled.

'I think it is,' said Walker. They appeared to be deep in conversation. 'I didn't think they knew each other that well. Do you think they're an item?'

'Don't know. They both live in the hospital accommodation.'

The pair didn't notice Walker and Madeline until they were almost upon them. Élodie's cheeks were coloured and her dark fringe had fallen over one side of her face.

Schäfer was talking, his voice low and urgent. 'He got what he—' Schäfer broke off suddenly when he became aware of Walker and Madeline nearby and stepped away abruptly from the young Frenchwoman. 'Dr Piper. Dr Walker. How are you this evening?'

'Fine,' said Madeline with a slow smile. 'Getting to know one another, are we?'

Élodie frowned and pulled her hair back off her eyes, tucking it behind her ear. 'We were just talking about a patient.'

Walker knew she was lying. He thought they'd been fighting. Maybe it was a lovers' quarrel.

Schäfer's gaze seemed to focus on something along the airbridge behind Walker. 'Here come the police. It appears they're looking for us.'

Walker thought he seemed anxious. He looked over his shoulder and saw it was Wendy – Barry – and Bianca then turned to check how Élodie was taking the arrival of the police. If anything, she seemed more annoyed.

'I'm glad I have you all together,' Darling said when he reached them. 'I'm sure you've heard about the train accident. We need to talk to you all about it.'

'Do you think it has something to do with one of us?' asked Madeline.

'We've interviewed the train driver,' said Darling. 'He says Shaun was pushed. This is an attempted murder case.'

'You're kidding.' Walker paused. 'I was going to say, who would try to kill Shaun, but I think a lot of people might want to kill him. Or hurt him, at least.'

'Well, they certainly did that. Lost a few toes, head injury, still unconscious. Tried to kill him, not just hurt him.'

'Do you have any idea who did it?'

'We have a few ideas.' Darling examined each face in turn. 'We think it wasn't a random attack, but someone who knows him.'

'Who?' asked Walker.

'You knew him.'

'So did you, Barry.'

'I only met him once.'

'And he cracked onto your girlfriend.'

'That would hardly call for murder.'

'Oh, I don't know, depends on how jealous you are.'

'Where were you on Tuesday afternoon, Kit?'

'Where I always am Tuesday afternoons – in clinic.'

'Until what time?'

'It was a short list for a change, so until about three. I spent the rest of the time in my office.'

Darling wrote in his notepad. 'And what about you, Madeline? Were you in clinic too?'

She paused before answering, as if she was straining to recall. 'Tuesday afternoon. No, actually. I went shopping.'

Walker looked at her in surprise. 'Whereabouts?'

Darling interrupted. 'If you don't mind, Kit, I'm the one asking the questions.' He turned to Madeline. 'Whereabouts?'

'Westfield Parramatta.'

'At three in the afternoon?'

'Yes, I wanted to buy some pyjamas.' She glanced at Walker. 'Chris is getting uncomfortable with me walking around in scanty clothing.'

'Can you prove you were there?'

'How would I do that?'

'Receipts. They're usually time-stamped.'

'Sure, I'll dig it out for you.'

'And we'll check the security cameras. Westfield have been trialling them in their carparks.'

'But I didn't drive. I walked through the park.'

'We'll check anyway. And Detective Bianca will get that receipt from you.' He turned to Peter Schäfer. 'What about you, Dr Schäfer?'

'I had an afternoon off. Dr Piper was away so there was no clinic. I went back to my quarters to do some reading.'

'That's in the hospital accommodation, right?'

'Yes.'

'Can anyone verify that?'

Schäfer glanced at Élodie before shaking his head. 'I don't think so. I didn't speak to anyone.'

Darling flicked a look at Bianca before continuing. 'Do you own a raincoat, Dr Schäfer?'

'Of course.'

'Can you describe it?'

'Long, black.'

'With a hood?'

'Yes, with a hood. I brought it with me from Switzerland.'

'The train driver says he saw Shaun being pushed by a person wearing a long dark coat with the hood pulled up. Like a monk. Couldn't see the face.'

Schäfer remained unreadable and said nothing.

'Do you own rain boots?' asked Bianca.

'Of course. And before you ask, they're short black Wellingtons.'

Bianca wrote in her pad.

'I think that's all,' said Darling, speaking to them all. 'We may need to interview you again. Dr Schäfer, we'll definitely need you come to the station at your earliest convenience.' He addressed Walker. 'Do you know where Pier Mathijssen is? We need to interview him too.'

Schäfer answered instead. 'This time of day, he's probably at his desk. He shares an office with me.'

Everybody left together, going in different directions, except Walker and Madeline, who waited behind. 'Did you notice that Wendy didn't ask Élodie for an alibi?' said Walker.

'Hmm, strange. Maybe he doesn't think her the murdering type.'

'Or maybe he's especially suspicious. It'll be interesting to see whether she ends up at the station like Peter.'

Madeline walked in silence for a while before asking, 'Chris, I came to your office when I got back from the shops. You weren't there. It was about four.'

'I might have gone to the bathroom.'

'I waited for half an hour. Then I went back to my office and came back to yours but you still weren't there.'

Walker crinkled his forehead, trying to recall. 'Maybe I'd gone home early.'

Madeline put a hand on his arm. 'Chris, if you've done

something, you don't have to worry, I won't say anything.'

'I've done nothing. Like I said, I went home early.'

'But you weren't there when I got home.'

'What's this, an interrogation? You're not my mother. I don't have to explain to you where I've been.'

Madeline examined him for some time before answering. He wasn't sure what she was going to say. 'You're right, I'm not your mother. I just wanted to say that I'll support you no matter what you've done. I just hope you'd do the same for me.'

'Like I said, I've done nothing.'

After another moment's silent scrutiny, she smiled and grabbed his arm in hers companionably and they continued along the corridor. 'That's all good then. Let's go home. I'll make you dinner?'

'Two-minute noodles?'

'No, I've found something better. Rice-a-Riso.'

Walker smacked his lips. 'Mmm. Pity I'm off to see Cassie. Your gastronomic masterpiece will have to keep til another night.'

Bianca and Darling found Pier at his desk, as Schäfer said. The tall Dutch doctor seemed happy to talk.

'Yesterday afternoon at 3 pm?' he said in answer to their question. 'I was here. We'd finished the clinic early.'

'Can anyone vouch for you?'

'Normally Peter Schäfer would, but he wasn't here. I saw him leave about two. But check with Élodie Segal. I gave her a short tutorial here at about that time.'

'I'll check with her,' said Bianca as she jotted a note. She looked up. 'Do you know Shaun Callen?'

'Is that the man who fell under the train? Madeline's old boyfriend?' He shook his head. 'No, never met him.'

'I understand you were in Manchester with Madeline Piper. I'm also led to believe that Shaun Callen spent some time there. You could have met him then.'

'Could have, but I didn't. Madeline and I didn't socialise. Our time only overlapped by a few months.'

Darling flicked back through his notes and paused on a page. 'Dr Mathijssen, we'd also like to ask you about your recent trip to Brisbane. We have a witness that puts you at Simon Krantz's office a few weeks before his death.'

Pier appeared puzzled. 'Me? I don't think so. I went to Brisbane but that was in April, over four months ago, just after I arrived in Sydney.'

'We have checked the flight records. You flew to Brisbane from Sydney about two months ago then returned three days later.'

He shook his head adamantly. 'I can assure you I was not in Brisbane two months ago. What was the date?'

Bianca flicked back through her notepad. 'Friday, fifteenth of June.'

'I was at the Opera House,' he said after a moment's thought. '*La Bohème*. I should have the ticket somewhere. I usually save them.'

'Did you go with anyone?'

'By myself. I got the ticket at the last moment.'

'So how do you explain the flight record?'

'Anyone could have used my name to buy a plane ticket. And they never ask for identification at the airport. That proves nothing.'

'Why did you go to Brisbane in April?'

'Sightseeing,' he said after a pause.

'Did you meet up with anyone?'

Again, he paused before finally claiming he hadn't.

As they walked away, Bianca said, 'It's true what he says. They never check ID at the airport. People often share tickets and don't even bother to update the name. Someone could easily have bought a ticket using his name.'

'Why would they do that?'

'To hide the fact they'd been to Brisbane.'

Darling grunted in frustration. 'There would be video

surveillance at security checkpoint. Which terminal was it?'

'Ansett, terminal two.'

'I think you'd better contact them and get them to send you the tapes.'

'Let's just hope they haven't wiped them.'

'Anyway, he was lying about why he was in Brisbane. He sure wasn't sightseeing.'

'Agree,' said Bianca. 'I'll check with Krantz's secretary again.'

CHAPTER FORTY

BARRY DARLING STOOD at the window of the Parramatta Police Station pondering the murder of Solomon Krantz. On face value the case seemed simple – a lawyer thrown off the escarpment at Katoomba. There were no witnesses but the situation was so unusual, clues should have been easy to come by.

Why was a lawyer from Brisbane in Katoomba, of all places? It couldn't be a coincidence that the hotel Krantz was staying at was booked out by staff from Western Meadow Hospital. And there was a note that had religious overtones. What were they missing?

Bianca sat at her desk behind him and he glanced at her. She was flicking through some papers. She was a hard worker and smart.

'Bianca, I feel this investigation into Krantz's murder has stagnated. We've got a lot of leads but they don't seem to be going anywhere. I feel an important clue is eluding us.'

Bianca looked up at him with large blue eyes. 'Like what?'

'If we knew what, we wouldn't be missing it, would we?' He spoke without acrimony and the young constable appeared not to take offense.

She held up a sheet of paper she'd been studying. 'I've

found this but I'm not sure whether it's anything.'

He moved to her desk.

'What do you think of this?' The sheet of paper was covered in untidy handwriting in blue ink.

'What is it?'

'Pier Mathijssen's notes. We took them as evidence in relation to his attempted murder. They were the notes he was taking the morning he was found unconscious.'

'So?'

'Look at this.' She held a photocopy of the letter that had been found in Solomon Krantz's pocket. 'They look the same to me.'

Darling frowned over her shoulder. 'You sure? They don't look anything alike to me. The handwriting is terrible in both Mathijssen's notes and the note on Krantz's body but I don't see how they match.'

'Exactly. Krantz's letter is simply atrocious. I wondered whether if it was made untidy on purpose.' She put the letter back on the desk next to Mathijssen's note. 'Accepting that, some of the letters appear to be the same style. See the "g" and the "r"?'

Darling peered at the two sheets. They looked too different to his eye. 'Maybe. Looks like any doctor's crappy writing. Could even be Chris Walker's. He has the same illegible scrawl.'

'I suppose so. I'll send Mathijssen's notes off to forensics to see what they think. See if they match.'

'Be my guest. We need to follow any lead we can. You know what they say – the Phantom will leave no stone ...' He tailed off when he noticed Bianca's puzzled look. 'Never mind.' Darling stared at the corkboard between their desks, covered with photos and lists. 'We're missing something, I know it. Let's go through what we've got again.'

She moved to the board and began to tick off the clues. 'First, we have the victim, one Solomon Krantz, a lawyer from Brisbane. We have concluded that he died from a broken neck after being thrown over the cliff at Echo Point by someone strong enough to do so.' She twisted towards Darling. 'So, probably a man.'

'One of his recent cases,' added Darling, 'was the will of Markus Schneider who had given all his money to a local bird sanctuary. Markus had inherited the money from his brother who died in Germany.'

Bianca took up the narrative. 'One of his last cases was the mother of Madeline Piper, Jean Holly. Piper claims she didn't even know that Krantz was in Sydney and there are no witnesses linking the two. As far as we can see, Jean Holly's probate went through without a hitch. Madeline Piper inherited everything and nobody contested the will.'

'Which means she had no motive to kill the lawyer,' added Darling.

'Unless he'd stolen some of it?'

Darling brightened. 'Is there any sign of that?'

Bianca shook her head. 'No. The figures all match. And no such claim has been made by Madeline.'

'Bit of a coincidence that Madeline knew Krantz though, and that of all places, they both happened to be in Katoomba when he died. She did say in the initial interviews that she had heard of him.'

'Maybe she didn't know him,' said Bianca. 'If the will went through without any issues, she may never have had to meet Krantz.'

'Maybe. But she should have at least said that he'd done her mother's will.'

'There is that,' Bianca agreed.

They both stared blankly at the board in silence.

Bianca stirred. 'Then we have the attempted murder of Pier Mathijssen. Someone slipped a potent sedative into his coffee when he was in the bathroom. Mathijssen claims Peter Schäfer was in the room where he'd been working but Schäfer denies it. Madeline Piper confirms that Schäfer was in a clinic with her at the time.'

'Why would anyone want to kill Mathijssen? We haven't found a motive.'

'Do you think Peter Schäfer and Madeline could be working together?'

'On what? Why?' Darling rubbed his jaw roughly. 'None of this makes sense.'

'Are they lovers? Did Schäfer kill Krantz for Madeline?'

'Kit said he can't understand why Madeline won't get close to him.' He smiled. 'Personally, I can't see what any woman would see in Chris Walker, but there you go.' When Bianca didn't join in, his smile faded.

'But we don't have a reason for Madeline to want Krantz dead,' said Bianca. 'She has all her money. And I just can't see her being a killer. And I can't see her with Schäfer. If I had to guess, Chris Walker and her make a better couple.'

'Maybe Kit did it,' said Darling, poker-faced. Then he laughed. 'This is getting ridiculous.' He looked back at the board. 'What else have we got?'

'There's the Brisbane connection. We've already spoken about Piper. You said you were going to check on Élodie Segal, why she went to Brisbane?'

Darling turned away to the window then shrugged. 'Turned up blank. It seems she really was just sightseeing.' He looked back. 'What did you find out about Pier Mathijssen? Did you check with Krantz's secretary?'

'Her description of the man who visited Krantz's office fits – tall, dark hair, foreign accent.'

Darling screwed up his face. 'Certainly sounds suspicious. But Pier is adamant he was not there. Do you have the video from the airport?'

'Just arrived,' said Bianca, indicating a parcel on her desk.

'Let's look at that shortly. What else?'

She pointed to a document near the bottom of the board. 'Okay, back to the letter in the deceased's pocket. It contained threats of retribution and some of the words are from the Old Testament.'

'Meaning the killer may have had a religious upbringing.'

'The letter had a postscript, followed by a more direct threat.' She leaned in and read from the letter. 'PS. I'll never forgive you for what you did.'

Bianca continued, 'Finally—' She stopped when Darling raised a hand.

He walked to the board and studied the letter closely then leaned back with a bemused look. 'Ha!' He spoke as if to himself. 'Why didn't I notice that before?'

'What?' She stared at the note.

'The PS. Look where it's placed. It's closer to the Old Testament stuff than the last line of the letter.'

'So?'

'So what if it's not a postscript? What if it's an initial? The killer finished the letter, initialled it, then added the last line later.'

'Maybe,' said Bianca uncertainly. She looked back at a list of names. 'The only person with those initials is Peter Schäfer. He hasn't been to Brisbane.'

'No? Have we asked him? Have we checked the airlines? We need to view the tapes from airport security.'

Bianca shook her head. 'There was no reason to ask him.' She opened the package on her desk and tipped out a VHS cassette. 'I'll check it now.'

'I'll call the hospital. I want Schäfer available for an interview. Now!'

Darling stared back out of the window as he waited impatiently for switchboard to page Schäfer. He knew he was onto something, he could feel it. He twisted the Phantom ring on his finger. He heard a click and looked back to see Bianca loading the VHS tape into the machine. She fast-forwarded through the tape, stopping every few moments to view a face.

Finally, the operator got back to him and he listened for moment. 'Damn,' he exclaimed, before hanging up.

'Sir,' called Bianca. 'Look at this.'

Fuming, he moved closer to the screen and examined the

face on display. The image was fuzzy but the face was easily identifiable.

'So it was Schäfer who went to Brisbane, not Pier,' he said.

'Did you get hold of him?

'He's gone,' he said. 'All of them. Can you believe it? They've gone back to the mountains to the same hotel. To finish their bloody retreat.'

CHAPTER FORTY-ONE

THE STAFF FROM Western Meadows were congregating again to complete the team-building that had been abruptly curtailed with the murder of Solomon Krantz, and Tania Forcett had managed to secure accommodation at the same hotel in Katoomba.

Spring was a lovely time to be in the Blue Mountains. The air was still crisp but the sun usually shone and the days were warm, especially in the afternoon. The gardens had burst forth in colourful splendour and many of the houses were open for tourists, so Walker had convinced Madeline that they should go to the mountains a day before the conference and had booked two rooms for an extra night.

Walker had decided to show Madeline one of the lesser-known tourist spots. He drove through the next village of Leura, past a golf course and on to a bush carpark, where they left the BMW. A short walk along a paved trail led them to Sublime Point Lookout.

The view of the valley from the escarpment was spectacular in the clear air. A sea of blue-green eucalypts covered the valley floor as far as the eye could see. The dip of Leura Creek led the eye away from the clifftop to the larger furrow of the Kedumba River that cut across the valley floor through dense forest. On the other side of the river a sandstone wall rose up in the middle of the valley.

'That's Mount Solitary,' said Walker, pointing to the long protrusion. 'Over there to the right is Narrow Neck plateau. And see that small rise in between? That's the Ruined Castle.'

Madeline squinted where he pointed. 'Looks like a couple of stones. Is it really a ruined castle? Who would live out there?'

'No, it just a pile of eroded rocks on the spur between Mount Solitary and Narrow Neck. But it's a nice walk. We'll do it first thing tomorrow. Takes about a day round trip. Great views back to the escarpment.'

'Looking forward to it,' she said.

They walked companionably back up the track to the car and made their way to the hotel. As they drove, Walker considered how comfortable he felt with Madeline now. He was glad they'd never got close physically. He just liked to be with her. He wondered if she felt the same.

'How are you going with Cassandra?' she asked.

For once, he felt relaxed taking about her. He didn't feel the need to pretend he wasn't interested in her. 'Good. Slow. I think Shaun really messed her around.' He paused. It wasn't just Shaun, he realised. He'd made a mess of things too.

'I think she's good for you,' said Madeline. 'You're well suited.'

Walker wondered why he wasn't uncomfortable speaking about another woman with Madeline anymore. In fact, he couldn't remember ever talking about his love life with a female friend in the past. Then he realised he'd never had female friends. His only close friends had been Wendy and Felicity, and Flea was his girlfriend and then wife. He was about to add *and Wendy is a dickhead* but he realised he didn't feel like that anymore. Wendy was his longest and probably only friend. But now he had Madeline. She felt like a friend.

Madeline cut through his reverie. 'What are you thinking about?'

'Cassie,' he said. 'And Wendy. And you.'

He could sense her smiling beside him.

'One big happy family?' she said.

Now he turned to her. She *was* smiling, her dimples creasing her fresh cheeks. 'I hope so.'

When they arrived at the hotel, they soon realised that half the team had the same idea as them and had come a day early to enjoy the mountains. Pier Mathijssen and Peter Schäfer had come together and were walking through the front door as they pulled up. While they were getting their suitcases out of the boot, Tania Forcett arrived in a silver Honda. Walker could see Élodie Segal in the passenger seat. When they entered the foyer, Holland Xavier was walking towards them dressed in jeans and a long-sleeved shirt.

'Everyone has the same idea,' said Walker to Xavier.

He nodded. 'I think we all need a break. It's a bit nippier than I expected though. I'm walking up to the shops to buy a fleecy top. I saw they're on sale at one of the outdoor stores.'

Madeline waved to Xavier as he left. 'Good luck.'

Just before dusk, Madeline and Walker went down to Echo Point to watch the sunset against the Three Sisters, a massive collection of sandstone rock pillars that thrust up out of the valley a bit more than a stone's throw from the escarpment edge. The low sunrays lit up the golden yellow rock set against the blue-green of the forest on the valley floor.

'Beautiful,' said Madeline. 'I missed it last time. Too much mist.'

Walker put his hand on the edge of the metal barrier and peered down over the precipice. 'Whoa! Bloody long way down. I reckon this is the spot that Krantz was thrown over.' He shook the fence. 'Sturdy enough. Whoever did it must have been strong to hoist him over.'

Madeline slipped her arm through his and stood beside him, gazing out over the valley. 'I don't want to talk about murders, Chris. Look at the beautiful view. Can't we just enjoy it?'

Walker cast his eye over the vista. He realised that for the first time in a long time, he felt happy.

CHAPTER FORTY-TWO

AFTER BREAKFAST THEY gathered in the foyer attired in bushwalking gear and carrying daypacks. Madeline wore long pants and a woollen jumper and Walker shorts and a fleecy jacket. Both had on stout walking boots.

Madeline indicated Walker's bare legs. 'Aren't you worried about leeches and ticks?'

'Ticks are unlikely this time of year. Leeches I can just burn off.' He smiled. 'My legs get hot when I walk. What we have to be careful of are snakes. We're coming into the breeding season. If you see something that looks like a stick on the trail, look twice before you pick it up or step on it.'

Madeline grimaced. 'Great! You can lead.'

'Gladly.'

The hotel provided bottles of water, a cut lunch and fruit, so they knelt together on the floor and proceeded to stow them into their packs. While they were there, Élodie came to the reception desk dressed in a tight red top and floral pants.

'You have a message for me?' she asked the receptionist.

'Yes,' said the young man. 'A telegram. International. I'll get it for you.'

While she waited, Élodie turned to Walker and Madeline. 'Going for a walk?'

'Yes,' said Madeline. 'To the Ruined Castle. We'll be gone most of the day. What about you? You're welcome to come.'

'Oh, no, thank you. I intend to have quiet day. I might have a look at some of the gardens.'

They waved their goodbyes to Élodie then made their way to Walker's car. As the drove off, Walker noticed in the rear-vision mirror that Élodie had come out of the front door of the hotel and was looking around, as if searching for someone. She held a piece of paper in her hand. Walker stopped the car in case she was after them. Maybe she'd changed her mind. After a moment's wait, he could tell Élodie had seen him but she ignored him, so he drove on.

Fifteen minutes later they arrived at the beginning of the walking trail at the top of the Golden Stairs and started off down the steep track. It was easy walking and the air was crisp and fresh and they babbled to each other about how glorious it was to be out in the bush.

'The air is so sweet,' said Madeline. 'I can feel it doing me good already.'

Walker led the way and when he reached a switchback on the trail, he paused to look down through a break in the trees. From here they could see the track winding down to the valley floor.

'There's someone walking down there,' said Madeline.

'Two people,' said Walker. 'Men.'

They stared at the two figures who appeared and disappeared behind the trees as they made their way along a track on the valley floor.

'They're coming the long way from the Scenic Railway or Furber steps,' said Walker. 'We could have gone that way but it takes another hour.'

Madeline squinted. 'Hey, it looks like Pier and Peter. I didn't know they were walking. We could have all gone together.'

'Strange,' said Walker. 'They knew we were going to the Castle. They must have wanted to go by themselves.' He turned to her. 'Do you think they wanted privacy? Pier and Peter?'

'Maybe. But not like you think. Peter's not gay.'

'How do you know?'

Madeline chuckled. 'I just know. It's a woman thing.'

Walker laughed. 'Oh yeah? You'll have to show me what you mean one day.'

She giggled. 'Some things can't be taught, Chris. You either have it or you don't.' She pointed down the trail. 'Come on, slowcoach. Get moving. You tired already?'

Walker turned back to the trail. 'Ha, I'll show you slowcoach,' and he set off at a good clip down the slope. To his surprise, Madeline kept up.

Twenty minutes later they reached a track junction on the valley floor. A sign indicated the Federal Pass in one direction and the Ruined Castle in the other, and Walker paused and looked up along the steep track from where they'd come.

'Easy coming down. Different story going up, Madeline.'

'Don't worry, Chris, I'll help you with your pack if you have trouble.'

He refused to take the bait and peered along the track to the right. 'We'll probably catch up to Peter and Pier at the Castle.'

'Leave them,' she said. 'We can walk at our own pace. We seem well-matched.'

Walker thought for a moment then grinned. 'We are, aren't we?' With that, he took off along the track. 'Watch out for snakes,' he called over his shoulder.

It was an easy walk along a level track through ferns and eucalypts. On occasions, the path was covered with shrubbery and Walker noticed Madeline slow down to carefully examine the path before setting her foot down. Knowing their propensity to bask in the sun, he didn't think snakes would be hidden on the shaded path, but he slowed nonetheless. A snake bite would put a dampener on what was, so far, a perfectly pleasant day.

After an hour of ambling they reached another fork in the track. The signpost said left was to Mount Solitary and right was to the Ruined Castle. They rested and had a drink from their water bottles and ate a piece of fruit each before setting out again. The track became steeper and large rocks more prominent, which they had to clamber over. Soon Walker was puffing and he glanced back to check on Madeline, but she seemed very comfortable.

The path began to peter out between tall blocks of granite that thrust upwards out of the forest floor and they had to scramble over piles of boulders. The last climb was steep, but finally they hoisted themselves up onto one large square block that allowed a panoramic view of the valley.

Pier and Peter were nowhere to be seen.

'Where do you think they got to?' asked Madeline.

'Not sure.' Walker peered south-east. A bushy saddle connected their point to a sandstone-capped protrusion about a kilometre away, with no clear path between. He caught a flash of white in the sunlight. He pointed. 'There. I think they're making for Mount Solitary.'

'Keen,' said Madeline.

'Makes for a long day's walk. Unless they're thinking of camping.'

'Do you think they would?'

'Hope they told someone if they are. It's easy to get lost in these tracks.' Then he shook his head. 'I don't think so. It's an early start for the workshop tomorrow. Probably making it a long day-walk.'

They sat side by side on the top of the large rock, their legs hanging over the edge, and unpacked their lunch. Munching on cheese and salad sandwiches, they gazed back towards Katoomba.

Walker pointed into the distance to a line of man-made projections perched on the edge of the escarpment. 'I think that's our hotel.' He moved his hand slightly to the right. 'That's Echo Point where that poor fellow was thrown off.'

Madeline was silent for a moment. 'Why do you say poor fellow? You don't know what he was like. Solomon Krantz could have been a total bastard.'

Walker turned to study her face. She seemed pensive as she chewed on her sandwich. 'True. I didn't know him,' he said. He looked back towards the yellow wall of the cliff face, now bright in the sun. 'He was from Brisbane.' When she didn't say anything, he continued. 'Did you know him?'

'Brisbane's a small town. Everyone knows everyone.'

'But did you?'

'*Knew* might be too strong. He did some work for my mother. I spoke to him on the phone once or twice.'

There was something about her tone that made Walker think of Shaun – what he may have done to her in the past. 'Madeline, can I ask you something?'

She turned to him, her wide eyes blue and questioning, cautious.

He spoke hesitantly, unsure of his words. 'It's about why we've never been ... romantic with each other. I know you don't find me repulsive. You seem to like me. So there has to be a reason.'

She continued to stare, saying nothing.

'Was it ... was it something Shaun did? Has he made you not like ... physical contact?'

Now she looked away. 'There is something, Chris. I'll tell you one day. But not now.'

Walker waited patiently for her to speak again, but after a long silence it became clear she was not saying anything else. He turned to follow her gaze. Dark clouds were building in the north. A storm might be coming.

Then he wondered what he'd been doing chasing Madeline. It was clear from the start that she was not interested in him in that way. Why had he persisted? There was no need. There was Cassie. He knew she cared for him. And he cared for her. They had been a couple. What was it that made him push people away?

He stood abruptly. He was annoyed with himself. Cassie was there all along and he'd turned away from her and left her, ripe for that psychopath to enter her life. If he'd been with her, the business with Shaun would never have happened. When was he going to grow up? He couldn't use Felicity as an excuse anymore. She was dead and buried a long time ago.

'I'm going for a walk.' Without waiting for her to reply he made his way towards one of the pillars of rock that surrounded them. The Ruined Castle was a collection of sandstone rock formations that rose up from the remains of an eroded saddle that had once connected Mount Solitary to the Narrow Neck promontory. The nearest column was about four metres high and looked to be about two metres round at the top. He could see natural hand and footholds in the weathered rock and he began to clamber up. The last part was vertical with a slight overhang and there were few handholds, but he finally managed to roll onto the uneven top with a gasp. He looked down from where he had climbed. *Wouldn't want to fall down there.* He stood up carefully on the small level area on top and looked out over the forest to the escarpment. He realised the double vision he'd had before had gone. And he wasn't getting the numbness in his hand. He tried not the think of what might have caused it. The old woman in the jungle in Papua New Guinea. How they must have survived with no provisions. Pushing away the memory, he peered down into the forest below. Someone was making their way upwards from the track below. A lone woman. Red top, dark hair.

'Élodie! What are you doing here?' he murmured to himself.

He rotated around to find Madeline to let her know that Élodie was coming. He saw her to the left. She'd managed to climb up onto the next pillar of stone about thirty metres away. The long spindly branch of a mountain gum was partially obscuring her. He was about to call out when he noticed someone was climbing up the side of her pillar. Madeline hadn't seen him. She too was looking down the slope and he figured she must have seen Élodie approaching. He turned his attention back to the climbing figure. It was Pier.

Pier hoisted himself over the edge and stood up. Walker was about to call out a welcome but something about Madeline stopped him. She had become stiff, wary. Walker thought Pier said something to her. He couldn't hear the words. She didn't answer. He saw her glance back over her shoulder as if searching for another way down. She turned back and faced Pier squarely, tensely.

She was speaking. He could see her lips moving but couldn't hear her.

Walker had a rising feeling of dread. Something was not right. He could feel the menace. He looked down quickly at his descent and the rocky terrain between his pillar of rock and Madeline's. It was too far. He wouldn't be able to reach her in time.

In desperation, he looked back down the slope. Élodie had arrived at the base of the Castle and dropped her pack. She had something in her hand. A gun! She was making for Madeline's pillar.

Pier and Élodie! They're in it together. They're the murderers!

Walker shouted out in desperation. 'Hey! Leave her alone.'

Pier turned his head in his direction then seemed to discount him. He took a step towards Madeline. She was on the edge. One shove and she'd be finished.

He stood before her, towering, threatening.

Panicking, Walker looked back at Élodie. She had now reached the base of Madeline's pillar, just where Madeline was perched on the edge. She raised the pistol.

'Madeline, get down. She's got a gun!'

All three faces turned to him. Madeline looked confused. Pier surprised. Walker saw the gun barrel turn to him.

A single shot rang out. A flock of cockatoos took flight from the trees. The shot echoed on and on, bouncing off the clifftops that surrounded them.

Walker felt nothing. She'd missed.

But when he looked back, Pier was on his side. Madeline was on her knees over him. Élodie had put the gun away and was now climbing up the side of the pillar.

Walker scrambled down his column, almost falling in his haste, only just managing to keep his balance when he jumped the last two metres onto uneven stones. He clattered over the rocks towards the other pillar, tearing his hands and knees. He climbed swiftly behind Élodie and reached the top just behind her.

She had her gun out again and had it trained on Pier and Madeline.

He thought that if he lunged at her, he could knock the gun away before she shot. But she was nimbler than he expected. She jumped to the side of the small plateau and pointed the gun at him.

Pier was sitting up now and Madeline moved away and carefully came to stand beside Walker, clasping his hand. Pier eased himself up. He didn't look injured.

Walker held Madeline's hand tight. He knew they couldn't escape. 'What are you going to do, Élodie?'

She ignored him and pointed the gun back at Pier.

'I'm arresting you for the murder of Gustaf Schneider in Munich in 1988.'

CHAPTER FORTY-THREE

THEY WERE GATHERED in the lounge area of the hotel, Pier perched alone in the centre of a lush Art Deco settee with a heavy, dark-timbered coffee table before him, as if to hem him in. Élodie Segal sat on an adjacent armchair, her legs crossed, seeming perfectly at ease.

Detective Darling and Constable Bianca were already at the hotel when the party arrived from the Ruined Castle, having driven up together early that morning.

After Élodie had confronted Pier on top of the stone pillar, the Dutchman did not put up a fight and had agreed to return to the hotel with her. Walker thought he looked resigned, maybe even relieved. Élodie had pulled a set of handcuffs from her backpack and put them on his wrists, his arms out front. Pier had led the way along the track with Élodie close behind, followed by Walker and Madeline. Peter Schäfer was nowhere to be seen.

When they arrived in the hotel foyer, Darling had demanded to know the whereabouts of Schäfer. 'It was he who travelled to Brisbane, pretending to be Pier Mathijssen,' said Darling.

'We have security camera footage to prove it.'

'He's still out in the bush,' answered Walker. 'Last I saw, he was heading towards Mount Solitary.'

'Mount Solitary,' said Darling with alarm. 'Is there another way out?'

'Why?' asked Madeline. 'Pier here is the culprit. Élodie has arrested him.'

It was only then that it appeared Darling noticed the handcuffs and Élodie holding Pier's arm. 'Pier?' He seemed stunned. 'But the letter. The initials.'

'Letter?' said Walker.

'Initials?' said Élodie.

'There was a letter in Krantz's pocket,' said Darling. 'A threatening letter. And the letters PS were at the bottom. At first we thought it meant postscript but now we think it's the initials of the author.'

'PS,' said Walker thoughtfully. 'I can see why you thought of Peter Schäfer. But there's someone else with those initials.'

'Who?' demanded Darling.

Walker turned to Élodie. 'Patrice Segal.'

'What?' said Bianca. 'Her name is Élodie Segal.'

'No, it's not.' Walker became insistent and moved towards her. 'What I want to know is, *who are you really?*'

The young Frenchwoman smiled and leaned back in her chair, appearing completely at ease. 'I *am* Élodie Segal, although my full name is Patrice Élodie Segal. But I've always been called Élodie. I'm an Interpol agent working with the New South Wales Police Service. I can assure you I did not kill Solomon Krantz. I've been searching for the killer of Gustaf Schneider for two years, tracking him from Munich.

'The murder was not witnessed and he covered his tracks well. We had only tenuous evidence of what the killer looked like. Gustaf had moved to an aged care facility. Someone posing as a doctor asked to visit him, claiming that Gustaf had made the request. The staff didn't get a good look at him but were convinced he was a doctor by the medical questions he asked on the phone before he came. We knew he was tall with dark hair. He spoke perfect German. Our investigations came down to four suspects. One lived in Belgium, another in Vancouver, and we have sent agents to investigate those. And the other two came to Sydney – Peter Schäfer and Pier Mathijssen. I've been following both of them. I became suspicious when they both came to be employed at the same hospital. I began to wonder whether they were collaborating in some way.

'Finally, I received a telegram this morning that confirmed that Pier Mathijssen killed Gustaf Schneider.'

'But why?' asked Walker, confused.

'Because his name is not Pier Mathijssen. He is Paul Schneider, the son of Gustaf Schneider. That is what the telegram confirmed this morning – that Paul Schneider had changed his name to Pier Mathijssen before he left Germany. We finally tracked down an ex-boyfriend. Paul had been estranged from his family for many years. He left home at age fourteen before finishing school. There was a falling out between them because of Pier's, or should I say Paul's, sexuality. His father destroyed all records of him – photos, school records, everything. We had never been sure of his appearance, just vague descriptions of a younger version of him from neighbours in Munich. Paul returned to Munich two years ago and killed his father for forcing him out of home. But no one saw it. His mother had died years before. It took all this time to work out that it was probably his son. But even then we couldn't trace him. Paul Schneider had ceased to exist years ago.'

Walker looked at the man he knew as Pier Mathijssen, who was staring numbly at the coffee table before him.

'Paul Schneider?' said Walker in a low voice. 'PS.' He looked at Darling. 'So he killed Solomon Krantz as well?'

Élodie interjected. 'He visited Solomon Krantz in Brisbane in April to find out about the money that had been willed to his uncle Markus. I followed him.'

'Did he kill his uncle?'

'No, there's no evidence of that. It seems he visited Krantz only to confirm there was no money for him, then left.'

'So why would Pier kill Krantz?'

Élodie paused. 'That's the thing. I know he didn't.'

'How can you be sure?'

'On the evening of the murder, I was tailing him. I can account for all his movements. He did not kill Solomon Krantz.'

'Who did then?'

'That I will have to leave for Detective Darling to solve. My work here is done. I will return to Europe with Pier …' she paused to correct herself, 'Paul Schneider.'

Finally, Pier – or Paul – stirred. He raised his face to those surrounding him. 'That *was* my letter. I did write it.' Then he raised his finger and pointed at Madeline. 'I gave it to her. She had the letter. I gave it to her in this very lounge room at the last retreat.'

Walker looked from Pier to Madeline, confused. 'Madeline? Why?'

'Because she's a thief. She stole my work when we were in Manchester. I started a study in lymphoma. A large trial. I wrote the protocol, got the funding, put half the patients on the study. I did most of the work. But then I had to leave. I knew someone was getting close to me about my father. I came to Australia. But she wrote the paper up and put herself as the first author. She only put on a few patients.'

Madeline looked livid. 'You fool, Pier, we've been over this a thousand times. Without me, the paper would never have been written. I analysed all the data and wrote the paper and got it published. *And* you were second author. The others there didn't even want to include you when you left us in the lurch, leaving so quickly. I made sure your name was on it. That's better than no paper at all.'

'You're a thief and you know it.'

'Hang on,' said Walker. He pointed at Pier. 'You drugged

Madeline at the Hero. She could have died.'

'Could have, but didn't,' spat Pier. 'Ask *her* about drugging people.'

'Drugging?' said Walker. 'What do you mean?' Then it came to him, the time Pier had been drugged with a sedative. He turned to Madeline, astonished. 'Did you put midazolam in Pier's coffee?'

'Forget about that,' snapped Madeline. 'Yes, I did get your stupid letter. And just like all your other ones, I threw it away immediately. Right here in this room. Anyone could have picked it up. Krantz could have picked it up himself.'

'So let me get this straight,' said Walker. 'Pier is really Paul Schneider and he killed his father in Germany. But he didn't kill Solomon Krantz.' He looked from face to face. 'So who did?'

'Where is Peter Schäfer?' demanded Darling. 'We have video footage of him traveling to Brisbane using Pier's name. He went to Krantz's office. His secretary has confirmed the photo we faxed to her.'

'But why would he kill Krantz?' asked Walker.

'I didn't,' said a voice from behind. They all turned to find Peter Schäfer at the entrance to the lounge room. 'I did not kill Solomon Krantz,' he repeated.

'So why did you go to Brisbane?' asked Darling.

'To ask about the will. For my mother. I wanted to know whether any had been left to her.'

'Why her?'

'Elisabeth Schäfer is the youngest sister of Markus and Gustaf. It was not fair that Gustaf left everything to Markus. That was family money passed down through generations. It should have been shared with all the surviving offspring.'

'But why pretend you were Pier on the flight?'

'I wanted to go as a family friend not as a potential benefactor. I did not want to cause any suspicion. I had no idea that Pier was actually my cousin.' He turned to him. 'It makes me sick thinking about it.'

All eyes went from Pier to Peter, comparing them. Walker had to admit they certainly had a strong physical resemblance.

Darling stepped forward. 'Peter Schäfer, we require you to immediately accompany us to the local police station for questioning regarding the death of Solomon Krantz. You can come on your own accord. If you do not, you will be arrested.'

Bianca moved to stand beside Schäfer. He raised his hands. 'This is a mistake. I will go to the station with you but it is all a mistake.'

CHAPTER FORTY-FOUR

IT HAD BEEN a beautiful spring day with cloudless skies and the evening air was still warm, so Madeline and Walker sat on kitchen chairs near the back door as the sun went down to celebrate the finish of the week. A large hole still occupied most of Walker's backyard since the archaeologists were still at work and, according to them, likely would be for months yet. Archie must have heard them in the yard and had jumped the fence to join them, taking up a place on the back step so he could overhear their conversation.

Walker had bought a bottle of chablis from down the road and Madeline had supplied a plate with cheese and Jatz. It had been an eventful week with Pier Mathijssen (Walker couldn't get the hang of calling him Paul Schneider) being packed off to Germany accompanied by Élodie Segal. Darling and Bianca were still trying to hunt down Solomon Krantz's killer. Walker knew Darling still suspected Peter Schäfer but everything so far had come up blank. Only time would tell.

'We still don't know what that solicitor was doing in Katoomba of all places,' Walker mused. He realised he didn't really care anymore but it made for interesting casual conversation as they slowly got drunk. The sun was warm on his face, things were going well with Cassie and everything was turning good in his world. And now he had a woman he could call a friend.

Madeline swished the wine around her glass. Then she said quietly, 'Chris, I have to tell you some things.'

'Oh?' His eyes were closed as he savoured the sun on his body and the feeling of the chablis in his belly. 'Are you going to tell me you've discovered something better than two-minute noodles and Rice-a-Riso?'

'No, not that.' He heard her take a sip of her wine. 'I wasn't quite truthful about knowing Solomon Krantz.'

'You said you'd spoken to him once or twice.'

'That's not exactly true. He was my mother's solicitor for many years. He came to the house a lot, actually. Mostly business. But sometimes he just came to see my mother. And me.'

'You?'

'He was not a nice man.'

Walker's eyes snapped open. 'Madeline, did he do something to you?'

She didn't speak for a few minutes. Walker wasn't sure what to say.

Finally she began again, her voice strained. 'Sometimes he'd come into my bedroom. He told my mother he was helping me with my homework. Mum probably enjoyed the break. I was quite demanding with my schoolwork. Always wanted to be the best.'

'What did he do?' When she remained silent, he added, 'You don't have to tell me. It's none of my business. But just know that I'm here to help if you need.'

She took a swig of her wine. 'He would put his hands on me. Just friendly at first. But then later, more personal. He did things, things a family friend shouldn't do. I was too embarrassed to tell my mother. I didn't want to be a burden. She had it hard enough raising me by herself. Eventually, I got the courage to tell him to get lost and he stopped. I still never told my mum. She liked him. She was happy when we had company. I didn't want to make her unhappy.

'But after she died, I went to see him about Mum's affairs. He started again. Threatened to hold up the money from the will if I didn't go along.' She looked at Walker. 'And threatened other things.'

'What happened?'

'He didn't get very far. I told him where to go. Then I came to Sydney. I was shocked when I saw him at the hotel. I thought he'd come to try his luck with me again. Then I realised the real reason.'

'What?' Walker was as gentle as he could manage.

Again, she paused, as if deciding whether to explain. Then, 'He was going to tell someone a secret about me.'

'About you? What do you mean? Who?'

She let out a short laugh. 'Oh, don't worry, you'll find out soon enough. No need to know everything at once.' She turned to the western sky and Walker sensed she wouldn't say anymore.

For a while they watched the sun slowly sink below the fence line. When it had finally gone, Walker piped up. 'There was another thing I was wondering about.' In the dim light, he saw Madeline raise her eyebrows.

'What were you and Pier talking about on top of that rock? Why was he trying to kill you? It can't have just been about the research thing.'

'He wasn't trying to kill me. He was just upset.'

'About what?'

'I knew he'd killed his father, for one. Or suspected it, at least. I'd read that same newspaper article about his uncle donating everything to the bird sanctuary. And I was one of the few people who knew his real name was Paul Schneider.'

'How did you know that?'

'We worked together in Manchester. I actually had the hots for him until I realised he was gay. We used to hang out together. One night I was around his place having a few drinks.

We ran out so he nipped down to the off-licence for some more. I'm a bit of a sticky-beak so I had a look around his flat, saw he had two passports, two different names but the same photo. Didn't think much of it at the time. None of my business if a person wanted to change his name. He told me he had a hard time being gay in Germany when he was young. I just thought he wanted to make a fresh start. It didn't twig until I saw the newspaper article.'

'So he was going to push you off the cliff?'

Madeline raised the glass to her lips. 'I don't think so. He really *was* more upset about the scientific paper. It meant everything to him. I now wish I'd just put his name first.'

'What did he say in the letter he gave you?'

'It was all religious mumbo jumbo about revenge and an eye for an eye and all that rubbish.'

Walker thought for a moment. 'I wonder who picked up the letter after you threw it away. If it was Peter Schäfer, why did he put it into Krantz's pocket?'

Madeline's face was now lost in the gloom but her voice was clear. 'I put it there.'

Walker didn't know what she meant. 'Why would you do that? Did you give it to him?' She said nothing. Then realisation hit him. 'You mean …?'

He couldn't see her face anymore, just a shadow. Her voice was almost a whisper. 'As I said, he was a very nasty man. I don't think I was the only girl he …' Her voice trailed off to a whisper. When she started again her voice was firm. 'He deserved what he got.'

'But you can't have …'

'I'm strong, you know that yourself. It's amazing how much energy hatred inspires.'

Walker stood abruptly, causing his chair to fall over. He swayed with the effects of the wine. Or was it the fact that she was a murderer? 'That's not what I mean. You can't be serious. I just don't believe you killed a man.'

'Why? We see it in our jobs every day. Life's cheap. Totally innocent people who have never done anything wrong die all the time. Only the bastards cheat death, get away with it, live longer than they should.'

'But that's different. We try to help people. Saves lives, not take them away!'

Finally she raised her voice. 'I'm sick of being out of control. It's as if what we do matters for nothing. Felicity didn't deserve to die. Neither did my mother. Most of my patients don't deserve it. Well, you know what? Krantz deserved to die. He was an evil man. He wanted to force himself on me. Now, and when I was a teenager. And other girls. He wanted to tell my secrets. He thought he could get away with it, thought I was defenceless. But he found out that I wasn't.'

'And that's it? That's enough?'

'It was enough for Krantz. Why should my mother lose her life and not him? She was everything to me. He was nothing.'

It was dark now, the sun had left. Walker couldn't see her face. He stumbled towards the door. 'I've got to go. Got to think.' He went into the kitchen.

Madeline stayed where she was. 'Okay, Chris.' Her voice was soft and calm. 'I'll be here when you get back. Don't do anything rash.'

He stumbled along the hallway and out onto the street. He could hear music and loud voices from the pub. He went the other way. He had to get away, had to go over everything and try to make sense of it.

He'd drunk a half-bottle of wine but now he didn't feel the effects. Madeline had killed Krantz. She was a murderer. He actually knew someone who had willingly killed someone. At least, killed them violently. He knew lots of people who had killed someone, him included. But usually that was when they were trying to do good. Trying to save someone's life but things had gone bad. The wrong drug used in a cardiac arrest, or couldn't get the emergency pacemaker in the atrium at 3 am and caused a fatal arrhythmia, or hadn't made the diagnosis of meningitis fast enough to start the antibiotics, or initiated someone's chemotherapy too late so they died earlier than they should have. Injected a terminally ill person with a sedative so they died today rather than tomorrow in agony. The list was endless. But Madeline had made a conscious decision to kill someone. On purpose. To end their life. That was different.

He would have to talk to Madeline, convince her to go to the police. She'd killed a man! But Krantz sounded like a nasty piece of scum. He'd tried to molest her when she was a young teenager then again recently. A paedo.

And she had said something else. Something about telling someone about her. A secret? What could be worse than murder?

He was mindless of where he went or for how long. Then he found himself standing outside The Rocks Police Station. He stared through the window. A young officer stood at the reception desk scribbling in a large book. Another came out and eyed him suspiciously as he made his way to a police car. Sergeant Bowls would know what to do. But if Walker told him about her, Madeline would be arrested. The young officer at the desk looked up and noticed him staring. He took a step towards the window, a hand upon the pistol on his hip.

Walker spun and made his way up a dark alley. He knew what he had to do. He would convince Madeline to turn herself in.

CHAPTER FORTY-FIVE

WHEN WALKER RETURNED to the house, Madeline was nowhere to be seen. Perhaps she was upstairs in her room. He went into the kitchen to make a cup of tea. He noticed one of the cupboard doors was open, and as he went to kick it shut, he saw a plastic bag sitting on the bottom behind the brooms and mops. He opened the bag. Inside was Madeline's raincoat. There was water in the bag. He couldn't remember her wearing it. He remembered her saying she'd brought it with her from Manchester. He pulled the raincoat out of the bag. It was leather. There was a hood. And it was wet.

'What the fuck!' he said coarsely.

He stuffed the raincoat back into the cupboard and closed the door. Who the hell was he living with? He felt as if all his strength had been wrung out of him. He put the kettle on and sat down at the kitchen table to wait for it to boil. Where was she? He'd wait for her and calmly convince her to do the right thing.

He noticed an envelope on the table. He picked it up. It was addressed to Madeline. It looked official. The stamp had a Brisbane watermark on it. He flipped it over. It had already been opened. He stared at the envelope blankly then raised his head. He could hear Madeline walking around in the bedroom upstairs.

He flicked the envelope open and peered inside. It contained a single sheet of paper. He checked again to make sure he was alone then carefully eased the contents out.

It was a death certificate.

Queensland
DEATH CERTIFICATE

DECEASED	
Name and surname	*Jane Bingley*
Occupation	*Businesswoman*
Date of death	*23 Jan 1990*
Sex and Age	*Female, aged 59*
Place of Death	*Royal Princess Alexandra Hospital, Brisbane*
Where born and, if not born in Australia, period of residence in Australia	Gunnedah *(1930)*
PARENTS	
Name and surname of father	*Joseph Bingley*
Occupation	*Labourer*
Name and maiden surname of mother . .	*Susan Holly*
MARRIAGES	
Where, at what age and to whom deceased was married	*Sydney, NSW 1955, aged 25, Lester Walker*
CHILDREN	
Names and ages	*Christopher Joseph Walker 33 years Madeline Jane Piper 28 years*
MEDICAL	
Cause of death	*Ruptured spleen from MVA*
Duration of last illness	
Medical attendant by whom certified . . .	*Dr R Harlin*
When he/she last saw deceased	*23 Jan 1990*

Walker stared at the document for some moments, trying to decipher its meaning. He heard a noise and saw Madeline standing in the doorway.

'Madeline, this is all wrong. They've got it mixed up. They've got your mother and mine jumbled up.'

She remained silent.

He stared back at the piece of paper, his mind numb. Slowly, he raised his eyes to hers. 'You're my sister.'

Still, she said nothing.

'You've known all along?'

At last, she spoke. 'Only after Mum died, when Krantz went through the will with me. He told me I had a brother in Sydney.

I was completely floored. He said he was going to Sydney to tell him. You. It wasn't until I saw him at the hotel that I realised he was really going to go through with it. It was too early. I was still in shock. Like you are now. I wasn't sure you should know. Ever know. I needed time to think.'

'About what? We had the same mother. You had to let me know.'

'Mum didn't include you in the will. You weren't even mentioned. I had to think about that. And I had to get used to having a brother. I was used to being an only child for all those years.'

'Why would she include me in her will? She didn't even know me. Didn't care about me. Never contacted me once to tell me she was still alive.'

'Krantz said he was going to tell you, encourage you to contest the will. He tried to use that to get to me. To force me to do what he wanted.'

'So is this what it's about? Money?'

'It's not about money.' She lifted her head. Her face had no expression. 'I'm not sure I want a brother.'

The kettle started to whistle and, like a robot, Walker watched Madeline go to the counter and pour the water into a mug over a tea bag and then set it down in front of him. He sat, dumbstruck, desperately trying to make sense of it all.

He took a sip of the tea. It wasn't hot enough. Madeline had put too much milk in it. He took another gulp. His mother had left him and never wanted to talk to him again, never see him, even after his father died. She'd had another child and wanted to live with her, not him.

A feeling of complete weakness came over him, body and mind. He felt like he was going to pass out and the double vision had come back.

He pulled himself upright and staggered towards the door. He just wanted to sleep. 'I'm exhausted. I have to lie down. This is all too much.'

'Sure, Chris. I'll stay down here.'

He dragged himself up the stairs, holding on to the railing with one hand and the mug of tea in the other. His legs felt like two rods of lead, numb and lifeless. Finally, he reached his room and crashed onto the bed.

He woke. How long had he been asleep? He looked at the clock. Less than an hour. He had to talk to Madeline, work things through. He still felt groggy.

He tried to get out of bed but his legs were stuck. He pushed the covers off and tried to swing his legs off the bed. They wouldn't move.

He looked at the mug of tea on his bedside table with a feeling of dread.

'Madeline!' he yelled.

He heard her footsteps on the stairs and the door opened but she remained in the dark hallway, just outside the room. He tried again to move his legs. They just wouldn't obey.

'Madeline, what have you done?'

She stepped into the room. 'What do you mean?' Her voice had a strangely flat affect.

'I can't move. I'm paralysed.' Walker knew, somehow, he had to move. He had to save himself. He tried to push himself up with his arms. At least they worked. But he was at the wrong angle. He was completely at her mercy.

'What are you going to do?' he said.

She moved closer.

He flopped back down. 'Is it about the will? If it's money then you can have it. I don't want it. I won't contest it.'

'Chris, what is the matter?' Her voice was calm. She leaned over him. He knew she was strong. Strong enough to throw a man off a cliff. Strong enough to strangle him. 'Don't excite yourself.'

'Madeline, you can't do this.'

'Just calm down. Don't make so much noise.'

'You've poisoned me. I'm paralysed.'

'Paralysed?' She looked down at his legs. 'Move them.'

'I can't.'

She pinched the skin of his thigh. 'Can you feel that?'

'Not much. Just.'

'So you can't move your legs at all?'

Walker shook his head. 'Madeline, please don't do anything you'll regret.'

'Do you have pain? Pain in your back?'

'No. What's going on, Madeline? What have you done?'

'Answer me. Do you have any pain?'

He shook his head.

'Try to move your legs. Lift them.'

Walker tried but his limbs would not move. 'What is it? Will I become completely paralysed? Will I stop breathing?'

'Shut up, Chris! I've done nothing. Why would I poison you? There's something wrong. I'm calling an ambulance.'

He fought to sit up, digging his elbows into the mattress, straining his head forward. His neck hurt. He had to get up. What was she doing?

She disappeared down the stairs. He could hear her on the phone. She was giving the address, telling them to come quickly.

He fell back onto the bed. She really was calling an ambulance.

If she hadn't poisoned him then it had to be something else. Then he realised what it was. It had finally caught up with him.

He closed his eyes.

His father had not killed his mother.

His mother had only just died.

He had a sister.

And she was a murderer.

And now he finally got what he deserved for the thing he had done.

Kuru!

The story continues in *Murder After Death*

AUTHOR'S NOTE

THE MAIN CHARACTERS in this novel are completely fictional. If you think you recognise yourself or someone you have worked with then you're wrong!

This might disappoint those who think this series is some sort of exposé of a Sydney teaching hospital. Of course, like any story, all characters and situations are necessarily based on memories of real people and events. But I can assure you that all main characters are the product of my imagination.

There are many historical names that are obviously real. I have never met any of these people, and any mention of them in the book is a construction of events from public records.

Many of the historical details are accurate, such as contemporary news items, names of songs and television shows, and the names and position of restaurants and pubs in Sydney in 1991. Some details are inaccurate and I intentionally departed from the facts for the purposes of this fictional story.

The medical cases are descriptions of events I or my colleagues have been involved with over the years, although the patient names are fictional.

Discover other titles by Howard Gurney

Path to Chaos series (fantasy)
Twin
The Thread Frays
Chaos

Dr Christopher Walker Murder Mystery series
Murder on the Ward
Death in a Chapel
Murder at The Rocks
Murder in the Mist

Thank you for reading my book. If you enjoyed it, please take a moment to leave a review at your favourite retailer.

Howard Gurney

www.howardgurney.com

@HowardGurney